Fic
H

Hart, Roy.

Remains to be seen

$15.95

DATE			

© THE BAKER & TAYLOR CO.

REMAINS
TO BE SEEN

REMAINS TO BE SEEN

Roy Hart

St. Martin's Press
New York

Library of Congress Cataloging-in-Publication Data

Hart, Roy.
        Remains to be seen / Roy Hart.
                p.   cm.
        ISBN 0-312-02971-3
    .   I. Title.
    PR6058.A694857R4   1989
    823'.914—dc19   89-30097
                                                            CIP

First published in Great Britain by Macmillan London Limited.

First U.S. Edition

10 9 8 7 6 5 4 3 2 1

CHAPTER 1

The doubts surfaced the moment the removal men had driven away. It was all a hideous mistake. The silence was oppressive, the dingy white walls hemmed her in, and even with all the doors and windows flung wide there was hardly a breath of air about the place. And the beamed ceiling was surely lower than she remembered. And her few sticks of gimcrack furniture didn't fit the rustic ambience, and the windows looked as if they hadn't been cleaned since Queen Victoria died. And what the agent had called an acre of mature garden was an impenetrable jungle of grass and weeds that would take her a hundred years to make it even *resemble* a garden. And now she was stuck with it all. A disaster. Hers, and paid for; and on Monday she had to get down to work again come Hell or high water.

She steeled herself to tackle the ramparts of cardboard cartons stacked up in the passage and the parlour, peeling the cocoons of newspapers from her cups and saucers and plates, knives and forks and finding homes for them about the kitchen. She was *not* going to be able to live with that old china sink. It would have to go. *And* that antiquated cast-iron range. For the time being she would do her cooking on her camping-gas burner and just light the range to heat her bath water . . . if, indeed, it would heat anything at all.

By five o'clock there seemed to be just as many boxes to unpack as there had been when she had started and her shirt was sticking to her back. The milk she had brought down from London had gone off in the heat. She tipped it down the sink and flushed it away.

'But what are you going to do, Cass?' Isobel had asked her.

'Moving out. Going down to the country. Your actual thatched cottage.'

'What? *You? You'll* never do it. It's 1976, self-sufficiency is out.'

And perhaps Isobel had been right, because already she was pining for London, to hear the familiar buzz of people and traffic, feel the bustle, even smell the reek of car exhausts and the sweat of humankind all pressed together on the Tube.

But it was no good looking back, and getting hysterical about it. This had been what she wanted. To isolate herself, to dump herself down somewhere where no more harm could come to her, to get away from funerals and solicitors and memories of bloody Steven. A quiet place to do some work and straighten herself out and generally get her act together. And, anyway, she couldn't go back to London for years. She simply couldn't afford it. She had burned her boats right down to their rudders.

At seven o'clock she wearily stamped a couple of packing cases to extinction on the tiled floor of the kitchen and managed to start a fire in the range. But by eight o'clock the water was still too tepid for a bath and at five past she discovered that the electricity wasn't working. In London that wouldn't have been a disaster. You picked up the telephone and rang the electricity people. Someone would come; eventually.

But, fool that she was, she had decided not to have the telephone installed down here because it would make her too accessible. And that, after buying this ramshackle place, was her *second* mistake.

'I'm Cassie Murcheson,' she said.

He said nothing, looking both at her and her Mini,

8

parked in the lane behind her, with withering disinterest.

'I've just moved into Box Cottage. Next door.'

'Really?' he said, only just not making it sound like 'so what?' Black-haired and black-bearded, he filled his cottage doorway from side to side and from lintel to doorstep. From somewhere inside wafted the smell of linseed oil and turpentine.

'Do you have a telephone?'

He shook his head. 'No. Sorry,' he grunted. He started to close the door.

She pushed the flat of her hand against it, her wrath rising. She had driven for *miles* in search of a phone box, but all the lanes had looked alike and she had finished up unwittingly driving a full circle. If only she had started off in the opposite direction . . .

'I've got no electricity.'

The pressure against her hand grew stronger. His shirt gaped. He had a hairy chest. She had never liked hairy chests.

'Try the electricity people.'

'*Please*,' she said, in a moment of wringing desperation. 'I only want to know where the nearest phone box is, for God's sake.'

Some of the pressure went off the door. 'Try the main switch.'

'I don't even know where it is.'

His eyes rolled upward. Bloody women, the expression said. Oh, he was a right pig was this one. King Kong made flesh; except, as she recalled, poor old Kong had at least had a few saving graces.

'Give me five minutes,' he said irritably. 'I'll be along.'

'Right,' she said. But already the door was closing in her face. 'Thanks.'

When she got back to the cottage, the fire in the range was all but out and the water was still no warmer. In near anger she fed in a mixture of crushed newspapers, wood and torn-up cardboard. The result was terrifying; a sort of

9

flash-fire that made the chimney roar like a jet engine and sent red-hot sparks floating up into the darkening sky in a cloud of dense black smoke, all of which boded ill for her thatched roof; until, blessedly, it burned itself out of its first gusto and just produced drifting grey smoke that at least looked harmless. And still the water had got no hotter.

Her neighbour's five minutes was nearer half an hour and it was half past nine, and almost dark, when he finally deigned to put in an appearance. Without a word, he opened the poky little cupboard under the stairs and squeezed the top half of his substantial bulk inside it. She heard a match strike, the rub of metal against metal, the click of a switch.

And there was light.

His massive unlovely behind backed from the cupboard. He stood up, pointedly flicking the cobwebs from his shirtsleeves.

'Your main fuse was out,' he said sourly, as if she should have known that all the time. 'And it was switched off at the box.'

'I'm grateful,' she said. 'Thanks for turning out.'

He shut the cupboard door.

'You'll have to get it rewired,' he said. 'It's all old cable in there. Dangerous.'

'I'll get it fixed.' Later. When she could afford it . . .

They were eye to eye, diagonally. His head almost touched the ceiling.

'I'll be off then,' he said, moving to skirt her in the narrow space.

'I don't suppose . . . ' she hazarded, blocking his way. The tired look came back into his eyes. ' . . . I can't get my water hot. Any ideas? It's a range. An old cast-iron thing. All the heat seems to be going up the chimney.'

Wordlessly he turned about and took the two paces to the kitchen, ducked under the door frame. He regarded the range with the same evident distaste with which he seemed to regard everything else.

10

'Have you tried it with the damper in?'

'No, I haven't . . . ' And what's a damper? But she decided that to ask him that question would only exacerbate an already fraught situation.

The damper was obviously something to do with the little iron knob sticking out between the base of the chimney and the top of the range. He pushed it in. The chimney creaked as it started to cool.

She wondered if he might be the local odd-job man and whether she ought to pay him something, or at least offer. His disreputable corduroy trousers were shiny at the knees, and splashed here and there with paint, his shoes down at heel, his wristwatch a battered old steel thing. And a razor wouldn't have done him any harm either . . .

'Do I owe you anything?' she ventured. 'I mean, if you do this for a living . . . '

Plainly he didn't. She had read of a lip curling, but had never actually seen one do it before, and hastened to make amends.

'Look,' she said. 'I'm sorry. No offence . . . I'm just grateful. That's all.'

'There's no need,' he grunted. Just make sure it doesn't happen again, his eyes said, more volubly.

Don't worry, old sport, she telepathed back. It won't.

'Well, thanks, anyway,' she said.

He jerked his head curtly and started back up the passage ahead of her. Without a word, not even a goodnight.

'And stuff you, too, mate,' she said, aloud, after she had closed the door behind him. 'Oaf!'

The bath was bliss. She hurt all over. It was Friday. Nearly midnight. Downstairs, apart from all the cardboard boxes in the kitchen, she was very nearly organised. Whatever wasn't done now could wait.

She lolled for an hour, replenishing the hot water whenever it began to feel chilly. It had been a long time since she had lolled anywhere, so very long since she had not been

11

on call for someone or something. And after that there had been the funeral, the business with solicitors, and just as she had got back on her feet after that dreary palaver, darling Steven had become bloody Steven and shot off to New York, with someone she hadn't even guessed about, and left only a letter that began Dear Cass and finished with a sorry, tucked behind the dial of her telephone, together with his doorkey and half a month's rent.

But if Steven's departure had done nothing else, apart from leaving her feeling betrayed, it had taken away the human race's power to surprise her any more. From that moment on, after the hurt and resentment had diminished enough, she had resolved to start afresh. Rearrange her geography. Take her favourite chattels with her and put them down somewhere where the world would leave her alone and there would be no memories except good ones. She had loved her old Dad, not cloyingly so, but as a friend, someone whose ear she could bend, someone who, pruning his roses, had only to say: Well, you know what I'd do, don't you, Cass? and the world would usually be set to rights in a couple of minutes. She missed him; he had left a gap. If Steven had stayed around and given her someone to lean on, she might have got over her father's death more easily. But Steven hadn't stayed and her father still hadn't gone away.

He would have liked this place, her Dad. An acre of wild land. Trees in the garden, a pond, an overgrown rockery. The malignancy that had taken him had stolen him in stages, slowly, lingeringly, and when he had finally gone she had hated God for the lousy way he had arranged things. She had hated God almost as much as, three months later, she was to hate bloody Steven.

The bath revived her. At one o'clock, in the larger of the two bedrooms, beamed, with a ceiling that sloped down towards the leaded casement window, she unpacked her few clothes. As yet she had no wardrobe, only a dress-shop display rail, on castors, purchased second-hand in the

12

King's Road; but with an old bedsheet draped over it, like everything else it would do for now.

She remembered distinctly packing her hair dryer . . . or had she?

In the other, smaller bedroom, she hauled her drawing-board on its wooden stand closer to the window, ripped away the sheet of corrugated cardboard she had taped to its working surface to protect it from the ravages of the removal men. Unpacked her paints, inks, brushes and air-brush equipment, and arranged them all in the chest of drawers that she'd had in her bedroom as a child, and her sheets of white board still in their wrapping paper, and for the first time in months felt like doing some work. On Monday she would start, whether the cottage was straightened out or not. On Monday she would face a blank sheet of Bristol board and suffer the usual terror of having to fill it with something.

By three o'clock, wound up tightly like a clock-spring, she found herself with the same kind of light-headedness that she last remembered feeling as a child, perhaps on a birthday when an ill-affordable new bicycle had arrived, or on that memorable day when her dear old Dad had at last come home out of the army after the war, an unknown, nut-brown stranger who no longer even looked like the photograph on the chest of drawers – the same one, beside her bed in those days, a man she did not remember in the flesh, except vaguely, last seen when she was two and not seen again until she was six and only sure he was who he was because he felt right and smelled right and had brought home more bars of chocolate than she had ever seen in all her short life. That had been thirty years ago. A lot had changed since then.

These nights, she slept in a single bed. The double one she had shared with bloody Steven had been given away to the Salvation Army.

She lay awake for a long time, and became aware again of the velvety silence and the heat. In London, there had always been an orange halo in the sky at night. Down here the dark was like a blackly gloved hand. She kicked down the bedclothes. Lay on her back, her front, her side, found each position more uncomfortable than the last. The occasional creak she heard was the timber of the old cottage giving up the heat of the day. At least, she hoped it was.

And when, at last, she did drift into sleep, it was to dream of bloody Steven stealing her new yellow Mini and making off with it along Ealing Broadway, with her in hot pursuit, barefooted and in her pyjamas.

She awoke at eight o'clock to the twitter of birds and the steady putt-putt of a distant tractor. It was Saturday, and even before she had half opened her eyes she had decided to take today and tomorrow more leisurely. Yesterday had been chaos, and she still ached from lugging all those boxes about. And she wondered what Freud would have made of that dream about Steven.

It was possible, she discovered, to make toast over a camping stove, the only qualifications being that one had to keep the bread briskly on the move and did not object too strongly to the taste of charcoal. Boiling a kettle was straightforward, but she'd always found black coffee foul when it was the first drink of the day. Top of the shopping list would have to be milk. If the weather continued the way it was, she could always stand the bottle in a bucket of water under the sink.

With her makeshift breakfast on the seat of a kitchen stool beside her, she sat in her father's old chesterfield in the parlour, with a pad on her knee, and totted up her resources. They were not vast. The sale of her father's terraced house in Fulham had fetched only fifteen thousand and a few hundred pounds. Shared between herself and sister Isobel, less solicitor's fees and funeral expenses and all the dreary etceteras, she had finished up with six thousand eight hundred and a couple of coppers. The cottage

14

had cost five thousand; the asking price had been five-five hundred but her father's voice at Cassie's shoulder had cautioned: You know what I'd do, don't you, Cass? Offer him five. It'll cost you another couple of hundred to do it up, won't it? Some spirited bargaining in the hall between her and the agent set the price at five thousand. And, of course, there were more fees, which brought the cost up again to five and a half thousand. Plus another eighty pounds for the removers, and a few other incidentals. The Mini had been an unmitigated luxury, bought in the heat of the moment because when Steven went their jointly purchased second-hand Cortina had gone with him.

A tally of her cheque-stubs showed that her bank account stood currently at one hundred and fifty-two pounds. The contents of her purse, tipped out on to the kitchen stool and stacked in neat piles of silver and copper – and a slender wad of notes – stood at twelve pounds, twenty-eight pence, and an Irish penny. Carefully nurtured, twelve pounds-odd might last her three weeks. And the floorboards would have to be stained rather than carpeted and the china sink would have to stay for a while longer and if winter came early she might even be able to do without a refrigerator . . .

And there was always work. And tossing her pride to one side and ringing Paul Criddle, her agent, for an advance, or even a loan, if the worst came to the worst.

At mid-morning, shirted and jeaned, she drove the Mini into the village and parked behind a couple of other cars on the verge near the war memorial. She was ill at ease the moment she slammed the car door and started across the lane towards the grocer's shop. She could feel the eyes, the turning heads. It was, for a moment, as if the entire world had frozen about her. Then everyone and everything came to life again and she decided it had only been her imagination. She was new here, a stranger, of course she was an object of curiosity. It would pass.

The shop was busy, boxes and sacks of greengrocery outside, its door caught open against the upraised corner

15

of a coconut mat, its dark interior smelling like the grocers' shops she remembered from childhood, a spicy sweetness that caught at the nostrils. She felt more glances, like cold knives at her back, as she quartered the shelves and the display racks in front of the counter. Bacon slicer on a marble slab at one end, cheeseboard with a wire cutter, butter pats like miniature cricket bats; the supermarkets that had conquered London were obviously still a long way from Newby Magna.

The queue at the counter diminished. The woman in front of her looked like the witch of Endor, a tartan scarf tied round her head, a few lank grey hairs showing, a face so lined that it looked like a spider's web. A man's raincoat, several sizes too large for her, was hitched tightly round her waist with a couple of turns of rope washing line. And she stank. That was the only word for it.

Neither the hag nor the shopkeeper spoke to each other. She gave him a list written on the back of a grubby envelope and he filled a paper carrier-bag with whatever it was she wanted. It looked like a regular routine. Still without a word she passed over three crumpled pound notes and held out a woolly-mittened hand for her change. And when she had shuffled out, in carpet slippers, Cassie noticed, she left a lot of her pervasive odour behind her.

'Morning, miss.' The shopkeeper, elderly, white-coated, viewed her with evident interest as she took the place of the hag in front of the bacon slicer.

She smiled brightly at the first human voice she had heard since the removal men had driven off yesterday afternoon. She discounted Blackbeard the pirate, from next door, as slightly less than human.

Eggs. Self-raising flour. A jar of peanut butter. Large Hovis. A small jar of Bovril. Three pints of milk . . .

'And three pounds of Edwards, please.'

Mr Haygarth, or so the sign over the door had read, came back in from the sunshine with half a dozen potatoes in a brass scale-pan. By the look of them, they weighed a

16

good few ounces more than the three pound weights he measured them against.

'That'll be fifteen pence,' he said, pouring them into her open string bag, and still, she observed, regarding her speculatively from under his eyebrows. The potatoes ought to have been nearer twenty pence, but she passed no comment. Mr Haygarth was obviously seeding the ground for her future custom.

He stacked up a few more packets beside the till for her.

'Anything else, miss?'

'I don't suppose you sell logs?'

No, he was sorry but he had no logs. But he did sell coke, by the 28-pound bag, eighty pence, and he could let her have a couple of wooden tomato crates for kindling – and no charge. The bagged coke was outside by the greengrocery and she could take all the wooden crates she needed from the yard beside the shop.

He totted up her account on the corner of a wad of wrapping paper. 'You the new young lady along at Box Cottage, are you?' he asked, still jotting down figures with a stub of pencil.

'Yes,' she said. 'Moved in yesterday.'

'Like it up there, do you?'

'Yes,' she said, to the top of his head. He had scored a line beneath the figures and was adding them up. 'So far.'

'Been empty for years, that place. Nice to see somebody in there again.'

'Thank you', she said. It was nice to feel welcome. Her bill had come to four pounds and six pence. The six pence was slashed through.

'Call it four pounds,' he said.

'No,' she protested. 'Really.' What she didn't need at the moment was charity.

He took her four pound notes and firmly gave her back the three two-pence pieces.

'Thank you, miss.' He fanned the notes to count them.

17

'Your husband's coming down later, I suppose, is he?' he enquired casually as he rang up four pounds on his ornamented brass till.

That was none of his business. She pretended she hadn't heard as she stuffed the rest of her purchases into her string bag, but shot him another bright smile as she swung the bag down by her side.

'Thank you,' she said.

'And thank you, too, miss. – And we're open Sundays. Ten till one.'

'Thanks,' she said. 'I'll remember that'.

'Morning, Mr Cambridge,' he said, as she turned away, to the customer standing behind her. 'What can I do for you this morning?'

And the most pleasant, throaty male voice she had heard in years replied, 'Good morning, Jake. Just a large cut white and half a dozen eggs – brown ones, please.'

And, despite herself, she took him in from the tail of her eye as she turned away and started for the door; and saw, to her astonishment, that it was Blackbeard. From next door.

She managed to pack six tomato crates on the back seat of the Mini. The bags of coke proved more recalcitrant. Twenty-eight pounds avoirdupois hadn't sounded all that much in the comparative cool of the shop. Out here in the blazing sunshine, having already dragged one across the grocer's forecourt and the grass verge, she tackled the second with gritted teeth. It wouldn't lick her, she'd do it if it took all day . . .

'Do you want a hand with that?' a gruff voice said, as a shadow fell over her.

She took in the paint-stained Hush Puppies, the tatty corduroys, and needed to look no higher.

'No, thanks,' she said. 'I can manage.'

And he stood aside and watched her manage, until something clicked ominously in the small of her back. There was

18

a definite snap higher up as she straightened up again.

'Have you got a car?' he said. He had his world-weary bloody-obstinate-women look on again.

'The yellow Mini,' she said, against her better judgement. 'Over there.'

'And that other bag's yours, too, is it?' His head jerked towards the lonely bag of coke she had already hauled to the verge.

'Yes.'

One of his great fists closed over the slack top of the bag and he walked a few yards with it then picked up the other one as easily.

'I'll bring it over,' she said, too late, following him across the road, hard put to keep up with him.

He didn't answer. He dumped both bags down while she opened the boot, then swung one in and packed the other in beside it. He stood away.

She slammed the lid shut and locked it. And now she would have to say thank you again, but even as she struggled to frame the words, he was gone, back towards the shop, in front of which his enormity straddled an elderly Lambretta and almost obscured it. He walked it forward until its stand sprang up, kick started it, then drove off towards his cottage, the back of his checkered shirt filling with air like a balloon, the Lambretta beneath him like a child's toy.

The man in the hardware shop knew about stoves that ran on bottled gas. A small one would cost her eighty pounds, plus the gas, plus the deposit on each of the bottles; she would need two bottles, one in use, one spare. The local plumber was one Albert Harmer. It was a relatively simple job. Block off the water pipes to the range, smash up the range with a club-hammer, drill a hole through the wall for the gas pipe and to install the new stove where the old one had been. A day's work at most. Twenty pounds, say, for labour.

She would have to think about it. It was a great deal of money and there was still going to be the problem of not having hot water once the range had gone. Perhaps she would have to keep the black monstrosity after all, at least until some money rolled in.

'Perhaps you'd like a word with Albert,' the man said helpfully. 'I'll get him to come along, if you like.'

It seemed to be a good idea; at the time; especially as Mr Harmer also did work as a jobbing gardener at weekends.

'Cassandra Murcheson,' she said, as the man jotted down her name in a duplicate notebook of some antiquity.

'And your address, Miss?'

'Box Cottage,' she said.

The man's face lifted, his gaze slowly glazing over. 'Oh, aye,' he said, weighing her anew. 'You've moved in *there*, have you? . . . All right, is it?'

'Yes,' she said. 'It's fine.'

'Oh, aye,' he said again, the glassy look still in his eyes, then bent back over his littered mahogany counter and wrote *Box Cottage* and underlined it with a sweep of his pencil that might have spoken volumes if she had been familiar with the language it was written in.

Remembering the incident with Blackbeard last night, she bought a torch, and half a dozen candles as an afterthought. Another pound gone.

'Good day, Miss Murcheson.'

'Good day. And thank you.'

At the doorway, going out, she stood aside for a hunched little figure shuffling in.

It was the witch of Endor again, still clutching her scruffy envelope.

CHAPTER 2

She was not at her best when Albert Harmer called at four o'clock. For two hours, on her knees, rubber-gloved and with perspiration dripping from her, she had attacked the oven of the range with soda and hot water and a packet of wire wool. In several places she had quarried through the grease and rust and found solid metal beneath. It looked promising, she could live with it. The oven was big enough to take a chicken and she was no great shakes as a cook anyway. She would save the money and buy a refrigerator. She dragged the gloved back of her hand across her forehead, and buckled to again with the fistful of wire wool. And it was then that Albert Harmer called.

She peeled off one of the gloves on her way to the door, thumbed back a switch of hair stuck to her cheek, wondered who it was outside and decided it couldn't be anyone important. Isobel was in Spain and the only other person who had this address was Paul Criddle, and he would certainly *never* come calling without an invitation.

What she saw first when she opened the door was a back view of long golden locks and a muscular pair of shoulders under a tight black tee-shirt. Only the width of the shoulders and the narrowness of the backside, jeaned like a second skin, proclaimed the gender of it as male and gave the lie to the hair.

'Good afternoon?' she said, to the back.

He turned slowly, looking studiedly surprised to find that his knock had been answered, and, steadily champing

21

at his chewing gum, took her in leerily, from damp sandals
to dirt-smeared face and wet rat-tails of hair. He was clearly
God's gift to womankind.

'Oh, hi,' he said, expanding both face and chest simul-
taneously. Clear blue eyes, a healthy tan and a casual toss
of his car keys to show off his biceps. 'I'm Mr Harmer
. . . Albert.'

She had expected someone older.

'I come to see about your range,' he said, still chewing,
in a slow Dorset drawl. 'Hear you want it ripped out and
a new one put in.'

'I'm not sure . . . 'she bit it off. She was sure. The range
was going to stay. But it seemed cavalier to turn the man
away having arranged for him to call. And he had called,
and promptly too, and there was still the matter of the
garden.

'You'd better come in, Mr Harmer.'

'Albert'll do,' he said, sauntering past her, still chewing
his gum and tossing his keys. She caught a waft of Old
Spice. 'In the scullery, is it?'

'Yes,' she said, closing the door and following him
along the passage and down the step to the kitchen.

He dropped to a crouch in front of the range, lower
lip jutted, nostrils dubiously flared, and eyed the range
like a surgeon deciding where best to make the first cut.
One brown knee peeked through a split in his jeans.

'Hear you want one of them bottled gas ones put in.'

'Yes,' she said. 'Well . . . for the moment just an esti-
mate.'

He was somewhere in his very early twenties, and awash
with his own ego. A sword and a wreath tattooed on his
left forearm, the word LOVE above it and PEACE below.
His wristwatch was a flashy gold affair, as was the identity
bracelet on his other wrist.

He rose. Sniffed.

'Course . . . they're rubbish, these old iron things . . .
About three days' work getting it out. Ninety for a new

stove. And thirty quid for your initial bottles of gas. Know what I mean?'

Which was, she estimated quickly, going to cost her forty or fifty pounds more than the man in the hardware shop had told her. And it would *never* take three days to take out that range.

'I was told a new stove would only be eighty,' she said.

'Well, course, I *could* get you one for eighty,' he conceded grudgingly. 'But buy cheap and get cheap . . . ' His chewing gum was rolled from one side of his cheeks to the other and he smiled sympathetically. ' . . . know what I mean?'

'I'll think about it,' she said.

'There's no rush. It just happens I've got a slack week next week. But after that, see, I couldn't tackle it for three or four weeks, maybe. Know what I mean?'

'There's no hurry,' she said. 'Really. It was only some idea of the cost I was after.'

'Well, now you've got it. Sleep on it for a couple of days, eh?'

'Yes,' she said. 'Thank you. I'll do that. . . . I'm told you also do a spot of gardening.'

'Weekends and evenings,' said Harmer. 'What's the problem? Want it landscaped, do you?'

'Well, no, not exactly. I'd like the grass cut down, the pond cleaned out and the rockery tidied up. A general clear-up so I can manage it myself afterwards.'

Still clinking his keys and champing at his gum, Harmer went to the open back door and took a pace outside to the garden.

'Bit of a tip, eh?' he said.

'Yes,' she agreed. 'It is rather.'

'Thirty quid,' he said. 'Special offer.'

'Done,' she said. Compared with the price he wanted to do the range, thirty pounds to tidy up the garden seemed extraordinarily cheap.

'Next weekend,' he said. 'Okay?'

23

'Fine.'

'Not been anybody seen to the garden since old Bill Monk was here.'

'Really?'

'Four years,' said Harmer. 'Shot himself. Twelve-bore. In the parlour.' He glanced quickly over his shoulder to await her reaction. 'Blood everywhere, there was.'

The cottage quickly lost a great deal of its appeal. 'You're kidding. . . . The agents didn't tell me that.'

'No. Well . . . they wouldn't, would they? They found him . . .'

'Look,' she interrupted. 'Thanks, but I'd rather not know.'

He smiled. 'Course. Understood. I expect you'll hear all about it eventually, anyway.'

'Yes,' she said. 'I'm sure I will.' She stepped back into the kitchen. Harmer followed.

'Just come down from London, have you?'

'Yes,' she said. 'Yesterday.'

Harmer took in the kitchen again with a single comprehensive glance of disapproval.

'Taken on a bit of a handful, though, I'd say. Been empty for years, this place. Needs a new roof. And probably a fair bit of rewiring. And those floorboards in the hall; felt a bit spongy. Know what I mean?' His chewing gum was revolved back to fill out the other cheek. 'Have it surveyed, did you? Before you bought it?'

'Yes,' she said, to his obvious disappointment. Thoroughly. The thatch was sound, the floorboards were free from dry rot and wet rot and all the other diseases wood was heir to. 'All over.'

'Ah, well, you're all right, then,' said Harmer. 'By the sounds of it. Reckon you'll stay, do you?'

'I don't see why not,' she said, smiling sweetly. 'Do you?'

'Used to be old Ralph Thorn's place, this,' he said. 'But I don't suppose you've heard that story either yet, have you? Being just down from London.'

24

'No,' she said. 'But perhaps some other time, Mr Harmer.' She stood a little to one side to give him a clear passage to the door; but he declined to take the hint.

'Got killed,' he said, lugubriously.

'Really?'

'In France. The invasion. They put his name up on the war memorial, up there by the church.'

She could feel it coming. Young Mr Harmer was setting her up for something. His amused blue eyes lifted slowly, ready to measure her reaction again.

'And he comes back occasionally to haunt the place, I'll bet,' she said.

Albert Harmer was clearly pre-empted. 'Oh,' he said. 'They told you that, then?'

'Yes,' she lied glibly. 'They told me that.'

'Ah, well then,' he said. 'Just so *long* as you know. Don't want you frightened off, like. Not before I've had a chance to fix that new stove for you, eh?' He smiled lecherously. She might have taken a more sanguine view of him if he had been a plain and simple country bumpkin; but Mr Harmer was neither plain nor simple, nor a bumpkin. Even in London, he would have been a sharp operator.

'I'll think about it,' she said. 'Give me a few days, I'll let you know. But the garden's definitely on.'

Still tossing his keys, he had started towards the door to the passage.

'Still swinging?' he enquired, over his shoulder as they reached the front door.

'I beg your pardon?'

'London,' he said. 'Still swinging, is it?'

'Oh, yes,' she said. 'Still swinging.' She held the front door open for him.

'Right, then,' he said, by way of farewell, going down the step and half turning. 'I'll be seeing you.' He smirked over his shoulder. ' . . . And give my regards to Ralph Thorn if you see him. Eh?'

25

'Indeed I shall,' she said. Her smile would have withered anyone less sure of himself than Albert Harmer.

At half past five she called it a day and lit the range. Coke was clearly the secret ingredient. With the trap off the top and the base of her tin kettle replacing it, a couple of pints of water boiled in less than five minutes. The water in the tank was hot enough for a bath within an hour and between times an experimental exercise with the frying pan produced a passable bacon omelette which she tackled with relish. It was, she decided, merely a question of knack.

She washed her hair, sprawled in the bath with a towel wrapped round her head like a turban. She still hadn't found her hair-dryer. The bathroom was little more than a cupboard, the bath a great cast-iron coffin of a thing with rust stains trailing down under the taps. She would tackle those tomorrow. More wire wool and elbow grease. The walls and ceiling looked as if they had been daubed with old-fashioned whitewash, peeling here and there. But that was another job for later. There was no hurry, no one she had to impress. And the kitchen at least was a decent size. The one at Ealing had been no bigger than a curtained-off ship's galley . . .

A length of string, and two nails hammered in to the ends of the wooden mantelshelf above the range, made a makeshift clothes line. At Ealing there had been a washing machine, but like the refrigerator it had been the property of the landlord. Primitive though it all was here, at least it was all hers.

Armed with a pair of scissors she reconnoitred the garden, cut herself the less tatty of the peonies and a few roses that had managed to survive in the wilderness of knee-high grass and brambles. The tumbled rockery was a tangle of creeping jenny and couch grass. The potting shed was in an advanced state of collapse, littered with broken flower pots and jam jars and cobwebs. An old spade and garden fork looked still serviceable. What she thought was a rusty

26

swordblade turned out to be a scythe without a handle when she had cleared away the rubbish around it. A heap of soil in the corner was potting compost, from which the paper sack that had once contained it had long since rotted away.

And it seemed that she owned six trees, four massive cypresses that swayed like huge feathers in even the merest puff of breeze, at the rear boundary of her land, and an apple tree and a plum tree closer to the cottage. And when the green sludge was raked from it she might be able to grow a few waterlilies in the pond. Her father would have worked wonders here: for her, even the pruning of roses was a mystery.

A couple of the jam jars rescued from the potting shed, once rinsed of grime, made good enough vases. The parlour almost looked like home with flowers in it.

For an hour then, as the sun set and the dusk gathered, she took herself upstairs, drew up her stool to her drawing-board, opened a layout pad and sorted out a fat felt pen from the chest of drawers. For a good five minutes her right hand shook and her mind went totally blank.

Come on, she raged silently to herself. Do it!

The first few lines were a torment. Mind and hand seemed to make no connection. It had been nearly four months. Too long.

An angry black slash from one corner of the paper to another. Flimsy sheet of paper ripped from the pad, scrunched into a ball, hurled into the waste basket.

The second attempt was no better. She went downstairs, made a coffee and stoked up the range. Took the mug of coffee upstairs and stood it on the window ledge while she tried again, wrestling to get some kind of coordination between brain and hand.

The effort showed. Two out of ten. *Must* do better!

It was determination that carried her through. The mug of coffee grew cold on the window ledge, and slowly, in the last of the pearly daylight, she began to become aware of the sounds coming in through the window, the rustle of leaves, the sound of a distant train, the rasp of crickets, the bark of someone's dog, and that her hand had steadied – she broke off briefly to plug in the lamp over the drawing-board – it was almost dark outside now.

She stopped only when she noticed the prickling behind her eyelids, and realised that she had five sheets of the pad strewn on the board beside her and another used one still on the pad and that none of them would have to be consigned to the waste basket. And from the sheet still on the pad, eyes twinkling, smiling mouth filled with fanged teeth and wisps of hair escaping from her tartan headscarf, was the witch of Endor, cobwebbed face and all. And it really wasn't bad.

She sat back on her stool. The coffee was foully cold and it was quarter to one in the morning and the moon was up, the air so crystal clear that she could see the craters on it with her naked eye, and she knew that the exhilaration she felt now would be gone in the morning, when she viewed the sketches again with a more objective dispassion. But not now, not tonight. In the bedroom, on the mantelshelf, was a packet with a solitary cigarette in it, and she was tempted to reward herself with it, however old and stale it was. But she fought the temptation away. There had been a time when she had not been able to draw a line without a cigarette in her other hand. But she had beaten that craving too, the way she had beaten her need of bloody Steven. Eventually. So no cigarette. The satisfaction was reward enough . . . What was *that*!

The sound froze her. Like the crack of a whip. From the garden.

For a few seconds she remained perfectly still, held her breath and listened for it to happen again; and when it didn't she wondered if she had heard anything in the first place or only imagined it.

But she had *definitely* heard something. It had sounded like a twig snapping. And definitely down in the garden.

28

She told herself not to panic. It was probably only a fox, foraging for its supper, totally harmless.

Except, she suddenly remembered, all the downstairs windows were open wide on their stays and she had left the back door open too, hadn't she? And if it wasn't a fox it might be something heavier, like a human intruder . . . and if it was it would probably be male.

It was important to do everything slowly. Mustn't panic. She got down from her high stool. Legs a bit shaky. The landing was dark, the hall and staircase even darker. She cleared her throat noisily. The stairs creaked as, a hand on each wall, she warily descended them into the Stygian black of the hall and fumbled for the light switch. The light momentarily dazzled her. She quickly secured her back by bolting the front door. Cautiously, she opened the door to the parlour, eerie with moonlight and dense black shadows, and reached round the door frame for the light switch. The curtains flapped in the breeze. The torch she had bought yesterday glinted on the mantelshelf. She felt better with the weight of that in her fist. It was heavy, and easily swung. She crossed the bare floorboards quickly, shut the window and latched it. All that was left now was the kitchen, across the passage. Heart still thudding, her foot found another creaking floorboard as she edged the kitchen door wider open and went down the step. Her hand rose for the light switch, the wavering beam of the torch sweeping into the dark corners beside the open back door.

And she saw it; in the fraction of a second between the torch beam striking it and her fingers finding the light switch, she saw it.

A feathery bundle of blood and feathers, on the back step.

With gritted teeth and averted eyes, crouched on her heels in the doorway, she packed the gruesome mess in newspapers. It was not a job to do at half past one in the morning. A plucked, trussed, headless chicken on

29

a butcher's slab was one thing; a feathered, fully grown cockerel with its throat cut, and its eyes wide open, was quite another. And it was still warm, so it had not been dead long; and from that it followed that it had not lain long on her kitchen doorstep either. And a cockerel with its throat slit could hardly have got here on its own.

It was heavy. As she picked it up to put it out of sight in a cardboard box its head lolled out from between the layers of paper and her gorge rose, and a mouthful of bile with it. She bundled it quickly into the box and folded the flaps on it and hurried outside with it to put it beside the dustbin.

It was then that her anger supplanted the revulsion. Someone had put it there. Someone had been. Someone had violated her privacy. Some bloody yokel who thought she was fair game for a practical joke in the middle of the night. The new townie, living on her own.

And it was anger, too, that took her into the moonlit garden, hammer in one hand and torch in the other, even though she knew that whoever it had been was long gone, her torch turning the grass and weeds to quicksilver as she resolutely swept it from side to side. She even found the courage to fling open the door of the potting shed, hoping to God it was empty, and it was.

Nothing. He'd gone. Of course he had.

She retraced her steps and skirted the side of the cottage, the torch beam still sweeping from side to side.

The front gate was open. She had left it shut. Or had she? She shut the gate and returned to the cottage, to the back step and its gluey pool of blood with wisps of feathers stuck to it. She could not leave it, she decided. Best clear it up now. It was not a job for the morning. She would never sleep with that on her mind.

She filled a bucket and began scrubbing. At first, the more she scrubbed the worse it looked, a spreading dark stain that resisted her every attempt to take the redness out of it. She swore at it and raged at it, and at herself, and at whoever it was who had got her into this foul mess in the middle of the night. Tomorrow she would go to the police; not that they would be able to do anything, but the sight of a bobby looking around her front garden might show the joker that she meant business.

She heard a thud. And again; rat-rat; and in the instant she shot to her feet, her every nerve-end taut and shrieking again.

Someone at the front door.

The soft double thud came again.

She dropped the scrubbing brush into the bucket, darted to the table and grasped the torch on her way by and leapt the last yard to the light switch and plunged the kitchen into darkness. And held her breath.

Thud-thud. Harder and more determined.

She took a more purposeful grip on the torch, started towards the door to the back garden to shut it and lock it, drew back again as she heard a footfall on the gravel path beside the cottage. Quickly she was in the passage and shutting the kitchen door. She reached out for the passage light switch and flicked it off and felt safer in the dark. There was someone in the kitchen. She saw a flash of torchlight under the door, heard one of her chairs go over.

She took a deep breath and raised the torch. As soon as the kitchen door opened she was going to take one good swing and scuttle upstairs and lock herself in her bedroom and scream for help as she had never screamed before in all her life.

She heard the light switch click on in the kitchen. Which meant that he was immediately behind the door now.

Heart flapping about in her ribs she raised the torch higher. A better plan would have been to dash upstairs in the first place, but it was too late . . .

The door handle turned, and he slipped cautiously upward, and out into the passage, a huge silhouette gripping

31

a torch, and even as she brought her torch down, with all her weight behind it and her teeth gritted together, and felt it strike hair and flesh and bone and the pain of the jar shot up her arm she realised fractionally too late that she might just have made a terrible mistake.

She switched on the passage light.

Blackbeard, his eyes dazedly out of focus, was shaking his head like a wet dog. The gleam in his hair, just above his left temple, looked, hopefully, like blood.

'You'd better have a damned good story, Mr Cambridge,' she railed, white-faced, legs still trembling, and striving desperately not to pass out. 'Because if you bloody haven't, I'll get the police to you, too. Got it?'

'Look . . . '

'Look nothing!' She pushed up her face so that it was almost in his beard. 'What are you doing in my bloody house, Mr Cambridge?'

'You could have bloody killed me.'

'Don't worry, old sport. There's still time.'

He put the palm of his hand to his forehead. It came away blooded. He looked at both it and Cassandra with equal disgust.

'Stupid little bitch. . . . I came along to see if you were all right.'

'What? At two o'clock in the bloody morning? I should chuckle.'

'Chuckle all you bloody like, Miss Whatever-your-name-is. In future you can go hang.'

She glared back at him. Her blood was cold now, and nobody called *her* a stupid little bitch *and* got away with it.

'Did *you* put that chicken on my back doorstep, Mr Cambridge?'

'Chicken?'

'With its throat cut.'

'Look,' he blazed angrily. 'It's late and I'm bloody tired

and I've just had a bash on the head. So if you don't mind, I'll go back where I came from.'

A trickle of blood built into a glistening bead at the outer edge of his left eyebrow, and dropped to his cheekbone and ran down into his beard.

'You didn't put a chicken on my doorstep?'

'I don't even know what you're *talking* about, for God's sake.'

She half believed him. Except that Steven had lied to her for months, and she had believed him, too.

'So why did you come along here at two o'clock in the morning and scare the hell out of me?'

He put his palm to his forehead again, looked at it testily then reached into his pocket for a handkerchief that he crumpled and pressed to the split she had given him.

'Because I thought you'd got a prowler in the garden,' he said. 'I saw somebody moving about out there with a torch.'

'When?'

'About ten minutes ago.'

'That was me. *After* I found the dead chicken on the doorstep.'

'Oh.' Credit where credit was due, the man certainly looked genuinely bewildered.

'And you're always up and about in the small hours?'

'I was working,' he said.

'It took you long enough to get here.'

'I thought about it,' he retorted. 'I tend to mind my own business.'

Her anger dissolved. He'd seen her scouring the garden with the torch, and perhaps he had taken his time getting here, but at least he had made the gesture.

The bump on his head was half the size of a gull's egg. Blood still seeped from the split along the crest of it. He winced as she dabbed at it again with antiseptic.

'It really needs a stitch.'

'Don't worry,' he said. 'I'll survive.'

She wrung out the handkerchief over the bowl of hot water, folded it into a neat pad and laid it over the bump like a poultice. One of his hands lifted to hold it there.

'I thought you were a burglar,' she said, filling two mugs with tea.

'I did knock,' he said. 'Three times. Remember?'

'I wasn't expecting a caller. Not in the middle of the night.' She pushed one of the mugs closer to him. Beneath him, her wooden kitchen chair looked like something from a doll's house. 'Help yourself to sugar.'

'Thanks.' He tipped a spoonful into his mug and stirred it.

'Sorry about the head,' she said, sipping.

He shrugged massively. 'It's okay.' The big green mug was almost lost in his hand.

'This business with a dead chicken,' he said. 'Did that really happen?'

'It's in a cardboard box,' she said. 'By the dustbin. Take a look if you don't believe me. It was lying there.' She aimed a finger at the damp patch on the back doorstep. 'I was scrubbing up the mess when you arrived.'

'And its throat was cut?'

'Definitely. Go on; take a look.'

He put his mug on the table. The chair creaked as he rose from it. Outside, he dragged the box closer to the light spilling out of the kitchen door. Paper rustled.

'It's a cockerel,' he said, down on his heels and looking over his shoulder into the kitchen.

'So what's the difference? How did it come to land on my doorstep in the middle of the night? It didn't bloody fly there, did it?'

He tipped the open box towards the light, grimaced. 'No,' he said. 'Damned right, it didn't.'

'So how did it get there?'

'God knows.' Still holding his pad down with one hand, he repacked the dead cockerel with the other and closed the flaps of the carton. He nudged it back into the shadows beside the dustbin with his foot. He came back in, ducking under the door frame.

'Somebody's idea of a joke,' he said.

'Some joke.'

He resumed his chair and checked his pad. The immediate bleeding seemed to have stopped.

'Don't suppose you've upset anybody, have you?' he said.

'Hardly. I've not been down here five minutes, have I?'

'True.' He unfolded the handkerchief and left it to float in the bowl and picked up his mug again. 'Spoken to anybody?'

'Only a couple. The grocer, the man in the hardware shop. And the local plumber; Harmer. And you.'

He gave that some thought as he took a mouthful of tea. 'Well, young Harmer's a bit of a yob,' he said. 'But he's mostly mouth.'

'I'm ringing the police in the morning.'

'Useless,' he said. 'All you'll get is old Tom Blake.'

'Better than nothing. I just want to be sure it doesn't happen again.'

'Get the police in, and it might. They're a funny old lot around here. If I were you I'd let it slide.'

She shook her head. 'If it happens again, they'll ask me why I didn't report it the first time, won't they?'

'True,' he agreed. 'But I still say you're wasting your time.'

He left at a quarter to three. By the front door.

'Thanks for coming along.'

'You're welcome,' he said. 'If you get in trouble again, give me a shout.'

'I'll do that.' She proffered her hand. 'And I am sorry I bashed you.'

'So am I.' He smiled wryly. 'Believe it.' His hand dropped away. 'See you about.'

'Yes,' she said. 'I expect so. Goodnight.'

She watched him down the path in the moonlight. He closed the gate quietly behind him and raised a hand.

Whoever had put that dead bird on her step, she decided, it had definitely *not* been Mr Cambridge.

CHAPTER 3

She had felt foolish as soon as she had stepped from the telephone kiosk outside the Carpenter's Arms. And now, at half past nine on Sunday morning, she felt even more foolish as she opened her front door to find not one policeman on her step, but two, one a portly middle-aged sergeant in uniform and the other a younger, leaner man in a smart, dark-blue suit and who she hoped earnestly was not a detective because that would be even more embarrassing.

'Miss Murcheson?' enquired the Sergeant. 'I'm Tom Blake. I took your call . . . And this is Detective Chief Inspector Roper. County CID.'

She shrank even smaller than she was.

'Look,' she said. 'I'm sorry. It was only a chicken on my back door step.'

'With its throat cut, you said, Miss.'

'Yes, but really . . . I didn't want to make any bother. I didn't expect two of you.'

'Don't worry about me, Miss Murcheson.' The hatchet face of the younger man smiled encouragingly. 'I'm only along for the ride. Purely unofficial.'

She relaxed a little. The Sergeant's voice was broad Dorset, the Inspector's broadly suburban London.

'If we could come inside, Miss . . . ' the Sergeant said.

'Yes,' she said, 'of course. I'm sorry.'

She stood aside, then followed them along the passage. 'To the right,' she said. Two visitors made manifest her lack of chairs. She fetched one from the kitchen. When she

37

crossed into the parlour with it, the Sergeant already had
his notebook out and the Inspector was looking out of the
window towards the back garden. The Sergeant insisted she
had the chesterfield, and took the chair from the kitchen for
himself. The detective stayed by the window, still looking
out and apparently uninterested in her name and address
as she gave it to the Sergeant.

'And now your complaint, Miss, please.'

In the cold light of day the complaint shrivelled into
triviality. The detective had turned, his behind perched
on the window sill, bored to death probably.

' . . . So you see it's nothing really, Sergeant. Just a
dead bird.'

'I'd say it was a fair bit more than nothing, Miss,'
said the Sergeant. 'I'd say it was trespass.' He continued
to catch up on his note taking. 'And if it happens again,
it's harassment. And that's a criminal offence. What time
was it, Miss?'

'One. . . . Before perhaps, a quarter to.'

'So the pubs were shut,' said the detective. It took
her a moment to work out the relevance of that.

'Aye,' said the Sergeant. Old enough to be her father.
Shiny knees on his navy blue trousers, bulging thighs and
a chest to match. He wrote slowly and with great care.

'And where were you, Miss? When this cockerel arrived?'

'Upstairs.'

'Asleep?'

'No,' she said. 'I was working.'

'And you think you heard someone in the garden?'

'No. Just a sound. It sounded like a twig snapping.'

'At which point you came downstairs, Miss, that right?'

'Yes.'

'And you connect the cockerel with the twig snapping,
do you, Miss?'

The stupid business seemed to be taking on the most hor-
rendous proportions. 'Well . . . I'm not sure exactly . . . '

'But this bird wasn't on your back step when you went

upstairs, was it, Miss Murcheson?' enquired the silhouette by the window.

'No,' she said. 'Certainly not.'

'What then, Miss?' enquired the Sergeant, crossing one podgy leg over the other and rearranging his notebook.

'I scrubbed the blood off the doorstep. . . . No, I didn't. I went out into the garden. With a torch.'

'Going to sort the gentleman out, were you, Miss Murcheson?' The detective again.

'Yes,' she said, grimly. She expected the detective to smirk, but he didn't.

'Not wise,' he said. 'But good on you. Did you see him?'

She shook her head.

The Sergeant licked a thumb and flipped to a new page of his notebook. 'How long was it between when you thought you heard the twig snap and when you came downstairs? Can you remember?'

He was, she decided, a nice old guy. Gravel-voiced; and a row of medal ribbons over his whistle pocket. Probably fought in the war, like her Dad.

'A couple of minutes. . . . I sort of froze.'

The old Sergeant smiled sympathetically. 'Don't blame you, Miss. I might have done the same m'self. Then you came back into the house . . . ' he prompted.

'Yes.' She struggled to remember and get everything into order. It wasn't easy. 'Then a neighbour came along. Mr Cambridge. From next door.'

'Telephone him, did you, Miss Murcheson? Or did he just happen along?' This contribution had again come from the silhouette by the window. For someone who had just 'come along for the ride', he seemed to be taking the matter even more seriously than the Sergeant. She had already forgotten his name. Draper? Cooper? Soper . . . ?

'He just turned up,' she said.

'I see,' said the detective, with much the same sinking intonation as when the man in the hardware shop yesterday had said 'oh, aye', when she had told him she had just moved into Box Cottage. 'This Mr Cambridge just turned up, did he? At half past one in the morning?'

'He'd seen me in the garden with the torch,' she said, hastening to the defence of Mr Cambridge before he became a prime suspect.

'So *he* was up too, was he?'

'Yes. He was working.'

'I see,' said the detective again, in that same ominous way that boded ill for Mr Cambridge. Roper, she remembered. His name was Roper. She sketched a brief outline of Mr Cambridge's early morning visit, up to and including the blow she had delivered with the torch.

'... And I really shouldn't have done that. The man had only come along to see if I was all right. He had knocked, after all.'

'How many times did you hit him?' asked the detective.

'Once.'

He smiled. 'Then I wouldn't worry about it, Miss Murcheson. Once was self-defence. *Twice* would have been aggravated assault. Did he call out as he came into the kitchen?'

'No,' she said.

'Then he should have,' said the detective. '*Asking* to get decked, wasn't he?'

She showed them the back step. Even after all that scrubbing in the early hours the bloodstains were still there.

The cockerel they would take away with them. As evidence. Because someone, somewhere, was a cockerel short this morning.

She took them up to the studio where she had been working last night, still feeling faintly ridiculous that the two of them were taking so much trouble. The detective went to the window and took in the view of her private Matto Grosso.

'How long have you been down here, Miss Murcheson?'

'The day before yesterday. Friday,' she replied, to his back.

He opened the casement wider and leaned out. 'So you haven't had time to upset anybody.'

'I wouldn't have thought so.' Of the two, she preferred the Sergeant. There was something about the detective . . . a shrewd knowingness about the eyes, the quick smiles that were just as quickly switched off again, and he was just a fraction too dapper. In London he would probably have passed unnoticed; down here in the country, he stood out like a gold tooth. He was in his middle forties, she guessed, the back of his smart dark suit creased from sitting in the car that had brought him here, his hair cut unfashionably short.

'And you didn't see anything?'

'No,' she said. 'Nothing.'

He partly closed the window the way it had been and let the net curtain fall back. He turned, took in the room, the witch of Endor on the drawing-board.

'That's good,' he said. His interest seemed genuine. 'This your job, is it, Miss Murcheson?'

'I'm an illustrator,' she said. 'I'm working on a book of space-age fairy tales.'

'Looks like Winnie Fox,' observed the Sergeant, equally appreciatively. 'Bloody good, that is, Miss.'

'Thank you,' she said.

'Who's Winnie Fox?' asked the detective.

'A witless old biddy. Lives along at Highview Farm with her father and brother. Never talks. Harmless enough, though.'

'Pose for it, did she, Miss Murcheson?' asked the detective.

'No,' she said. 'I saw her a couple of times while I was out shopping yesterday. She just registered.'

'You didn't speak to her?'

'No.'

'She wouldn't have answered anyway,' said the Sergeant.

'Who else did you speak to?' asked the detective.

'The grocer, man in the ironmonger's . . . and yesterday afternoon the local plumber called.'

'For what? The plumber?'

'For a quote. I was thinking of having the range in the kitchen taken out. And having him sort out the garden.'

'What's his name?'

'Harmer, I think.'

The detective raised a questioning eyebrow at the Sergeant.

'Albert Harmer,' said the Sergeant. 'The local fly-boy.'

'Villain?'

The Sergeant shook his head. 'Not *that* sort.' The two of them seemed to have a special private argot when they wanted to exclude her.

The detective meditated, hands in his trouser pockets, eyes on his beautifully polished shoes.

'Look,' said Cassanda, as the silence became very nearly palpable. 'I'm wasting your time . . . '

The detective ignored her.

'Show yourself in the garden, Tom,' he said. 'Front and back. And pay a call on Mr Cambridge. Make a lot of noise. Let the buggers know we're about.'

'Right,' said the Sergeant. Tucking his notebook away, he went downstairs. The front door opened and closed.

'Would you like a cup of tea?' she asked, to bridge the ensuing silence.

The electric-light smile was switched on again.

'I would indeed, Miss Murcheson. Thank you.'

She made two mugs of tea and readied another for the Sergeant.

'From London, are you, Miss Murcheson?'

'Ealing.'

The detective sipped from his mug, relaxed, his jacket unbuttoned and the ankle of one leg resting on the knee of the other and displaying a navy blue sock with grey diamond clocks up the side. No wedding ring, she noticed. Spotless fingernails. Pity, though, about the yellow nicotine stains on the first and second fingers on his left hand.

'It's a nice little place you've got,' he said. 'Lot of possibilities. Settling down here, are you?'

'Yes,' she said, 'probably.'

'Me too,' he said. 'I've only been down here a few years m'self.'

'You're from London too, by the sound of it.'

'Willesden,' he said. 'Just across the way from Ealing.'

One thing led to another after that, although she would never be sure what trick he had used, or if he had, whether he had in fact interrogated her, or merely drawn her out with that beguiling smile and his obviously ready ear. She found herself telling him what the cottage had cost, and what it was likely to, and how she had come by the money for it, and how she had bought the Mini and wished now that she'd settled for something second-hand, and that her sister had two kids and lived in South Mimms with her husband who was a solicitor. And how there wasn't a great deal of money in illustrating and it had taken her years to get her foot in the door and it was only just lately that she had managed to scrape a living from it at all.

And Roper listened to her little machine-gun bursts of confidences, aware that this was probably the first long conversation she had had for days, and that Miss Murcheson was perhaps already regretting her move from London and into this isolated place. And he was aware too that she was intelligent, an accurate observer, and tough. And although there was little of her, what there was was lean and purposeful and woe betide anyone who upset her. She was about thirty-five, he guessed. No make-up apart from lipstick, no jewellery, no arty clothes . . . and no nonsense. And more upset about the business of last night than she cared to admit.

She rose to fill the other mug as Blake came in from the back garden and wiped his boots.

'Any luck?' asked Roper.

'I saw Ted Cambridge,' said Blake. 'He didn't see or hear anything until he saw Miss Murcheson in the garden with her torch.'

'Did he mention that she hit him?'

Blake smiled. 'Hardly,' he said. 'He's six foot six and built like a barn. But he's got a lump on his head like a duck's egg.'

Blake put the cockerel in its cardboard box into the boot and joined Roper in the front of the white Escort.

Roper looked at Blake along his shoulder as the Sergeant tossed his cap over to the back seat and sorted out the ignition key. 'Well,' he said, 'what d'you think?'

'Just like the last time,' said Blake.

'Worth looking into, then?'

'Definitely,' said Blake.

Newby Magna police station was a brick cottage with a blue lamp above the door and a radio aerial strapped to its chimney stack. Tom Blake and his wife lived above it, and had since Blake had been posted here soon after the war.

Sunday lunch was over. Blake, a belt and braces man and only a few months off retirement, sat in his shirtsleeves and with his tie off in one armchair, and Roper in the one nearest the window with a box file on his knees and a cup of Mrs Blake's coffee on the arm beside him. From the kitchen came the clatter of crockery as Mrs Blake saw to the washing up.

The papers in the box file went back four years, to 1972, mostly carbons and photocopies, their edges tattered and stained, the corners inside the box black with dust and the outside not much cleaner.

From the bottom of the box Roper drew out carefully three flimsy sheets of buff paper held together with a rusty paper clip. They were carbon copies of Occurrence

Reports, typed, and erased and overtyped here and there where Blake had thumped the wrong key.

Roper put them on the arm of the chair. The next batch of papers were photocopies of Blake's crude sketches of the incident in question, together with a plan of Miss Murcheson's parlour, carefully dimensioned, the body lying face down, with its head in the hearth, a shotgun, twelve-bore and with both barrels discharged, lying eighteen inches away from the body's right foot and with both triggers attached to the big toe of that same right foot with thirty inches of nylon fishing line. A toppled chair close by.

Next came a photocopy of the pathologist's report, six sheets of it. Body believed to be that of William Arthur Monk, retired civil servant, aged approximately sixty years. Height five feet seven and one half inches, weight eight stones and six pounds. Well nourished, etc, no diseases except the usual onslaught of anno domini, incipient arterio-sclerosis, a touch of high blood pressure. Mr Monk ought to have lived for another twenty years, except . . . that he had died of shotgun wounds, self-administered, both barrels in his mouth and the triggers – hair-triggers because both pawls and sears of the firing mechanisms had been filed down until the gun would fire at a touch on the triggers tied together to fire as one, and the other end of the nylon gut looped to fit Mr Monk's big toe, which that gentleman had only to twitch after he had made himself comfortable in his wooden chair beside the fireplace . . . both the top of Mr Monk's head and the cranial contents thereof had been scraped from the parlour ceiling . . . etc.

'And it says here that only Monk's prints were on the gun – and then only around the trigger and the butt.'

'Right,' said Blake.

'But to load a shotgun, you have to break it open,' said Roper. 'Which means he had to grip the barrels. So why no prints on the barrels? And what about the cartridge-cases?'

45

'Clean,' said Blake. 'Not a dab on 'em. Everybody reckoned he'd cleaned the gun and loaded it with gloves on.'

'Carrying hygiene a bit too far, I'd say,' said Roper.

'Aye,' agreed Blake. 'But it all fitted, you see. He was a very tidy man, old Bill Monk. Kept the place like a new pin.'

Roper turned up the next few tattered sheets, another set of photocopies. The verdict of the Coroner's jury, unanimous and a foregone conclusion in the circumstances: suicide while the balance of the victim's mind was disturbed.

The wad of papers closer to the top were Blake's own, copies of memos he had sent subsequently to County Headquarters and one to the Chief Constable, the last dated nearly two years after the inquest. Blake had obviously worried at the case like a terrier, and no one had wanted to listen to what a mere village bobby had to say about it.

Roper scanned the memos, and decided that they were far more interesting than the CID officers of the time had cared to admit.

'When did Monk make his first complaint?' asked Roper.

'About a week after he moved into Box Cottage,' said Blake, around the pipe he was lighting. 'Kept seeing this soldier in his garden.'

'This Ralph Thorn?'

'Couldn't have been, could it?' Blake's face was briefly wreathed in pungent blue smoke. 'He'd been dead over twenty years. His name's on the war memorial up by the church.'

'So someone pretending to be Thorn's ghost,' said Roper. 'Putting the frighteners on Monk.'

'Could have been,' said Blake. 'Except that Bill Monk didn't believe in ghosts. He reckoned it was more than likely an army lad bent on a bit of burglary. Bovington Camp's only three miles up the road. Ten a penny soldiers are, up there.'

'But these soldiers always made sure Monk saw 'em. Burglars don't do that.'

'Right,' said Blake, chewing his pipe from one side of his mouth to the other.

'Did Monk have a shotgun licence?'

Blake shook his head. 'And he wasn't the kind to have a shotgun either. All he ever did was a bit of fishing, and he wasn't much good at that. He was a townie. Retired down here from Streatham. Worked in the Foreign Office. Clerk, I think he was. Nothing fancy.'

'And he filed his next complaint when the rabbit arrived.'

'Throat cut and tied to his doorknocker with a snare-wire,' said Blake. 'And a note. Told him he was dead . . . or very soon would be. Note was pinned to the rabbit with a wooden meat skewer.'

William Arthur Monk's tribulations had continued. His water supply had been turned off at the Water Board's tap on the verge outside the cottage, his downstairs windows had been smeared with blood . . . cow blood. The over-head cables carrying his electricity supply were cut and he awoke one night to find a bonfire blazing in his garden and a chicken tied to a stake in the middle of it and screeching and fluttering in its death throes.

The torment had lasted throughout the winter prior to his death. According to Blake, Mr Monk was of tough stock. He set snares and traps, and bells on lengths of trip-wire. He had bought his retirement cottage and intended to stay in it.

'Could he have bought the shotgun on the sly to protect himself, d'you think?' asked Roper.

'I don't think so, somehow,' said Blake. 'I was up there every other day practically. He used to show me all his precautions, the wires, the bells. He'd even rigged up a net with half a dozen bricks in it in his apple tree. Anybody walked underneath it in the dark . . . and zap! I had to make him take that down before he killed some-body. I got the impression he was even enjoying himself inventing his secret weapons.'

But then Mr Monk's only daughter had died. And two

days later, Mr Monk had ostensibly shot himself. And it was the daughter's death, in a traffic accident in South Shields, that had swayed the jury and not the evidence given at the inquest by Sergeant Blake.

'The old boy was shattered,' said Blake. 'But I know for a fact he was going up for the funeral, because I collected a black suit from the cleaners in Wareham for him. And there were two packed suitcases up in the bedroom when we found him. And only that morning, he'd started work clearing up that rockery at the back of the house. He'd even shown me the packets of seeds he'd sent for. He was going to plant them after the funeral. He told me so that very morning. Before the shotgun business.'

Roper sipped meditatively at his coffee.

'And it had happened before?'

'Twice,' said Blake.

According to Blake, Box Cottage had been part of the Moxley estate, the Moxley family having been the squires of Newby Magna since the middle of the eighteenth century. The First World War had heralded the initial downward slide of the Moxley fortunes and the next war saw them reach rock bottom. In 1947, Old John Moxley sold up and took himself off to Portugal, where he died in 1948.

Before the war, old Moxley's estate manager had been one Ralph Thorn and his home and office had been Box Cottage. In '39 Thorn had volunteered for the army and only returned to the cottage when he had been on leave. The last occasion had been during the Christmas of '43. He had never come back after that, and was now only a name on the village memorial. The first tenant to buy the freehold when Moxley sold the cottage in '47 was a retired schoolteacher from Bristol. She and Tom Blake had arrived in Newby Magna within a few days of each other.

'Florence Gomersall, her name was,' reminisced Blake. 'Lovely old girl. A proper memsahib, she was. Used to ride one of those sit up and beg bikes with a basket on the front. Anybody got taken sick, you'd see Miss Gomersall's bike leaning against their front fence inside the hour.'

If any complaint could ever have been levelled against Miss Gomersall, it could only have been about the perpetual ramshackle state of her garden, front and back. Miss Gomersall had been a devoted nature lover and apart from a small flower bed, and a handkerchief of lawn upon which to open her deckchair, the remainder of her land was made over to the purpose for which God had intended it, or so Miss G. used to say. For the birds, the flowers, the insects and the local rabbit and hedgehog population, Box Cottage remained open house for sixteen years.

Miss Gomersall was finally carried off to hospital in Wareham in the winter of '63 and, like Ralph Thorn, was never seen in Newby Magna again.

'Buried in Weston-super-Mare, old Miss Gomersall was. She must have been eighty, very nearly.'

' . . . And, as I remember, there was a squabble over the old lady's will. Nieces and nephews. Dozens of 'em. I think it all finished up in court. Took a couple of years, and it was the best part of another one before the place was put up for sale again. And nobody wanted it in the state it was in, did they? You'd have needed a machete to hack your way to the front doorstep.'

It was now 1966, reckoned in Newby Magna time as the Year of the Hippies.

'Like a bloody invasion it was,' said Blake. 'Motor bikes, old bangers, a charabanc. Must have been a couple of hundred of 'em.'

For a week, the hippies had swarmed over the village like ants, making camp in one farmer's field after another, lighting their cooking fires wherever the fancy took them and leaving a trail of litter and beer cans and playing their transistor radios at full bore in the small hours and generally making a nuisance of themselves. And then a gang of them discovered Box Cottage empty and decided it was better than sleeping in a makeshift tent in the middle of a field.

'And when the others moved on, that lot stayed. Claimed squatter's rights. About a dozen of 'em. Couldn't shift 'em.'

But a month or so after the main body of hippies had packed their tents and gone, things began to happen in Box Cottage. Smoke bombs in the middle of the night, the chimneys stuffed with wet straw, dead animals with their throats slit found on the kitchen doorstep in the mornings, and one day an iron spring trap with serrated teeth had closed on a girl's leg while she had been picking mint in the back garden. The hippies decamped.

'Did you ever find out who owned the spring trap?' asked Roper.

'Never,' said Blake.

Box Cottage stayed empty, and almost derelict, throughout the following autumn and winter, but was sold at last around the Easter of '67. The new tenants were a retired engineer and his wife from London. Within a week they had called on Blake's services. Three nights running, the wife had seen a figure flitting about the garden. It had looked like a soldier, a soldier from the war, in a khaki battledress and a forage cap, by the cypress trees, staring at the cottage. When she shouted at him, the soldier seemed to disappear into the ground; or so she told Blake. It was from this incident that had sprung the myth of Ralph Thorn's ghost. The couple, however, were not put off. They had the cottage painted and the husband managed to restore the front garden to a semblance of order, cutting the hedges and hacking the grass short enough to run a mower over it. It was when he began to tackle the back garden that the war of nerves began again. Snared rabbits hanging in bushes, wet straw stuffed down the chimney of the range during the night, filling the cottage with coke fumes and putting the wife in hospital for two days. Within a year, the engineer and his wife had moved on.

The cottage stayed empty for two years; until 1970. The next tenant, and the last before Cassandra Murcheson, had

50

been the late Mr Monk, who had died of shotgun wounds by his own hand, or so the Coroner's jury had decided.

'Follows a pattern,' said Roper. 'But if somebody wants Box Cottage to stay empty, why don't they burn it down?'

'No idea,' said Blake, lighting his pipe again. 'But somebody does, and that's for sure.'

CHAPTER 4

Seven o'clock came with a jolt. She had thought it was only five, until she had noticed the distinct reddening of the sky to the west. She had spent the afternoon in a fever of work, her only concession to last night having been to make sure that all the doors and windows downstairs were locked and bolted. The witch of Endor had been transposed to a sheet of white board, her skinny legs astride a vacuum cleaner and her raincoat flapping behind her as she sped through black space in hot pursuit of the mighty Hu-Ra in his intergalactic war-schooner.

Tomorrow she would cut the first of the acetate masks and spray in the black background, but not now, not tonight. It was always best to finish the day on an emotional high, while the creative juices were still flowing. And, besides, she was hungry, her lunch only a snatched cup of coffee and a couple of biscuits and that was hours ago.

When she went downstairs, the kitchen was like a furnace, which was one of the penalties of having the range alight and the kitchen sealed shut on a hot summer evening. She opened the window and wedged the door wide with an old brick to let some air in. It was a beautiful evening, the occasional breath of breeze scented with grass and flowers. Deep down in the garden, a wood pigeon suddenly launched itself skyward from the undergrowth, briefly startling her, and on creaking wings lifted itself over the trees and away towards the setting sun. That was freedom.

With a lighter heart than she had felt in a long time

she bent herself to the practicalities of eating, wondered if her pressure cooker would blow up if she tried it out on the range. It didn't, and while it cooked a couple of potatoes she opened a tin of corned beef and cut up a tomato. And perhaps afterwards she would go for a walk, as far as the village and back, then read for a while and listen to the radio. She was beholden to no one any more.

At eight o'clock she closed the front gate behind her and started towards the village, the evening still balmy, the ground underfoot still exhaling the heat of the day. She walked briskly. Blackbeard's upstairs windows were all open. There were no curtains. His front door, like hers, was greatly in need of a coat of paint. And his tattered hedge hung out over the grass verge. He, too, obviously wasn't houseproud.

Somewhere not too far away, someone was using a lawn-mower. That was something else she would have to buy. And a pair of hedge shears.

The lane steepened and narrowed. The people she met were all walking from the opposite direction and mostly elderly, the men all in suits, the women wearing hats. Of course. It was Sunday. They were coming from church. A few smiled at her, most pretended to ignore her, although she could feel their eyes on her back as soon as she'd passed them.

The hardware shop sold seeds. A lawn-mower was eight pounds fifty, a pair of shears was two pounds thirty-five. There was a scythe in the window too. She had never seen one intact before. There had not been much call for scythes in Ealing.

There were still a few Sunday newspapers hanging up in a rack outside the shop. She bought herself a *Telegraph* and slipped her coins through the letter box.

The old grey church on the other side of the green was Saxon, a graveyard beside it and woodland behind. She wished she'd brought a sketchbook with her. With the golden evening sun slanting across it and the dense black shadows in its porch and deeply recessed windows it screamed out to be committed into a watercolour or two. The vicar, or perhaps he was the curate, was pinning up a poster on the notice-board beside the lychgate. He was wearing bicycle clips under his belted black cassock. And white socks.

She ambled across the lane, towards the granite obelisk of the war memorial on the verge a few yards to the right of the church gate. The upper bronze tablet commemorated the men who had died in the Great War. Arnold J.A., Baker C.G., Bowers K.E., Carpenter B.J., and finally Wilkins A.B. Twenty-six of them. It seemed such a little place to have lost so many young men. In the last war there had only been two. Moxley P.G. and Thorn R.W. The name of Thorn rang a bell . . .

'Hello . . . Miss Murcheson, is it?'

It was the same man who had been pinning up the notice beside the lychgate. He was wheeling a bicycle. Spectacled, bearded, fortyish and earnest.

She returned his smile. News obviously travelled fast in Newby Magna.

'Yes.'

He stuck out his hand. 'Colin Moxley,' he said. 'I'm the incumbent, as they say.'

'How do you do,' she said, resisting the need to flex her fingers when he had finished shaking her hand with a little more enthusiasm than was necessary.

'Looking for a name in particular?'

'No,' she said. 'Just looking. Lovely old church.'

'Yes,' he said, casting a fond eye over it himself. 'Saxon. Stands on the site of a wooden one. Been one here since 970. A couple of the gravestones date back to the first Elizabeth. The scorch marks on the north wall are where the Roundheads made a bonfire of the altar-cloth. It's steeped in history. Absolutely *steeped*.'

She was not too sure what to say next in the face

of such enthusiasm. And the Reverend Moxley seemed disposed to stay.

'There's a Moxley on the war memorial,' she said, for want of something better.

'My father. I was born here, in fact. My grandfather was the last squire. Sold out after the war. And that chap Thorn, down there at the bottom, was my grandfather's bailiff . . . or steward . . . or something. And you live in Box Cottage. . . . Which is where *Thorn* lived. Now *isn't* that a coincidence?'

'Small world,' she observed tritely.

'Yes,' he said. 'Isn't it? It was the newspaper, by the way.'

'I'm sorry?'

'Your newspaper. It isn't opened. So I guessed you'd just bought it. And since you wouldn't have walked from the next village to buy a newspaper at this time of a Sunday evening, I guessed you'd be our new arrival. QED.' The garrulous Mr Moxley beamed hugely through his beard. Cassandra bracketed him as nice, a category into which few men had fallen since the departure of bloody Steven.

'Shades of Father Brown,' she said.

'Father . . . ? Oh, yes . . . the ecclesiastical detective.' Look, she would have to come along and meet his wife. And there was a coffee morning in the church hall every Wednesday. Ten thirty to midday. And a bazaar next Saturday, also in the church hall if the weather was inclement and outside if it held. And there was a drama society, every Friday that was, from seven thirty until whenever, and they were desperately short of victims. And the WI met every other Thursday.

She declined all the offers as gracefully as she could. Had he not taken the cloth Mr Moxley would have made a wickedly efficient salesman.

'I'm down here to work,' she said. 'I shan't have a great deal of time.'

'I say, you don't write, do you? . . . My wife runs a little Poetry Circle . . .'

55

She laughed. 'No, I'm sorry, I don't do that either. I'm a commercial artist. Illustrator. I don't even write letters unless I have to.'

A new light glittered in Moxley's eyes. 'Now *that is* interesting, Miss Murcheson. *That* is *incredibly* interesting.'

Because Mr Moxley was writing a book, oh, quite a modest little volume, a potted history of the church and the village to put on sale with a few postcards in the church porch. A few sheets of foolscap, photocopied and stapled together, with a green paper cover and with a pen and ink drawing on the front, it had to be a pen and ink drawing because photographs didn't photocopy all that well, and perhaps another drawing inside, somewhere in the middle. And there was a mention of Box Cottage in the draft text, perhaps she would like to see a carbon copy of it, the vicarage was only a couple of hundred yards along the way, and she could meet Geraldine at the same time.

She finally slid her doorkey into the lock at a few minutes after ten, a copy of Mr Moxley's history of Newby Magna sticking out of her shoulder bag and a solemn promise made to him to illustrate his little book. There was no hurry, he assured her. He had set himself a deadline for next spring. Geraldine Moxley had been equally breathtaking, tall and lean and angular and effusive, hauling out cheese and biscuits and coffee before Cassie was scarcely in the door. It had been good, though, to talk, and neither Moxley nor his wife had even mentioned religion or enquired if they might expect to see her in church.

She closed the front door and fumbled for the light switch in the passage. The cottage was stiflingly hot and there was a faint smell of coke fumes. That range was really going to have to go, eventually.

She took a leisurely bath and brewed some coffee. Took the coffee into the parlour and spent half an hour browsing through Moxley's draft. It was chatty, like its writer. Newby

Magna was mentioned in the Domesday Book. Twenty-four hides, land for twenty ploughs. Forty villagers and tweenty-five smallholders. Three slaves. One mill at thirty-one shillings and eightpence. Meadows, twenty-one acres; woodland; eighty pigs. Value in entire before 1066, £20. Ranulph Wulfmer holds the church of the manor . . .

The name of Moxley was mentioned several times . . . the present Moxley Hall, now a nursing home, had been built in 1803 . . . during the First and Second World Wars it had been converted into a convalescent hospital for wounded officers . . . Box Cottage . . .

Her downward scanning eyes flicked upward again.

. . . reputedly haunted by the ghost of Ralph Thorn, estate manager to the Moxley family for the decade before the last war. Ralph Thorn was killed during the invasion of Normandy in 1944. Newby Magna's other ghost is that of Lizzie Fisher, executed for witchcraft in 1607 . . .

What rubbish! But she read on and decided that all in all the Reverend Moxley had not done a bad job, and that a couple of lightweight sketches with her name underneath them wouldn't exactly tax her abilities nor take up too much time and might even enhance her standing among the locals. Geraldine Moxley had given her a few plants to put in the rockery. Had that been a hint to tidy up the garden? It was probably the untidiest patch of the village, that garden . . .

At eleven thirty she locked up downstairs. An early night, her first for a week. Cleaned her teeth, got into her pyjamas, couldn't remember if she had shut the studio window before she had gone for her walk, felt the draught as soon as she opened the door and knew that she had left it open, right hand reaching round the door frame for the light switch . . .

Oh, dear God . . . ! Blood . . . No. Not blood.

Someone had splashed an entire pot of scarlet ink all over the walls. And the ceiling.

And the witch of Endor on her vacuum cleaner. And

her drawing-board. And the floor. And all over her new packet of boards. And everywhere else that mattered.

She paced the parlour floor, trembling with black rage. She had succumbed to that last cigarette. It was dry and foul and metallic. But credit where credit was due, the village bobby had got here within minutes of her hauling on the Mini's handbrake after her drive to the telephone box.

'Have you touched anything, Miss?'

'I haven't had bloody time, have I?' she spat back. 'I went straight up to the village and rang you.'

'What time did you go out?'

'Eight o'clock.'

Blake noted that in his pocket-book. 'And you were back when, Miss?'

'Tennish,' she said, irritably, still pacing stiffly. 'Look, Sergeant, that was a day's work up there. It was money in the bank, you know?'

'I do understand, Miss,' he said calmly. 'And I don't like it either. But perhaps if you sat down we could talk about it. Did anyone see you go out?'

'How the hell do I know?'

Blake sighed. 'Put it another way, Miss: who did you see?'

'A few people coming from church. No one I knew. And the vicar.'

'Mr Moxley?'

'There's more than *one*?' she retorted. God preserve her from woolly headed thief-takers.

'Yes, Miss,' replied Blake. 'Mr Moxley and Mr Venables. Mr Venables has retired, but the old boy still reads a lesson from time to time.'

'Mr Moxley,' she said, and felt her anger dissolve about her. 'And his wife.' She perched herself on a plywood tea-chest that was presently doing service as a chairside table. 'And I'm sorry.'

'Quite all right, Miss,' replied Blake equably, still jotting. 'Volunteer you for anything, did he?'

'Yes.'

Blake smiled. 'Then you *definitely* met Mr Moxley. . . . So you were out for two hours. More or less. And didn't shut your back upstairs window.'

'I honestly thought I had.'

'Which is why I asked you if you'd touched anything, Miss.'

'No. I don't think so.' As she recalled, she had stormed into her bedroom, dressed, poured herself into the Mini and driven hotfoot to the kiosk outside the Carpenter's Arms. All she had done after that was storm about and wait for Sergeant Blake to arrive. 'Do you really intend doing anything about all this?' she said.

'Yes, Miss,' replied Blake, gravely. 'I fully intend doing all I can about it, don't you fret yourself.'

He left at a quarter past midnight, having warned her to make sure that all her downstairs doors and windows were shut, and her bedroom door.

The police came at eight o'clock the next morning, Sergeant Blake, the detective inspector who had called yesterday and another plain-clothes man who was carrying a black attaché case.

The Inspector cast an impassive eye around the studio.

'Anything stolen, Miss Murcheson?'

She shook her head. 'I don't think so.'

'Sergeant Blake tells me you might have left the window open when you went out last night.'

'No. I didn't.' She had thought about that for a long time last night. She had *definitely* shut the window before she'd gone out.

'You sure?'

'Positive,' she said.

The other plain-clothes man was over by the window. He had put on a pair of white cotton gloves and was experimenting delicately with the catch and the stay of the left-hand casement.

'Found it, Mr Roper,' he said. 'Near the bottom of the frame. Lead's been levered out with a chisel. Then pressed back again. Down here.' A white finger indicated a diamond-shaped pane halfway between the catch and the stay.

'What does that mean exactly?' asked Cassandra.

'If he's right, it means someone put up a ladder, took a pane of glass out and reached inside,' said Roper. 'And Bob's your uncle. Easy, eh, Miss Murcheson?'

'But why, for Christ's sake?' she exploded angrily. 'I don't even have anything *worth* stealing.'

Roper looked down at her, and she could feel herself being shrewdly assessed.

'Got anywhere you can go for a few days, Miss Murcheson?' he asked at last. 'Friends? Relations? Anything of that sort?'

'I'm not going anywhere, old chum,' she retorted. 'I nearly broke myself paying for this place. Here I am and here I bloody stay. Okay?'

His face stayed set. He looked down at his shoes. 'I think, Miss Murcheson,' he said, gaze slowly coming up again, 'that you and I ought to go downstairs. I think there are a few things you ought to know about this place . . . before you make up your mind.'

'It's made up,' she said. 'I'm not going anywhere.'

He stood aside from the doorway. 'I still think we ought to talk about it, Miss Murcheson.'

Roper watched her come briskly in from the kitchen with two mugs of coffee, her dark hair drawn back into a plastic clip this morning. No lipstick, jeans, a check shirt and white sneakers. And angry. Most other young women in Miss Murcheson's circumstances would be concerned for their safety, but Cassandra Murcheson was clearly made of tougher stuff.

She handed him a mug.

'Thank you,' he said.

She took a sip of her coffee, eyed him four-squarely and for several seconds over the rim of her mug. 'I'm still not sure I believe all this,' she said.

'It's all on the level, Miss Murcheson. Tom Blake's got a file as thick as your wrist on this place.'

'The estate agent never mentioned any of it.'

'No. . . . But he wouldn't, would he?'

She shrugged. 'No, I suppose not.'

A moment of silence. A trapped bee buzzed frenziedly between the window and the net curtains, until it found its way into the garden and the silence fell again.

'Mr Monk could have been murdered, Miss Murcheson.'

'But the inquest said otherwise, didn't it?'

Game to the end was Miss Murcheson, Roper decided, or just plain obstinate. But then so was he.

'So you're going to stick it out?'

'Yes,' she said. 'Bet your life I am. I've poured almost everything I've got into this place.'

A floorboard creaked upstairs; DS Morgan still quartering the studio for fingerprints. Blake was out in the garden, looking for ladder marks.

'Do chief inspectors usually see to piffling little jobs like this?' she asked.

'It isn't piffling, Miss Murcheson. Somebody wants you out of here. Which means you're a threat to somebody.'

'Rubbish,' she retorted scornfully. 'I've never threatened anybody in all my bloody life.'

'Then give me another motive for all this malarky. . . . Just a practical joke, d'you think?'

'It may not happen again. I mean it could just be a flash in the pan, couldn't it? Some lout from the village who gets his kicks out of scaring women.'

'It could be,' agreed Roper. All things were possible, many were probable, and few things, he had long ago learned, were what they seemed. Miss Murcheson had had a dead cockerel left on her back doorstep on Saturday night, on Sunday night her cottage had been criminally entered and a room vandalised. It would be interesting to know what tonight would bring, if it did.

Roper glanced up as Blake came in from the garden. 'Any luck?'

'Two dents in the grass,' said Blake. 'About a foot apart and four feet from the wall. Look like ladder marks.'

Roper put his mug on a tea-chest and levered himself out of the chesterfield. 'Show me.'

Cassandra followed the two of them out to the garden. Blake dropped to his heels beneath the studio window and parted a tuft of grass. Roper crouched beside him. The depression was new, blades of grass ground into it. There was a similar depression a foot or so to the right, and a few flattened areas of grass nearby that might have been footprints.

'Yours?' asked Roper.

'No,' said Blake. 'Mine are the ones close to the wall.'

'Get Sergeant Morgan to take a couple of photographs, and some measurements.'

'Will do.'

'Do you own a ladder, Miss Murcheson?'

She shook her head. She was still standing on the path, tough and resolute; and immovable.

It need not have been much of a ladder, but someone must have carried it from somewhere, and risked being seen if he'd come by way of the lane. So the chances were that he had entered the property from the back, through the tangle of hedge behind those trees; and, if he had been sensible, waited for the dark. And, given that latter premise, he must have known his way about.

'What's at the back?' he asked Blake.

'Just behind the hedge there's a drainage ditch,' said Blake. 'Then another hedge. Then fields.'

'Where does the ditch run from?'

'The village,' said Blake. 'Almost. And it runs down into Colnbrook stream about half a mile east of here.'

'Wet or dry?'

'Dry,' said Blake. 'It takes the floodwater from the fields. Doesn't get filled much before Christmas as a rule, and then only if we have a really wet autumn.'

Roper and Blake went down the path as far as the cypresses. At a distance the hedge had looked impenetrable. A closer examination showed that there were several places near the ground where a small man could have crawled between the roots and hauled a ladder through after him.

'Here, for instance,' said Roper, plucking at the knees of his suit and crouching again. The grass here had recently been trampled down and something hard and heavy had scraped against the bark of the hedge sufficiently roughly to have stripped a patch off and left the bone white sapwood showing a couple of inches above the ground. When Roper put a finger to the scar it was still moist.

He sat back on his heels, elbows on his knees.

'Small man,' he said. It might have been a woman, but he didn't think so. 'A lightweight. And he owns a ladder. And his land probably backs on to that ditch. Anybody we know, d'you think?'

Blake shook his head.

'Could be any one of a couple of dozen,' he said. 'About ten properties back on to that ditch. And there are a couple of places where you can get to it from the side roads.'

'So he drove from somewhere? – or walked from somewhere? – with a ladder? – late on a Sunday night, just to leave his mark? Not on your life, Tom. It wouldn't have been worth the risk, would it?'

'Depends on the motive,' said Blake.

Roper rose. If he was right, the motive was a long-standing one. It had been sufficient to scare off two other tenants, and the hippies, and perhaps led to the death of Mr Monk. Only the schoolteacher, Miss Gomersall, had been allowed to live in peace at Box Cottage. What had rendered her beneath the villain's notice was still not clear, perhaps she had not posed a threat like the others, whatever that threat was; or perhaps the threat had not existed during Miss Gomersall's time, but only later.

'I want a map, Tom,' said Roper. 'Large scale. One that shows the ditch from end to end. And marked up to show which landowner owns what house and field on either side of it. Can you fix that?'

'Give me an hour,' said Blake.

'And tell Morgan I want him down here with a camera and tape measure.'

With another coffee and a cigarette . . . her last one, she had promised herself . . . she watched from the parlour window as the arcane fan dance went on down the garden. The detective sergeant was on his stomach in the grass and taking a photograph of something under the hedge while the inspector crouched beside him talking. What they were talking about she didn't know. Sergeant Blake had gone off somewhere in his car. It all looked very businesslike, but she couldn't help wondering if they were actually *doing* anything or merely trying to reassure her that they were taking her seriously. Although she thought the Inspector was. He looked the sort who would turn every last stone, and he was excruciatingly polite. A bedside manner, she supposed.

She watched them walk slowly back, the Inspector with a stick he had picked up somewhere and with which he was pushing aside the grass ahead of him like a park-keeper ready to spike up litter. Beside the apple tree he stopped and pointed down with the stick. The Sergeant bobbed down on his heels and sighted his camera at whatever it was, rose again, and the two of them stood for a minute or two with their heads together and occasionally glancing at the upstairs windows. She found it infuriating, and would have given her eye-teeth to be able to lip read.

When they came in, the two of them knocking grass from the soles of their shoes against the back door step, they were no more forthcoming.

'Have you found anything?'

'No, Miss, not a great deal,' said the Inspector.'Except that we think we know how jack the lad got into your garden. That ditch along the back.'

'You mean you're guessing, or you know?'

'It's all a guess at this stage, Miss Murcheson. But we'll be in touch.'

She saw them out. This had been going to be the day of the Great New Start, the day she had promised herself and Paul Criddle that she would be getting down to work again. It looked unlikely.

Blackbeard called so soon after the police had driven away that she was almost convinced that he must have been watching from one of his upstairs windows. He was still wearing his bump with the crust of dried blood over it. He had a parcel under his arm, flat and about three feet by two and wrapped in newspaper.

'I saw the police rummaging about in the garden,' he said. 'I came along to see if you were all right.'

'Yes,' she said. 'I'm fine.' Then almost in the same breath immediately changed her mind. 'No. I'm *not* fine. Somebody broke in here last night.'

'What? Again?' His concern looked genuine. 'I'm sorry. Not much of a welcome, is it?'

'I didn't think much of it myself.'

'Anything stolen?'

'No. They just left the place in a bloody mess.'

'Vandals.'

'Yes,' she said. 'Probably.'

He stood diffidently for a moment. Then took the makeshift parcel from under his arm and held it out.

'Something for the parlour wall,' he said, offering it to her. 'If you don't like it, I'll go back and fetch another one. Or you can come along and pick one for yourself. I've got plenty.'

As she took it, she felt a picture frame through the

65

paper. It was difficult to be gracious. Over the last few years, apart from her father, few people had ever given her anything that they hadn't taken back again.

'Thank you,' she said. She assumed it was a peace offering of some sort, and supposed she ought to make a gesture of her own. 'Look, I'm still in an unholy mess in here, but if you'd like a cup of coffee you're more than welcome.'

'No,' he said. 'It's okay, thanks. . . . And if you don't like the picture, just say. I'm hard to offend.'

She watched him go back down the path, returned his curt wave as he closed the gate behind him and went from sight behind the hedge.

She opened the parcel on the kitchen table. She had half expected a print or a ghastly amateur landscape of some sort. Only it was neither. It was a Constable . . . no, of course, it couldn't *possibly* be . . . but it certainly *looked* like one. A lush landscape of trees, with a church in the foreground . . . the church along the lane, with the evening sun on it, the way she had seen it last night except that there was no war memorial in front of it and the old cottages in the distance didn't have TV aerials strapped to their chimneys. The whole was in an ornate gilt frame. And only the smell of linseed that came from it, and the fact that it did not bear a signature, showed that it wasn't an original but a masterly pastiche. And she wondered if Blackbeard had painted it himself. The frame alone had to be worth ten pounds at least and it looked like an antique, repaired here and there, but skilfully done.

She had never been a great fan of Constable, but a tentative trial against the parlour wall gave a splash of much needed colour, and even a touch of homeliness against the raw whiteness. She thumped the wall with the heel of her hand. It felt hollow. Probably lath and plaster. Which meant that if she was careful she could knock a nail in without too much trouble. She had hammered in all the nails back at Ealing. Bloody Steven had also been pretty nearly helpless when it came to DIY.

She sighted up the picture and marked the wall more or less at the point where the nail was going in, collected a hammer and a suitably hefty nail and drew a wooden chair close to the wall to stand on.

The first two taps sent hairline cracks radiating out from the nail point, the third drove it in unexpectedly to the head and the hammer dented the plaster. No matter, the picture would cover it. She reversed the hammer and yanked the claw into the plaster to hook it behind the nail head. It took her three attempts, each more vicious than the one before, before she finally managed to get the vee of the claw behind the head of the nail. Her first upward heave was fruitless. The nail did not budge and the dent in the plaster deepened and showered crusty white fragments over her feet; and revealed not wooden laths but old red bricks, and with another curse at the recalcitrant inanimate she reversed the direction of the hammer handle and threw all her weight downward on it.

The nail gave, and so did a square foot of plaster and bricks that exploded all over her. And her upper front teeth arranged themselves on her lower lip to hiss the only possible expletive suitable for the occasion.

But she never uttered it.

There was a face looking out of the hole. And there was hair, blonde hair. Only it was not quite a face. A lot of it was missing.

'Jesus,' she whispered softly, and on buckling legs climbed down from the chair before she fell from it.

CHAPTER 5

She had to hand it to the man; Blackbeard had been
a tower. He had driven into the village on his moped,
telephoned the police for her, and then made her a mug
of thick black coffee while the two of them waited in the
parlour for the police to come. Sergeant Blake had arrived
shortly afterwards, and then Chief Inspector Roper and his
assistant and, just now, a civilian, a doctor Something or
Other, and a young woman with a briefcase and another
man, presumably another detective, who had brought up
the rear with what had looked like a bag of carpenter's
tools.

'What d'you think they're doing now?'

Blackbeard cocked an ear to the racket going on in
the parlour. 'I'd say they were knocking the wall down,
wouldn't you?'

The operation, however, was a little more delicate than a
clumsy demolition job. The area of floor beneath the hole
in the wall had been cleared of furniture and a tarpaulin
sheet laid over it to catch the debris of plaster as it was
carefully chipped away to reveal the bricks beneath and
the hideous thing that was wedged behind them. Doctor
Something or Other was Dr Weygood, a Home Office
pathologist, the young woman who had accompanied him
was his assistant and the man who had followed her into the
cottage with the bag of tools was the Coroner's Officer who
had collected the tools from County Headquarters on his
way here. It was DS Morgan who was presently wielding

68

a hammer and cold chisel to chip the plaster away down to the skirting board.

'How long d'you think, Doctor?' asked Roper, as Weygood came up beside him in his white overalls and tugging on the second of his rubber gloves.

'Years, I should think,' said Weygood tartly, tucking the cuff of his overall into the wrist of the glove. Dr Weygood was not pleased to be here. He had been about to tee off on the eighteenth hole, and for the first time in his golfing life had only been six over par. And then the clubhouse telephone had rung. Dr Weygood was not a happy man at this precise moment. 'Years and bloody years.'

'It's in fair condition,' observed Roper.

Weygood sniffed. 'Mummified,' he said. 'If we handle it properly we might get it out in one piece.' From his tone, it sounded to Roper as if Weygood cared not a jot one way or the other.

'I still haven't figured out why it's so high up,' Roper said to Blake.

'I can't, either,' said Blake.

But as Morgan wielded his chisel steadily downward it soon became obvious that the bricks half a dozen courses from the floor were far older than the ones that had already been stripped of plaster, and whereas the newer ones were clumsily laid, the old ones had been laid by someone who had known his business. They were also smaller, yellower bricks, and the mortar between them had been mixed with more lime, in the old way. The woman had been bricked up in what had once been a shallow cupboard, or perhaps a recess in the wall to take a few wooden shelves. And yet, surely, the wall was not thick enough to hide a body between this face and the face in the kitchen.

Roper paced from the parlour window wall to the vertical edge of the new bricks. Two and a half paces.

Then he went into the kitchen. Murcheson was sitting in a chair by the range and Cambridge, the neighbour, was

69

standing over her and holding a match to a cigarette that she was holding between trembling fingers.

He backed against the outside wall, then took two and a half paces forward. They brought him in line with the green wooden door of the pantry.

'Do you mind if I look inside this, Miss Murcheson?'

'Do what you like,' she said. 'Frankly, I don't give a damn.'

The side walls of the pantry were of brick and plaster, and the outside about two feet six deep. But the inside was shallow. Only eighteen inches at most. Roper reached in and tapped the rear wall. It looked solid enough, but sounded hollow. It was wood, tongued and grooved planking papered over and painted white, and here and there the paper was split. Running a finger across it he could feel the vertical joins between the planks underneath the splits in the paper. Under the top layer of paper, there seemed to be several others.

He returned to the parlour. Morgan was levering out more bricks around the hole, Weygood fussing about him irritably and muttering, 'Steady, man. Mind what you're doing. We want it *out*, not *in*!'

Morgan levered the brick out and handed it down to Blake who put it to one side on the tarpaulin. The mortar was weak and crumbly, and four more bricks quickly followed the first on to the tarpaulin.

'That'll do,' said Weygood. His assistant passed him a torch and he climbed on to the chair as Morgan stepped down from it. He shone the torch into the hole. 'White,' he said. 'Blonde. The roots are dark so it's probably peroxide. Her front teeth are all her own. Good condition. Somewhere between twenty and forty. Dehydrated. Tissues of left cheek missing between molar and lower ridge of mandible; disintegrated, I'd say. Anno domini.' The torch clicked as Weygood switched it off, and he climbed down from the chair. 'What I can't make out,' said Weygood. 'Is why she's still upright.'

'No, sir,' said Roper. 'I can't either.' Because, once rigor mortis has passed, a dead body is about as stiff as a rag-doll, and even though it was wedged into the tight space between the wooden planks and the bricks that particular body should have subsided by now. And it hadn't.

Morgan, back on the chair, chiselled at crumbling mortar and extended the hole downward, still passing each brick down to Blake to stack with the others on the tarpaulin. While Weygood's wrath began to abate in the face of his professional interest.

She . . . it, was wearing a red woollen coat with a tie belt, with shoulder pads, very wide and high. Apart from some dust on the shoulders, the coat was as new as the day it was bought, and as vividly red. The blonde bedraggled hair was shoulder length. A string of pearls, probably fake, hung around the shrivelled flesh of the neck that looked as brittle to the touch as old parchment. The length of rope around her chest was at first a mystery, across the chest of the coat and beneath her armpits and obviously knotted behind her. It was Morgan reaching into the hole and feeling about inside who resolved the mystery.

'She's lashed to a piece of timber,' he said to Roper. He reached lower. 'And the belt of her coat's tied to it as well.'

Morgan widened the hole and then began to work downward again. She had worn stockings. Nylons. And chunky, high-heeled black shoes. Wartime, thought Roper. His mother had had a coat like that, and a pair of shoes exactly like that. Bought with ration coupons that were even more precious than money in those days. The nylons would have been equally hard to come by. And the coat was quality. And the white dress underneath was silk. Parachute silk; silk dresses usually were in those days. Black market parachute silk. Precious stuff and only worn for high days and holidays.

'Enough,' said Weygood, and took Morgan's place at

the hole and shone his torch about. 'I suggest you take a good look now, Mr Roper, or forever hold your peace. Once we try to move her she'll probably crumble to dust.' He stood aside and handed Roper the torch.

The nyloned ankles had given way and the shoes with the feet inside them were set at an obscenely wrong angle; the flesh was wrinkled at one side and split at the other. The only smell was a musty one. There was no sign of a wound, at least at the front of the coat. Perhaps, if there was one, it was at the back.

And then Roper saw the dusty handbag, to the left of the feet and up against the front corner of the aperture where Morgan had still to attack. He reached in carefully for it.

'You okay?' asked Blackbeard, his hand briefly squeezing her shoulder as he passed behind her to put the kettle on the camping stove again.

'I'm nearly out of cigarettes.'

'They'll stunt your growth.'

'I don't give a monkey's.'

He offered to drive back to the village and get her another packet. But she preferred him nearer than that. The warm hand that had just squeezed her shoulder had not been unpleasant. He was the first man to touch her since bloody Steven.

'Did you paint that picture yourself?'

'Yes,' he said.

'Is that what you do? Knock out fakes?'

'Not fake,' he said. 'More "in the style of".'

'That a living?'

'No,' he said, shrugging as he swilled out the mugs under the tap. 'But it gets me by.'

'I don't even know what your name is . . . your first one.'

'Edward. . . . Ted.'

'I'm Cassandra . . . Cass . . . What d'you think they're doing in there now? It's gone very quiet.'

72

'Dozing, perhaps?'

She smiled thinly. 'God, I hope not. I want them out of here. *And* that bloody corpse.'

Wearing a pair of white cotton gloves, Roper had unclipped the brass clasp of the crocodile-skin handbag and one by one was carefully removing its contents and laying them out on top of a tea-chest. A linen handkerchief, still folded as if it had just come off the ironing board, a yellow silk M monogrammed into a corner. Another handkerchief used and crumpled. A powder compact, gilt with a mother-of-pearl inlay on the lid, a cylinder of lipstick, a diminutive phial of perfume – Californian Poppy, God, it was years since he had seen the newspaper advertisements for that stuff; three interwoven safety pins. A cellophane packet of Woolworth's hairclips; two missing. A jeweller's leatherette ring-box, lined with blue velvet, empty. A red leather purse with two brown ten-shilling notes inside it and some silver and copper coins, and tucked between the coins the return half of a green Southern Railway train ticket, from London Victoria to Brighton, dated May the 27th, but no year.

He gently eased open the zip-fastener of the central compartment and found treasure trove. A half-used sheet of clothing coupons. A wartime buff identity card with frayed corners. He opened it as carefully as he had inched back the zip. The M was for Marjorie. Steadman, Marjorie Alice. 18 Elliston Crescent, Brighton, Sussex. Born 18/2/24.

Ergo: she was no longer an *it*. She was the late Miss Marjorie Alice Steadman, done in and stashed away by person or persons unknown, and a very long time ago.

A black and buff ration book bore the same name and address. Issued at the office of the Ministry of Food in Brighton, January 1944. A half, roughly, of its coupons either cancelled with a rubber stamp or an indelible pencil, or clipped out. She had last used her meat coupons during Week 21, whenever Week 21 was. A complete sheet of clothing coupons tucked away inside, black market, probably, like her nylon stockings. What nobody had in those days, unless they were naughty, was two sheets of clothing coupons at a time.

'Would you give us a hand, Mr Roper?'

Weygood was waiting to take the body down. Sergeant Morgan looked decidedly queasy.

'Here,' said Weygood. 'You'll want these.' Morticians' gloves, red ones, elbow length. Roper took off his jacket, draped it over a chair back, and tugged the red gloves over the cotton ones.

'How about photographs?' he asked Morgan, as he drew on the gloves. 'Got enough?'

'About a dozen.'

'Good.'

He and Weygood would take the foot end of the wooden plank to which the body was tied, Blake and Morgan the head end. ' . . . and we'll take it out *feet* first. And get the board horizontal as quickly as we can. And *gently* on to the rubber sheet. Now, as I *say* . . . lift!'

They lifted. One of the feet crumbled away from the ankle and hung there in the nylon stocking.

'Now *out*! . . . Slowly . . . *slowly*!'

The foot slid sideways and hung over the plank, swinging like a pendulum in the stocking. The shoe clattered to the floor. Roper heard Morgan's gorge rise.

'Steady . . . steady . . . '

There was hardly any weight beyond that of the plank. Roper had read somewhere once that even the Archbishop of Canterbury was sixty-odd per cent water. Miss Steadman, desiccated, weighed next to nothing.

'Does *somebody* have an eye on that foot?'

Roper reached across for it and held it aside as the very late and very dead Miss Steadman, still lashed to the plank, was finally laid on the rubber sheet.

'Right, gentlemen,' said Weygood. 'Now you can look all you wish.'

Like a tender lover, Roper untied the belt of the red coat and unfastened the three large buttons. Weygood cut the rope across the chest with a scalpel. Roper parted the coat.

He grimaced.

Marjorie Steadman had died of a single shotgun wound. Discharged within a few inches of her chest. A single hole that had ripped through skin and bone. A bloodstained circular felt patch stuck to the shattered breast bone had been the shot's wadding. Powder scorches on the dress and around the wound. Not a great deal of bloodstaining, considering; red once, black now, with grey edges. She had probably been blasted off her feet. Death would have been almost instantaneous.

Some powder marks and scorches just inside the lapels of the coat. So she had been wearing it. Open. So she had probably just been going out somewhere. Or had just come back from somewhere. Perhaps she had just arrived from Brighton, except that her train ticket would have only taken her to London – or was there another ticket somewhere? No one would ever know. Marjorie Steadman had been dead for too long for interest in her murder to be anything more than academic. Which was a very great pity.

While Weygood and the Coroner's Officer made copious notes and discussed the arrangements for the body's removal to the mortuary, Roper returned to the time capsule in the handbag. What he drew out next looked like a wallet, but it was a photograph holder, leather, fitted with two sheets of thin glass. Under one was a snapshot of a man and a woman, he coy, she looking as if she had a smell under her nose, posing on a white step in a doorway, and, just perceptible in the shadows behind them, an aspidistra in a pot on a bamboo table, and a flight of stairs. A terraced house. Roper wondered if it might be the house in Elliston Crescent. Number 18. The other snapshot was of a soldier, forage-capped and battledressed, the three pips of a captain on his shoulders. Big chap. Good-looking by any standards, and he'd known it. All his front teeth on show and his chin up, booted feet astride and hands behind his back clutching his swagger cane. Marjorie Steadman's wartime boyfriend, or lover, or whatever. It would be interesting to know what regiment he had been in, but the badge on his raffishly tilted forage cap had been photographed from end on. The background was the same terraced house. So he might have been her brother. Or perhaps she had taken him home to show him off to Mum and Dad during one of his leaves. Nothing tucked behind the photographs. Pity.

A buff envelope. Sealed. Unaddressed. Something inside it. He held it up to the window. Something . . . definitely . . .

He slit it open. A mint-new marriage certificate. Brighton Registry Office, May 27th, 1944, the date when Miss Marjorie Alice Steadman, Spinster, of 18 Elliston Crescent, Brighton had changed her name and title and married her handsome captain.

Thorn, Ralph Edmund, Captain, Wessex Yeomanry, c/o Box Cottage, Malt Lane, Newby Magna, Dorset.

'How do you feel, Miss Murcheson?'
'I'm okay. Really.'
She didn't look it.
'I can have a doctor here in ten minutes.'
She shook her head.
'Perhaps you ought to spend a few days with a relative.'
'I'm not leaving. Too much work to do.'
'You're in shock, Miss Murcheson.'
'I'll get over it.'
And she probably would, but certainly not today and certainly not tomorrow. And the worst time would be in the dead hours tonight. It wasn't every day that a young woman found a body bricked up in her parlour.
'I've suggested she comes along to my place,' said

Cambridge. He was at the range, putting the kettle on for more coffee.

'I think that's a good idea, don't you, Miss Murcheson?' said Roper.

But she wasn't having that, either. 'All I want to know is how much longer that thing next door is going to be here.'

'About a quarter of an hour. There's a van on its way.'

'Thank God for that,' she said. Then she relaxed a little. 'I don't suppose you've got a cigarette, have you?'

'I smoke cheroots. But you're welcome.' He fished out his cheroot packet and lighter. She plucked a cheroot from the packet and he struck his lighter.

'Don't inhale,' he said. 'It's certain death.'

She smiled. She was almost pretty when she smiled.

She took in a mouthful of smoke and let it seep slowly out again. 'Do you know who she was?'

'A Mrs Thorn,' said Roper, tucking his lighter away. 'I found a brand new wedding certificate in her handbag.'

'A man called Thorn used to live here. Ralph Thorn.'

'Yes,' said Roper. 'Sergeant Blake told me. He was killed in the war.'

'Perhaps he comes back to look for her.'

'Yes,' said Roper, smiling. 'Very likely. Or maybe he even killed her.'

'And we'll never know.'

'No,' said Roper. 'I very much doubt it.'

'You won't investigate'

'Shouldn't think so. The marriage certificate was dated only a couple of weeks before Thorn died. And she died either before he did, or soon afterwards. She had a ration book, you see. For that year. 1944.'

'Ah.' She understood. She was old enough to remember ration books, and identity cards and all the other paraphernalia that went with them.

Cambridge brewed up more coffee. Roper took a mixed selection of mugs on a tin tray back to the parlour. Mrs

Thorn, née Steadman, was now merely a lump under a red rubber sheet. A couple of days in the air and what flesh remained on her bones would be turned to dust.

By one o'clock of the afternoon, the body was across at the mortuary and Roper and DS Morgan were alone in the cottage. Cassandra Murcheson had finally been cajoled by Cambridge to walk along to the Carpenter's Arms for a drink.

Morgan was making a dimensional sketch of the recess in the wall on a new page of his notebook. Roper, his behind perched on the arm of the chesterfield, was smoking a cheroot.

Every foot or so up the sides of the recess were wooden blocks, clearly shelf supports once, secured to the wall by way of iron flooring nails and whittled wooden plugs. Where the shelves were now was anybody's guess. The recess was about two feet wide, the sides, top and floor plastered, the plaster hacked away near the front to provide a key for the mortar and plaster for the subsequent bricking-up operations.

And Roper knew that the case was a dead one before an investigation had even got off the ground. Mrs Ralph Thorn had been dead for thirty years. She was history, NFA scrawled across her file. No Further Action. She had lived for a mere twenty years, according to her marriage certificate, which wasn't, in Roper's book, exactly a fair deal for anybody, regardless of the circumstances, whatever she had done to deserve it, and even if she had.

A wartime marriage that had gone wrong. Plenty had. If Thorn had killed her, then the two of them had only been at the honeymoon stage. A marriage in Brighton, perhaps a hasty one, then a train up to London and another one from London down to Dorset, then *bang*! Then Thorn goes back off leave and gets himself killed in Normandy. Case closed. If he'd been found out, it had been a hanging charge in those days. But a war had been

78

going on for the best part of five years and people went missing all the time, and nobody had noticed the going of poor Marjorie Steadman, or, if they had, their complaint had probably long since been consigned to the archives.

'I reckon it was a bookcase,' said Morgan. 'That hole.'

'Could have been,' agreed Roper. 'Big books, though.'

'If he was an estate manager, he'd have had account books and ledgers, wouldn't he? They're big, as a rule.'

'Yes,' said Roper. 'Right.' And Morgan probably was, but Roper was more interested in the late Marjorie Steadman, and the tiny slice of history encompassed by the contents of her crocodile-skin handbag, and why she had died and what might have happened in Box Cottage one night – or day - between Ration Book Week 21 and D-Day, 1944. He himself had been ten years old, still in short trousers, but the war was still a vivid memory burned in, always would be.

And whether Marjorie Steadman was decreed NFA or not, Roper would have given his eye-teeth to piece together whatever cataclysmic event had taken place at Box Cottage in 1944. Had she lived, she would still have been barely fifty. Someone somewhere knew her. Friends, relations, old boyfriends, neighbours. Someone would remember her, perhaps even had a photograph of her. It wasn't all that long, thirty-two years, in the scheme of things.

'I'm fit if you are, gov,' said Morgan, breaking in again.

'Yes,' said Roper. 'I've done too. You get the gear back into the car. As soon as Miss M. comes back, we'll shove off.'

Roper climbed into the Escort beside Morgan. It was half past one.

'D'you reckon she will spend the night there?' asked Morgan, sorting through his keys.

'From what I've seen so far, I don't doubt it,' said Roper.

'Rather her than me,' said Morgan, as he slid in the ignition key. 'Gives me the creeps, that place.'

* * *

79

It gave Cassandra Murcheson the creeps too, and by half past nine that night, with the dark slowly enfolding the cottage and the woodwork creaking, she began to wish that she had taken up Blackbeard's offer – his sofa or his bed, and a key to the door for whichever room she chose. She tried to read, upstairs, of course; the Inspector had asked her to stay out of the parlour at least until tomorrow lunchtime. Which had not proved, so far, to be difficult. She could not, in fact, have dragged herself in there if she had tried. Perhaps tomorrow, or next week, she could have that ghastly recess bricked up again. But she would always know, always remember.

She kept glancing down into the garden – the plain-clothes sergeant had carried the chesterfield upstairs for her – and at some indeterminate time realised that she could no longer see the branches waving against the sky and that she was in full view of whoever might be lurking down there. Which was ridiculous, because nobody was lurking down there, but her imagination was running at full stretch tonight and she was even too scared to go downstairs and make herself a cup of coffee, which was equally ridiculous because all the windows were shut and locked and Blackbeard had put a bolt on the back door and the front door was bolted as well and the whole place was sealed up like a fortress.

She lit another cigarette, her thirtieth today. It tasted dry and dusty and the print she was trying to read had begun to blur and her eyes stung. She *had* to have a drink, she *had* to go downstairs, she *had* to snap out of this futile, mindless state. Tomorrow she would have to drive into Dorchester and find an art shop and buy some new boards. She *had* to work . . .

She reached the landing. All the lights were switched on downstairs, but they didn't help. There seemed to be shadows where there hadn't been last night . . .

At the bottom of the stairs, she kept a tight grip on the finial of the newel post. Then her heart started bumping faster and harder and fear gripped her stomach like a mailed fist because there was someone on the front step not a yard away behind the flimsy door and what sounded like a set of knuckles was rapping softly on it, and her legs wouldn't move like the running away nightmare she had had over and over as a child and there was a pale shape – a face, trying to peer in through the single lozenge pane of glass, and when her voice came at last it almost choked her . . .

'Who is it?'

'Ted,' a muffled voice growled back from the other side of the door. 'Ted Cambridge.'

And with trembling hands and relief bubbling up inside her like gas in a bottle of lemonade she was shooting back the door bolts and taking the catch off the Yale. And he'd got a sleeping-bag under his arm, and was carrying a bottle of Guinness and a book and she had never been gladder to see a man in all her born days . . .

'Sorry,' he said, stepping in and past her. 'I'm bedding down in your kitchen tonight. If you've any objections you can make them in the morning. Okay?'

'Jesus,' she said. 'You're a bloody gem, you know that?' And there was a sharp prickling behind her eyes that was difficult to stave off and only just was she able to fight off the equally strong temptation to fling her arms around him and kiss him, beard or no beard and hairy chest or not.

'Good,' he said. 'Fancy sharing a beer?'

CHAPTER 6

Roper was in his office at seven the next morning, an hour early. There was a raft of paperwork to clear, a court appearance at eleven thirty; and tomorrow he was off on a week's leave, a few days of *dolce far niente*, driving around the county looking for the odd bargain or two in the antique shops or wherever else he happened to find them.

He plugged in the electric kettle and lit his first cheroot of the day and hung his jacket over the back of his chair.

By eight o'clock, he had ploughed through a third of the paperwork, by a quarter past nine three-quarters of it, and if nobody committed another felony before ten o'clock, he might with luck find the bottom of his in-tray. From time to time he suffered the intrusion of yesterday's affair at Box Cottage. Last night it had nagged at him like a hollow tooth. His Super was inclined to drop the case. It was thirty years old, and, like Roper, he had guessed that the murderer had been Ralph Thorn, dead himself now for as long.

'We'll wait and see what Weygood comes up with, eh, Douglas?' It wasn't worth the trouble, his tone had hinted, go away, I don't want to know.

But Roper *did* want to know. He had never put his hand to anything and then dropped it halfway through. It wasn't his style, and the discovery of a murder from thirty years ago was given to few. It fascinated him, it was history, there had been somebody once called Marjorie Steadman, in the round and breathing; and at half past nine, the remainder of the paperwork briefly put aside, he was spreading across his blotter the glossy coloured photographs that DS Morgan had taken yesterday at Box Cottage. Weygood was starting his post-mortem examination about now. It would, indeed, be interesting to see what he came up with.

She hadn't eaten a proper breakfast in years. Eggs, bacon, tomatoes, a slice of bread as thick as a doorstep and still warm enough from the baker's oven for the butter to melt on top of it. Blackbeard had woken her at ten o'clock. He had already been up to the village on his moped for the bread and a newspaper. She was in the papers this morning, although she had seen no reporters as yet. She supposed the police had told somebody.

'Food okay?' he said, putting a mug of tea at her elbow.

'Great,' she said. She was to cooking what Florence Nightingale had been to the space race, and cheerfully owned to it. They had talked into the small hours last night. She had shown him a few of her sketches and samples, and he'd said she was *bloody* good and he hadn't talked the usual arty crafty claptrap about composition and line, but about selling the work you turned out and all the shysters that littered the way and gave you twenty pounds for something you'd taken a month to knock out then sold it for nearer a hundred without doing anything but put it on show in a window. And she had told him about her Dad – and bloody Steven. Blackbeard's last woman had left him with eight of his best pictures. He had been living just outside Bristol then. He had moved next door soon afterwards, and kept his nose clean since. Back in February, he'd had the luck to get a portrait commission, but there had been no other commissions since. On average, he earned about twenty pounds each for the copies he churned out. The Impressionists mostly. Degas, Lautrec, Monet, that sort of thing. It was a living.

'I'm going into Dorchester this morning,' he said. 'Anything you want?'

'I thought of going in myself, if you fancy a lift.'

He fancied a lift. Nor was he too proud to let her treat him to a pub lunch. When they banded up again at two o'clock, she had bought her boards and he had managed to find a couple of second-hand canvases in a junk shop. He had also had a haircut and his beard trimmed, and looked a damned sight better for both.

Roper tidied his desk. All that had been in his in-tray was now stacked up in the out-tray, his desk calendar was set for eight days hence and the contents of his ashtray were now in the waste bin. It was six o'clock in the evening, the sun was shining and he could taste freedom in the air. He would see no more of this cramped little office for a week, was locking the right-hand side of his desk and dropping his keys back into his pocket when the knuckles rapped briskly on the glass panel of the office door. He did not recognise the silhouette . . .

'Come in!'

Praise be, it was Dr Weygood, a slightly more enthusiastic Weygood than Roper remembered from yesterday, his young lady assistant behind him in the passage.

'Oh, . . . you were just off, Mr Roper. . . . I'm sorry.'

'No, sir. Come in,' urged Roper, already pulling up another chair to the front of his desk. It wasn't often that HO pathologists paid calls on humble chief inspectors. He rang downstairs for a pot of tea and three cups and saucers while Miss Mead delved deeply into her briefcase and brought out a mass of papers of assorted sizes which she passed across to Weygood's lap as that gentleman hooked on a pair of half-moon reading glasses.

'I haven't been able to come up with much, Mr Roper,' Weygood conceded, riffling through the papers. ' . . . But Josie here, Miss Mead, is fairly sure that the dress the body was wearing was a wedding dress.'

84

'Therefore,' Weygood went on, 'if it was, we have a date of death. A most precise one, in fact.'

'The 27th of May, 1944?'

'Exactly,' said Weygood.

The train ticket in Mrs Thorn's handbag had been dated May 27, easy now to fill in the year.

'What was she shot with?'

'The gunsmith says the wadding patch was definitely from a twelve-bore. Fired from about a foot away.'

Mr Monk, Roper recalled, had shot himself with a twelve-bore.

From his papers, Weygood sorted out a wad of photographs, hastily printed but good enough for the time being, and handed them across the desk. The clothes had had to be cut from the body piece by piece and reassembled with pins. Above the loop of the coat was the wartime Utility Mark: CC41, on a white cotton label. A photograph of Mrs Thorn's – although Roper still thought of her as Marjorie Steadman of Brighton – Mrs Thorn's shrivelled left hand showed both a diamond engagement ring and a gold wedding ring. Her few items of underwear were also made of parachute silk, lace edged, probably home sewn. Both her handbag and shoes, Miss Mead guessed, were pre-war. The shoes were too well put together for wartime and bore no utility mark. They might even have been Mrs Thorn's mother's. The crocodile-skin handbag was genuine hide. It would have cost at least five pounds, even before the war. A week's average wages then, or perhaps more; two weeks for some.

The photographs of Marjorie Steadman's body, naked and crumbling apart on Weygood's table, were stomach churning enough to only skim through. Most of the dead bodies Roper had seen in the last twenty years had either been still warm or had at least looked like human remains. Poor Miss Steadman, dead at twenty, had been in her makeshift tomb for thirty-odd years, and looked like it. It was only the abundance of bleached blonde hair that proclaimed she might have once been a woman, and perhaps pretty on her wedding day, which, fate had decreed, had also been her last day, poor girl.

Miss Mead proposed that Mrs Thorn must only just have arrived from Brighton that day, because of the train ticket, still in the wedding dress, which surely she would have taken off within an hour of arriving at the cottage. And perhaps there had *been* no wedding reception, but she and her husband had got straight on to the train after leaving the registry office. The food shortages of the war and the haste of the marriage often precluded receptions in those days.

She was very bright was Miss Mead, decided Roper.

'She was also pregnant,' said Weygood. 'Can't tell you how long. But I guess somewhere between eight and ten weeks.'

Which would have made the wedding even hastier, especially in the stricter moral climate of 1944. Perhaps even a shotgun wedding, in the euphemistic sense, and Thorn had not wanted to go through with it.

'There would have been luggage,' proposed Miss Mead. 'She would have had a suitcase at least, wouldn't she?'

Yes, she would have, thought Roper. And where was it? No young woman went on her honeymoon without a change of clothes, even in wartime.

Over their cups of tea, Weygood read out the gist of his notes. Mrs Thorn had died of a shotgun blast straight into her heart. Several lead pellets, deflected by the bones of her rib-cage, had entered her left lung and upper left top of her liver. The shot had disintegrated her sternum, but from the small amount of blood staining on her dress and the lining of her coat she had died instantaneously. Her last meal might have been a tomato sandwich; there had been tomato seeds in her upper bowel.

But, of course, it was hardly worth pursuing an investigation; her putative killer was dead himself, and had been for many a long year. Carbon dating was possible, but it would take six weeks at least and was an expensive operation and would take up valuable time while the experts could be doing something more useful. There was no statute of limitation on murder investigations, Weygood knew that, of course, but thirty years . . . well . . . it was a *very* long time, wasn't it? And he was really not disposed to continue with the matter any further unless he had instructions to the contrary from the Home Office. It was a question of time and expense and budgets, especially budgets. And, anyway, her clothes and the contents of her handbag told far more of the story than any further autopsies ever would. That *was* the nub of the matter, wasn't it? Identification, time of death, manner of death, and even the date. There were not many bodies dead for thirty years of which that much was known so precisely, were there?

'No, sir, quite,' agreed Roper, reluctantly, over his tea-cup. And by half past seven Roper's boss, Chief Superintendent Mower, had driven across fresh from his dinner and listened to it all with his chin propped on his hands and drew a similar conclusion to Weygood, and so, at eight o'clock, over the telephone, did the Assistant Chief Constable. Marjorie Steadman was to be the subject of a No Further Action file.

'Unless something else crops up, Douglas,' said Mower. 'We don't have the time. Have a good leave, eh?'

At half past eight, that same Tuesday evening, he was tugging on his handbrake behind the yellow Mini parked half on the grass verge outside Box Cottage.

Miss Murcheson answered the door, although she took some time.

'I'm sorry,' she said. 'I was upstairs working. Do come in. Would you like a cup of tea?'

'No, Miss, thank you. I only came along to see if you were all right, and to let you know that you can use your parlour again.'

She was fine, she told him, a bit jittery whenever she

passed the closed door of the parlour, but she was sure that would pass. And she had been into Dorchester this morning and bought some new materials, and had some lunch, and Mr Cambridge had slept in her kitchen last night; and, Roper, listening and watching, decided that she was talking too much and too fast and that she was glad of someone for company, even if he was a policeman.

'Perhaps I will take you up on that cup of tea, after all, Miss Murcheson. I won't stay long.'

'It's okay. I was about to pack up for the night anyway.'

'You're sure?'

'Yes. Really.'

In the kitchen she put the kettle on the range and spooned a couple of measures of tea into an old china teapot.

'Have you found any more clues?' she asked. ' . . . Or whatever you call them?'

'She's a No Further Action. A file job.'

'I think that's sad,' she said. 'It makes it like she never existed. D'you take sugar?'

'Two. Thank you. . . . We think it was a wartime thing. About the end of May '44. She was wearing her wedding dress; that's only a guess, mind.'

'Poor cow.'

Which were equally Roper's sentiments. He filled in a few more details over their mugs of tea.

'So it was probably her wedding night.'

'Yes,' he said. 'We think that's very likely.'

'What do you do with them in cases like that? Bury, or cremate, or what?'

'Cremate.'

'So she goes up in a puff of smoke?'

'I'm afraid so.'

She stretched her mouth. 'I think that's rotten. You know?'

So did Roper. And he detected in Cassandra Murcheson a fellow spirit, that her interest in the body in her wall was born of more than ghoulishness, and that her sympathy for Marjorie Steadman of Brighton was wholeheartedly genuine, and if Marjorie Steadman had only died yesterday Miss Murcheson would have been no less earnest.

And she was going to stay. She was adamant. If she left now she would be kicking herself in six months' time. It was just a question of hanging on until she had purged herself of the memory of that face staring out through the gap in the bricks. After all, if she had chosen to hang that picture somewhere else, the body might have stayed in the wall for ever and she would never have known about it, and nor would anyone else. What would have happened then?

'I admire your philosophy, Miss Murcheson.'

'It's not a philosophy. It's a financial necessity. I'm bloody nearly broke.'

'Any more problems, and you contact Sergeant Blake. I've told him to keep an eye open.'

'Thanks,' she said, burying her nose in her yellow mug again. 'But I still think it's rotten that nobody's ever going to find out who killed her. I mean, it might not have been her husband, might it?'

Roper saw his entrée. He bided a moment. Then said quietly:

'I thought of having a go myself. Off the record. Have a nose about.'

'Can you do that?'

'No,' he said. 'Not officially. But I've got a spot of leave coming up and not a lot to do with it.'

'A sort of busman's holiday?'

'Sort of. Could get my knuckles rapped, mind. I thought I'd drive across to Brighton tomorrow. Then perhaps have a look around the cottage here. I can't get a warrant.'

She shrugged. 'You wouldn't need one. And I won't tell. You won't lose your woodcraft badge on my account.'

He smiled despite himself. He liked her flip style. As high as two pennorth of coppers, as they used to say, and still gutsy enough to crack the mighty Cambridge over the head with a torch and to spend another night in this place when she didn't have to. There were plenty of men, DS Morgan for one, who would have baulked at that. He was surprised that some enterprising man hadn't snapped her up years ago, or perhaps a few had and had not been able to come to terms with her fierce independence.

'Who pays for the wall, by the way?' she asked, practically.

'We do. You get a couple of quotes.'

'And you settle for the cheapest one? Right?'

'It's the ratepayers' money. We have to.'

'My heart bleeds . . . speaking as a ratepayer.' She spoke without rancour, and made Roper smile again. It was no wonder that Cambridge had found a way to sleep here last night. They'd make a good pair, Murcheson and Cambridge.

At the front door again she proffered her hand, and although Roper rarely shook hands he made Miss Murcheson one of the rare exceptions.

At ten o'clock in the morning Brighton was still quiet. He came in from the Preston Park end and parked outside the station, with all the car windows wound down, while he unfolded a street map over the steering wheel to get his bearings. He had always had a soft spot for Brighton, raddled old harlot of a town that it was; and if he had a pound note for every time he had fished off the Palace Pier as a lad he would not have needed to draw his salary this month. Elliston Crescent was a quarter of a mile to the west, the older part of the town, or rather it would have been if the speculators hadn't moved in.

It took him almost a quarter of an hour to beat the one-way traffic system that seemed to take him in every direction except the one he wanted. But it was still there, Elliston Crescent, as it had probably been for the last hundred years, a cramped, mean little street with solid front doors that let straight on to the pavement, prim net curtains at all the windows, and here and there a sign

90

that proclaimed VACANCIES which looked to Roper more like flags of despair than banners of hope. It was a good mile from the sea and one felt that however brightly the sun shone it had never penetrated the sombre greyness of Elliston Crescent.

He parked outside Number 10. A peeling front door, dustbin on the pavement, a briefly lifted curtain. He wound up all the car windows and locked all the doors; it was that kind of street, Elliston Crescent.

Number 18 still looked like the photograph he had found in Marjorie Steadman's handbag. And it probably would until the bulldozers came. He passed it the first time. The next house had a For Sale flag nailed to an upstairs window frame, a Sold sticker plastered across it like a triumphant afterthought. Four houses further along, he turned about and walked slowly back again. Number 18 was better kept than most, its net curtains draped rather than merely hung, a table behind them with a vase of flowers on it. The door was new, Philippine mahogany with a brass knocker, a brass letter flap and a bottle of milk still on the step.

He braced himself, rapped twice on the brass knocker, heard a dog bark, a woman's raised voice telling it to oh, shut up! and a slammed door as the dog was put away, then a footfall along the passage.

The door was opened against a chain, and half of a woman's face peered round the edge of it. Young, about twenty-five, blonde, and plumply cheeked.

'Yes?'

'My name's Roper, madam . . . '

'I'm sorry. I don't buy things at the door. Sorry.'

'I'm not selling anything, madam,' Roper assured her hastily. 'I'm a police officer – but I'm not exactly on duty.' He produced his warrant card – and if a passing Brighton flatfoot saw him doing this and reported him back to Superintendent Mower there'd be merry hell to pay. 'If I can just ask how long you've lived here – and if you've ever heard of a family called Steadman? They'd have lived here during the war. The forties.'

She shook her head vaguely. For her, the war had only been a few pages in her school history books. 'No. Sorry. We only moved in at Easter.'

'Then I'm sorry to have troubled you,' said Roper, tucking his card away again. 'I don't suppose there's anyone left in the street who might remember them?'

'No,' she said. 'Sorry. Except you *could* ask at Number 16. Next door. Mr Newson. I think *he* lived here then. But he's very deaf. You have to shout.'

'Thank you. You've been very helpful, Mrs . . . ?'

'Hope.'

' . . . Mrs Hope. Thank you.'

And well named, he thought. Under the estate agent's flag, the adjacent front door was a far shabbier affair. Peeling paint, cast-iron letter box going rusty for want of use, lion's-head door knocker, tattered net curtain on a length of sagging string across the window. It took three double raps, loud ones, on the ring through the lion's nose before there was any kind of response, and that only a sideways twitch of the moth-eaten curtain. And then, finally, the shuffle of carpet slippers just behind the door.

'Mr Newson?'

A pair of rheumy eyes peered closer. He had to be the best part of eighty, shrivelled and bent and leaning on a stick, his upper half draped in a bagged out seaman's blue jersey, his legs in a pair of creased and sagging grey flannels aged enough to have been made with turnups.

'Eh?'

Roper opened his mouth to shout Mr Newson? louder but the old fellow was already hoisting the frayed hem of his pullover and turning up the volume control of his deaf aid and pushing the earpiece deeper into his ear.

'Mr Newson?'

'Aye. That's me. Arthur Newson.'

'The name's Roper, Mr Newson. Mrs Hope, next door,

said you might be able to help me. I'm looking for a family called Steadman.'

Newson puffed out his cheeks in amazement. 'Gawd,' he wheezed. 'The *Steadmans*? My *sister's* people they were. They're all dead. Blimey, yes. Years and years ago.'

Roper felt the old familiar prickling of the skin . . .

'Your sister's people, Mr Newson?'

'Aye. Alice. My sister, she was. Next door. Number 18. Lived there for years.' The frail frame under the pullover was seized by a wrack of coughing that had a dreadful sound of the terminal about it; but Newson was tougher than he looked and after a few more wheezes and hawks and the production of a grubby-looking handkerchief that was sure evidence that he did his own washing, his breathing returned to the original wheeze and the crimson suffusion left his cheek. 'You was saying . . . ? Look 'ere, if you want to come in you can. I don't get a lot of company. And I get cold standing about on the doorstep. Come on.'

Much against his better judgement, Roper took the single step into the narrow dingy passage that smelled of old beeswax floor polish and damp wallpaper and the sourer odours of human decrepitude. A ragged tabby cat with a missing ear suddenly appeared from nowhere like a startled wraith and scuttled to safety up the dark of the stairs.

'That's Mrs Mogg,' explained Newson, shuffling ahead in his moth-eaten carpet slippers towards his kitchen. It was warmer in there, he confided. Outside, the temperature was up in the seventies. The kitchen, with a fire crackling in the grate and its window closed, was like a furnace.

Newson gestured to a ricketty-looking kitchen chair with a perforated plywood seat.

'Fancy a cuppatea, do you, son?'

'No, sir,' said Roper, having observed the bottle of yesterday's stale milk on the table. 'Thank you very much.'

Newson lowered himself creakily into an armchair that might once have been red but was now reduced to an indeterminate brown with dark greasy patches where his head and elbows had rested. When Roper offered him a cheroot, the old man rolled it beside his vacant ear like a cigar, although he probably couldn't hear it. Roper lit it for him, then his own as he settled on to the sheet of perforated plywood and cautiously tested its integrity.

'What were we on about . . . ?'

'Your sister, Mr Newson. Alice Steadman.'

'Ah. Yes. Her. Alice. What about her?'

'She had a daughter, Mr Newson.'

The old man considered that behind a veil of smoke. 'Aye,' he said. 'Marjorie. My niece, *she* was. Lovely girl.'

'Was?' said Roper, encouragingly. 'How d'you mean was, Mr Newson? Die, did she?'

Newson took his time replying. For the moment, he was more interested in sucking out the full flavour of the cheroot. The hearth beside his slippers was littered with brown-stained cigarette ends, home-rolled.

'She went,' he said. 'In the war.' He took the cheroot from his mouth and gave it a leisurely scrutiny. 'Nice, these,' he said.

'Went where, Mr Newson?'

'No idea,' said Newson. 'No idea, son. Sister and her husband, they never knew either.'

The girl had got herself married. An officer. Married here in Brighton. Went off on her honeymoon. That was the last anybody ever heard of her.

' . . . But I wasn't about then,' said Newson. 'I was on one of them convoys across to Russia. And that was a bloody cold job an' all.'

Newson briefly digressed to Archangel and Murmansk, and it was several minutes before he came back again.

' . . . I heard about it all from George,' he said. 'When I come back. Marjorie hadn't even written a letter, see? She'd just gorn. Down west somewhere. Honeymoon. Never come back.'

'Did the Steadmans ever go to the police?' asked Roper.

'Think *she* did. Once. But the war was on, see? Every-body was on the move all the time. Know I was.' A brief fit of coughing shook him again. Even during the war, Roper guessed, the old boy would have been well into his late forties or early fifties. He'd won a George Medal on the convoy, or so he'd told Roper. And he probably had.

Roper waited for him to wipe his nose on the terrible handkerchief. 'So what did the family think had happened to her, Mr Newson?'

Newson's red-rimmed eyes narrowed.

'I'd heard there'd been trouble. Strict she was, my sister Alice. Chapel, she was. The tin one up Clark Hill. I heard Marjie had got herself in the family way. With the officer lad. Everything got done on the quick. I don't even think Alice and old George went to the wedding. It was one o' those special licence things. That's what I heard. From George, though. Not Alice. I heard it from George. She was a very bitter woman, our Alice. Nobody could ever tell her anything. Led old George a dog's life, she did. Lashed him to death with her tongue, she did, old George.'

Newson hunched forward over his stick. He was in full spate; the poor old chap probably hadn't talked to anyone for days.

'She died soon afterwards, mind. Punishment from God, that was. For the way she made old George suffer. Me, I stayed single.'

'When did they die, Mr Newson? D'you remember?'

'Coronation year, the last one . . . '53, George did. Alice turned up her toes the next year. She's probably still nag-ging the poor old bugger. Up there.' Newson jabbed the handle of his stick in the direction of the ceiling.

'How about other relatives?'

'Just me,' said Newson, with a touch of pride. 'I seen 'em all out. Seen 'em all out by twenty years. Always looked after m'self, see. Never had anyone to nag at me. Adds years to a man's life, that does. You married, son?'

Roper shook his head. 'No, sir.'

'Well, you take my advice, son. Don't. And bring up your children to do the same. Eh? Eh?' Newson went into cackles of laughter.

Roper smiled patiently. So the Steadmans were all gone, apart from this old uncle of Marjorie's, and he didn't look as if he had all that much time left himself.

Roper ran a finger around his shirt collar and unstuck his trousers from his knees. With a pair of tongs, Newson reached into a brass scuttle and put another knob of coal on his fire.

'Would you have any family photographs, Mr Newson? Old snapshots, that sort of thing?'

'Never went in for 'em,' said Newson, to Roper's disappointment. 'But I do have an envelope that used to belong to old George. That's got a few pictures in, if I remember right. I'll show you, if you like. There's an old wardrobe in the front bedroom, and a case on top. You can fetch it down, if you've a mind. If you're *that* interested.'

It was undefiled gold, that envelope. Manilla, foolscap, frayed at the edges and with its bottom hanging out, a George Six stamp on it postmarked May 3rd, 1938 at four o'clock in the afternoon, addressed to George Steadman Esq. From a seed company in Haslemere. And Roper sat there doing his courteous best to mask his impatience while Newson's shaking old hand extracted its contents one by one, explaining each – at very great length – before passing it over to Roper, who by now had his jacket off and his necktie loosened and his shirt collar unfastened. Newson, by this time, was on his third of Roper's cheroots; and he had still not asked what Roper's business was, and with any luck might not.

And this, he read from the pencilled note on the back, was taken at Bognor in '38. And that was Alice, with her tongue tucked inside her mouth for once, and the bloke was old George. And that was Marjorie in the middle. She'd have been about fourteen that year, young Marjorie. Lovely kid . . .

Mrs Steadman had never been young. Under her black, wide-brimmed straw hat, with a couple of glass cherries for decoration, her shadowed face was vinegar. The floral-print dress, almost to her ankles, was cheap but stylish, her button-across-the-instep shoes primly heeled. Old George was in his Sunday-best dark suit and a cloth cap. He, too, was well into his forties. The girl between them, against the promenade railings, was clear proof that genes sometimes skipped a generation. At fourteen, Marjorie Steadman, dark haired in the faded photograph, had indeed been a 'lovely kid'.

And this was old Alice again. A studio photograph in a brown folder. Hair bobbed. A string of seed pearls. A sepia toned picture from the early twenties. And this was old George again, in ill-fitting khaki, and puttees and glistening boots, and looking happy because he was still most of the First World War and three more years away from meeting Alice.

And this . . . what the hell's this?

Newson's hands were clumsily unfolding and straightening out a flimsy sheet of pink paper with bands of white paper tape pasted across it. Oh, it was nothing, just an old telegram . . . something old George must have kept . . .

'May I see that, please, Mr Newson?'

Newson passed it over.

Mum and Dad, Roper read. *Ralph on embarkation leave. We want to get married before he goes back. Need to talk about it. See you Saturday, late afternoon. Love Marjorie.*

The telegram had been sent from Portsmouth Central Post Office on the 23rd of May, 1944, only four days before the wedding.

At twenty, in those days, Marjorie Steadman would have been a minor, and would have needed her parents' permission to marry. And there had indeed been something to talk about.

'Do you know what she was doing in Portsmouth, Mr Newson?'

'War work, I think. Munitions factory. And this one, I reckon that's a wedding picture, don't you?'

It was certainly a wedding picture. The registry office doorway for a background. A white pillbox cap with a feather sticking jauntily out of it, *the* dress, the one made of parachute silk, and *the* handbag, made of crocodile skin, and *the* shoes. And Marjorie Steadman clinging to her handsome young captain's arm as if a thousand wild horses wouldn't have dragged her from him. And the captain looked equally amorous. And yet . . . perhaps less than twelve hours after that photograph was taken . . .

It didn't feel right somehow. Intuition . . . something . . . nudged Roper's elbow and whispered to him that it just wasn't right. As a professional student of human nature he knew that he still had a lot to learn, but he had learned enough in forty-odd years to know that when a man and a woman look at each other like that they are more than good friends.

'Do you think I could borrow this picture, Mr Newson? I'll guard it with my life and get it back to you in a couple of days.'

The old man regarded him shrewdly. Then smiled, equally shrewdly.

'You're a bloody copper, aren't you, son? Stands out a bloody mile, it does. And I reckon you might know something I don't. Eh?'

'Do you take a newspaper, Mr Newson?'

No, he didn't take a newspaper. And he didn't hold with television. So Roper bent the rules a little, and told Marjorie Steadman's uncle a little more about his niece than he would have gleaned from either, and that too long a time had passed for the police to do anything but skate over an investigation. Unless something new came up, which was unlikely. And Newson sat there wistfully examining his cheroot and smoking it thoughtfully in between times, as if he had known all along what had happened to young Marjorie.

'And you're doing something about her on your own, are you, son?'

'Sort of, Mr Newson.'

The old man sat there considering, shuffling through all the memorabilia on his lap, old George and old Alice and young Marjorie, and then weighed Roper carefully again before he made his mind up.

'Here,' he said. 'Take the lot, son. I want 'em all back, mind. . . . But let me know what you find out, eh? I'd like to know before I turn me toes up. Just between you and me, eh? And if you could leave a couple o' those smokes o' yours behind . . . I can't get out far, see.'

Roper left him the remainder of the packet. It was little enough for the gold dust in that envelope.

CHAPTER 7

Cassandra Murcheson knelt on her hearthrug with the contents of the envelope spread all around her. Chief Inspector Roper sat in her father's chesterfield. And much as she tried to restrain her emotions, she found her eyes prickling at the backs, because, although she would never own to it, deep down inside, under the tough veneer she put on, she was as soft as most other people, and all these pictures of a family long gone affected her almost as much as the telephone call from the hospital that night when they'd rung to tell her that her old Dad was dead. And even though she had no connection with Marjorie Steadman, except the awful one, she felt that she had.

'What was he like?' she said. 'The old uncle?'

'Just an old man. Sharp, though. He guessed I was a copper.'

'Did he mind? When you told him about everything?'

'Yes, I think so,' said Roper. 'I think he was very fond of the girl.'

'Well, he would be, wouldn't he?' She took up the wedding picture again. The girl, by any standards, was pretty, the captain, Ralph Thorn who had lived here once, the kind of man who would be able to bowl almost any woman off her feet. And she was experienced enough to know that when a man looks at a woman like that, what he wants to do most is to get her into bed, not kill her. Not on your life.

' . . . what do *you* think?'

He shrugged. 'No evidence either way. Wish there was.'

100

'Oh, come on,' she scoffed. 'Speaking as the chap who drove all the way to Brighton today to talk to an old man you couldn't really care less about.' She held up the wedding photograph. 'If *he* killed *her* I'm the cat's mother.'

Roper smiled. 'Let's just say I'm working on it.'

And he would, she thought. Behind that professional smile, he would gnaw at the murder of Marjorie Steadman like a dog at a bone, whether his bosses told him he could or not.

'I know somebody who'd give his right arm to see those pictures,' she said.

'Oh? Who's that?' Hope rose again. Because whoever was interested in these photographs and tatty pieces of paper might be someone else worth talking to.

'The vicar,' she said. 'His name's Moxley. He grew up here during the war.'

Moxley was fascinated. He went across to his old roll-topped desk in the corner of his study and took out a magnifying glass. His two children were playing on a swing in the garden and his wife was in the kitchen making a pot of tea. It was four o'clock in the afternoon.

Moxley pored over the wedding picture again, tilting it towards the window and quartering it under the magnifying glass.

'Yes, by gum,' he said enthusiastically. 'That's *just* how I remember him. I was devoted to him. . . . He bought me my first cricket bat and set of stumps. Yes, that's *just* how he looked. *Exactly*.'

'But you never saw his wife?' asked Roper.

'No,' said Moxley. 'Sorry. I didn't even know that he'd married. But of course I was only a child then. Seven or so. . . . May I see the others?'

'Please,' said Roper. 'Help yourself, Mr Moxley.'

Moxley sorted through the other photographs, asked who this was and who that was. ' . . . The mother looks a tough nut.'

101

'She was Chapel,' said Roper. 'Strict, as they used to say.'

'Ah,' said Moxley, with a most unecclesiastical smile. 'I think I would have guessed that. And who's this?'

'The father. Army. First World War.'

'Ah,' said Moxley, totally absorbed. 'My word . . . my word . . . '

The vicarage was only a tiny place, dark and early Victorian, and most of the furniture looked either second-hand or on loan from a church store, if there was such a thing. There clearly wasn't a lot of money to be earned in a country parish. Through the open window came the shouts of the children, two little girls, from the kitchen an occasional clatter of crockery. On the desk in the corner was a clerical calendar with the saints' days on it, a *Crockford's*, a battered bible, open, and a pad of lined writing paper with a ballpoint lying across it. When Roper and Cassandra Murcheson had arrived, Mr Moxley had been writing next Sunday's sermon. Now it looked as if the furthest thing from Moxley's mind was the writing of a sermon.

'Fascinating,' he was still saying. 'Absolutely . . . '

He was forty, Roper guessed, and still young enough to be zealous, although he was no holy-roller. Outside, beside the front step, had been an old black bicycle with a basket on the front and a pair of cycle clips hooked over the handlebars, obviously Moxley's. That, too, had looked second-hand.

Roper rose as Mrs Moxley came into the study backwards with a tray full of china and a plate piled high with biscuits. A tall, rangy woman, with spectacles and a quick nervous smile, and an upper-crust voice that must have cost her parents a small fortune. Roper took the tray from her and laid it on the corner of the table.

'I say, darling, you should see these,' said Moxley, his enthusiasm still unabated. ' . . . *That's* Ralph Thorn, would you believe.' And Mrs Moxley barely had time to thank Roper before her husband had dragged her round to his

102

end of the table and was pressing the magnifying glass into her hand. ' . . . and that's his wife, apparently . . . and her father . . . '

And Cassandra Murcheson, who had walked over with Roper, shot him a sidelong what did I tell you? look. And Roper sent her one back to tell her how dead right she was. She was a smart young woman, was Miss Murcheson.

'Did you ever go to Box Cottage in Thorn's time, Mr Moxley?'

'Oh, yes,' said Moxley, sitting back in his chair and plucking off a pair of National Health reading spectacles. 'I practically *lived* there. If my mother wanted me, all she had to do was to send one of the housemaids along to Box Cottage. Although,' he added hastily, 'lest you think otherwise, it was all very proper. We were friends. My father was killed in France in '39. . . . And when my mother told me one night that Ralph had been killed in France as well, I cried. Heartily. He was such a big jolly man, you see. I thought he was immortal. But children do, don't they?'

'Yes, sir,' agreed Roper. Mrs Moxley was pouring the tea, then passing round plates. 'Did you know Thorn, Mrs Moxley?'

'No,' she said. 'No, I didn't. I'm from Suffolk. I didn't see Dorset until I met Colin.'

'We . . . or rather Miss Murcheson here, found Marjorie Steadman bricked up in a recess in the parlour wall,' said Roper.

'Yes,' said Moxley. 'We heard it on the bush telegraph. Tragic, quite tragic. . . . For you too, Miss Murcheson. . . . It must have been dreadful for you. In fact I was coming across this evening to see if we could put you up for a few days . . . if, well, you know . . . '

'The recess is in the wall on the door side of the room, Mr Moxley. We thought it might have been Thorn's bookcase.'

Moxley pinched his nose between his thumb and his

forefinger, and closed his eyes and puckered his forehead. 'Yes,' he said, at some length. 'Do you know, I think it was. . . . A bookcase, I mean. I can remember large books with brown backs . . . like account books, or ledgers. He used to collect the rents for my grandfather . . . that sort of thing. I used to ride round with him in the trap collecting them. And I recall him sitting at the table in the parlour counting it all afterwards.'

'Do you know if he had a shotgun, Mr Moxley?'

'Yes, indeed,' said Moxley. 'Several. I can remember when he went into the army . . . he came up to the house, our house, that is, and handed them over to my grandfather for safe keeping. For the duration of hostilities, as they used to say.'

Which awakened Roper's interest in yet another direction, because if Ralph Thorn had shot his wife with a shotgun, where had he got it from?

'*All* his guns, Mr Moxley?'

'Yes, I would have thought so. He was a responsible man, Inspector. I hardly think it was likely he'd have left one behind in a cottage that was going to be locked up for Heaven alone knew how long.'

'But you were only three or four years old at the time, Mr Moxley,' said Roper. 'Are you sure your memory is that good?'

'It isn't all memory, Inspector,' said Moxley. 'I'll show you something.' And he slid his chair back on the carpet and went over to the desk in the corner. From underneath a mass of papers in the centre drawer, he carefully lifted out a foolscap-sized book in blue marbled covers from which many of the leaves looked well on the way to falling out altogether. He carried it carefully across to the table, sat down again and opened the book about two thirds of the way through it. In silence then, between a delicate finger and thumb, he lifted and turned over some half a dozen pages, until he found what he was looking for.

'Ah,' he exclaimed softly. 'Here. See?' And turning the

book round, he slid it along the table to Roper. 'Friday, September the First, 1939.'

It was a very old book, looked like an estate diary, written up in copper-plate by a loving hand, not a day-by-day diary but a record of important events on the Moxley estate . . . a birth . . an engagement between two servants . . . an excellent harvest . . . *Thorn brought me his guns today for safe keeping. Tomorrow he is off to Aldershot. Like all the young men he is eager to go, and, like me, he thinks that a war is inevitable and that the Germans will never leave Poland now. But he was his usual cheerful self and thinks that if there is a war it will be over by Christmas. We had a drink together and shook hands. We shall miss him greatly. He is a good man and we all pray that he returns safely.*

The date in the margin was 1/3/1939.

'Now if you turn to the June of '44 . . . ' said Moxley.

The pages were crisp with age, the loose ones frayed and stained at their edges.

'The twelfth, I think,' said Moxley.

And the twelfth it was. Pasted to the page was a telegram. *Dear Mr Moxley: Regret to inform you that Captain Ralph Thorn killed in action, June 8th, 1944.*

The date of origin of the telegram was June 12th, 1944. It had been sent from London, SW1, by one R. C. Gregg (Capt.), War Office Records.

We are all desolated, Roper read, beneath the telegram. *Especially young Colin. So now there are two names to be added to the war memorial. What a terrible waste! I have asked Christopher Leach to make special mention of Ralph in his sermon on Sunday.*

Sad, thought Roper. One and a half terse lines of telegram, the bottom line of a man's life.

'Do you know why this telegram was sent to your grandfather, Mr Moxley?'

'No idea,' said Moxley. 'Except that Thorn was more or less part of the family. And I don't think he had any relatives. So perhaps he'd nominated my grandfather as his next of kin.'

It was possible. Except.

'But Mr Thorn *did* have a next of kin, Mr Moxley. He was married, wasn't he?'

'Well, yes,' agreed Moxley. 'But only a couple of weeks before he was killed. Perhaps Army Records hadn't got round to changing whatever it was they had to change in circumstances like that. . . . I'm sure you were in the forces yourself, after the war, of course; you must remember how cumbersome it was to have your records amended. I know I do.'

It was true. Military record keepers were like the mills of God. They ground slow, and exceeding small, but only at their own pace. But between Thorn's marriage and the date on the telegram nearly three weeks had elapsed, and that, to Roper's mind, did seem a mite too long, even in the maelstrom of the biggest war that men had ever known.

'Could you bear to part with this book for an hour, Mr Moxley?'

Moxley grimaced. 'Frankly, I'm not keen, Inspector. I'm sure you understand. It goes all the way back to 1925. It's irreplaceable. Totally. If I had a copy . . . '

'I'll get it *all* photocopied for you, Mr Moxley. The lot. All I want is a copy of this telegram. And I do know the value of the book, sir. If I had the time, I'd like to read it from cover to cover myself.'

Moxley looked across at his wife. And whatever semaphore she sent him back evidently did the trick.

'And you'll make a copy of all of it for me?' Even vicars, Roper observed, had trouble keeping the glitter of acquisition from showing in their eyes.

'All of it, sir,' said Roper. 'It'll only take a couple of hours. And it won't be damaged. I give you my word for it.'

The last of Moxley's doubts were resolved. He beamed ecstatically. 'But that's tremendous. Splendid. You've absolutely no idea. I've wanted it copied for years, but we've never been able to afford it. And I won't rush you.'

'Then tomorrow,' said Roper. 'I promise. You'll have it back tomorrow.'

It took several moments for the Reverend Moxley to clamber back down from the dizzy heights whence Roper's offer had sent him. Mrs Moxley poured more tea.

'We understand Thorn served in the Wessex Yeomanry, Mr Moxley.'

'Yes, indeed,' said Moxley. He shot to his feet again and went to the same drawer of the desk from which he had taken his grandfather's estate diary. He returned with an old tobacco tin which he prised open and handed across to Roper. 'When I was a little boy, what's in there were the most valuable things I ever had. Here. He gave me these on his first leave.'

Four tarnished military brass buttons and a cap badge on a bed of old cotton wool. As a lad during the war, Roper had had a similar collection himself.

He snapped the lid back on and returned the box to Moxley. 'Thank you, Mr Moxley.'

'Do you want to borrow those, too?'

'No, sir, thank you.' Roper had learned more about Ralph Thorn in the last half-hour than he had ever hoped to. He had some measure of the man himself, the date he had reported to Aldershot, the name of his regiment and the exact date he was killed. If Ralph Thorn had died only yesterday, Roper could scarcely have found out more about him in so short a time and with all the machinery of the law at his elbow.

For another half-hour, patiently, like a locksmith, Roper tried a few more keys in the wards of Moxley's childhood memories. Moxley was sure, yes, quite sure, that Thorn had come home on leave for the Christmas of '43. Moxley had never seen him again. Of that he was equally sure. And if his grandfather had known that Thorn was about to be married, he would surely have said. And he had not. There was nothing in the diary, you see. No mention of Ralph between that Christmas leave and the telegram.

Old Grandfather Moxley, had he known of anything about Ralph Thorn, would have committed it to the diary on the day of its occurrence. To Grandfather Moxley, Ralph Thorn became the son that the old man had lost in the early days, before Dunkirk.

Roper took out a notebook, not his official pocket-book, and a ballpoint, from inside his jacket, and wrote a brief précis of the last hour. It didn't amount to all that much, but was certainly a sight more than he had ever hoped for. Pen poised over a new blank page he said:

'Can I tax your memory a bit more, Mr Moxley? Who lives in the village now who might remember what went on here during the war? People around the fifty and sixty mark; Ralph Thorn's contemporaries, let's say.'

Moxley's brow furrowed. 'Oh, that's difficult. It's been a shifting scene down here since the war. . . . Well, there's old Jake Haygarth; runs the grocer's. . . . And Denzleman. He's the ironmonger and DIY shop. His father had it before him – used to run the village smithy in the old days as well. Sydney Denzleman, he is, by the way. . . . And the Foxes over at Highview Farm. Father, son *and* daughter. They'd certainly remember. The old man has to be ninety if he's a day – but I doubt you'll get much out of the daughter, Winnie. She's a little on the slow side, not to put too fine a point on it, poor woman. Oh, and yes, there's Mrs Harmer; Sarah. Her mother used to be a housemaid up at the house in my grandfather's day, so she ought to be an absolute *mine* of information.'

But there were very few others. Before the war, the population of Newby Magna had been enough to fill Moxley's little church three times over. Now it would barely fill it the once, which it rarely did, alas, except at Christmas and Easter and Harvest Sunday, and the occasional wedding.

' . . . But then we live in changing times, don't we, Inspector?' said Moxley, rallying again. 'And we have to keep up with them, don't we?'

'Indeed we do, sir,' said Roper. He declined Mrs Moxley's offer of yet another cup of tea. 'But if I could use your phone before I go, sir?'

'Yes, of course,' said Moxley. 'It's in the hall.'

Roper carried two jugs of bitter and a brace of cheese rolls out to the garden behind the Carpenter's Arms. At a table, under a striped umbrella advertising lager, DS Morgan was scanning through the Moxley estate diary. At his elbow was the envelope that Roper had brought back that morning from Brighton. Roper put down a jug and one of the plates in front of him.

'Cheers,' said Morgan.

'Pros't,' said Roper. He sipped at his bitter. 'What do you think?'

'Like you,' said Morgan. 'It's gold dust. . . . Only how do I explain what I'm doing on the Xerox if Treacher comes bowling in?'

'You tell him,' said Roper. Treacher was the County Admin. Sergeant. 'And if he cuts up rough, refer him to me. You can tell him I'll pay for it if he likes.'

'It'll cost you,' said Morgan. 'There are two hundred sheets here. Double sided. Plus what's in that envelope.'

'Not if we get a result, it won't,' said Roper.

He let Morgan chew through half his roll. A steady reliable copper was DS Morgan. When Roper had first come down from London a few years ago Morgan had made it plain that he was going to reserve judgement on him until Roper had got the dust from the Met off his suit. Roper had had to work hard on Morgan.

'There's something else I'd like you to do, Dan. A phone call. Army Records. See if you can get photocopies of anything they've still got on Ralph Thorn. When he took his leaves, that sort of thing. And he'd have had to have his CO's permission to marry. That ought to be on a piece of paper too, somewhere. Anything they've got.'

109

'You're really enjoying all this, aren't you?' said Morgan, around another mouthful of roll.

'Bloody right, I am,' said Roper, picking up his own roll and breaking it in half. 'Aren't you?'

It was nine o'clock. Her eyes ached and she decided to call it a day. Black space had been air-brushed in, Hu-Ra's war-schooner meticulously detailed and the witch of Endor's flapping raincoat given its first wash of dirty brown. Come tomorrow at this time it might even be finished, and it would then be one down and only six, plus a jacket design, to go. And then, God willing, she might even receive a cheque.

Going downstairs no longer held any trepidation for her. She had taken a dinner break this evening, the plate balanced on a cushion on her knees, in the parlour. Sat there with cold deliberation. She had never been superstitious. The dead were dead, her old Dad certainly was, and the hole in the wall, eyesore though it was, was merely that, a hole in the wall. Nothing was going to spring out at her, and when the bricks had been put back she was sure that, eventually, the image of that half of a face she had seen would recede. But she was, however, glad that she had not seen the rest of Marjorie Steadman; although, like the police inspector, she would have liked to know what had happened here all those years ago.

She put a kettle of water on the range. She almost had the infernal black thing licked by now. She fed it twice a day, and once more before she went to bed, kept the damper half in and the front trap shut. In its way it was very nearly efficient. And in the winter it would probably keep the entire place warm.

She took her mug of coffee and a book upstairs. The parlour was all very well in the daylight, but the night-time was a different kettle of fish altogether. Blackbeard had offered to bed down in the kitchen again tonight, but she had declined. She had to face the place on her

110

own sometime, and the sooner the better. But then, as the darkness came and the evening cooled, she began to wonder if she had done the right thing; because the old timbers of the cottage began to creak and crackle again and by ten o'clock she caught herself several times reading the same words twice or skipping a line, so that she lost the flow, or looking out of the wwindow at her row of cypresses as they swayed and rustled in the breeze. And the moon tonight really did seem to have a face hewn in it. And, apart from the rustle of the trees, the silence almost had a texture to it, thick and black and woolly.

It was nerves, she told herself, and too much imagination. Because suddenly she was strung as tightly as a violin string. It was time for bed. There was nothing wrong with her that a good night's sleep wouldn't cure. She closed her book and rose to shut the window.

And saw her Dad. Down in the garden. In the moonlight.

Her Dad the way she remembered him from the war, forage-capped and battledressed. Only he didn't have a face, at least not a proper one, just a featureless oval floating between the khaki battle-blouse and the fore and aft cap. And it glowed, the face. And her legs turned to water, even though she didn't believe her eyes, it couldn't *possibly* be her Dad. She blinked, and afterwards it was *still* there. But it wasn't her Dad, because if he were ever able to come back – which he wasn't – he would never come back and scare the life out of her . . .

She watched it drift closer to the cottage. Her moment of fear had passed, there was a rational explanation for all this: and her fingers were crabbing sideways along the window ledge for her coffee mug, which was the nearest heavy object to hand only she wished it was her hammer.

Her fingers curled about the mug, drew it covertly closer along the wooden shelf. Then in a single swift movement the mug was over her shoulder, then winging its way down to the garden; only it was too late. The face had gone; it was all pale moonlight and black shadows down there

111

again and she heard her Habitat mug shatter to fragments on the stones of the rockery. But what she also heard was feet scuffling quickly through the grass and the frantic rustling in the hedge behind the trees, and what sounded distinctly like a gasp of human pain, or at least she hoped it was, she most dearly hoped it was.

Five minutes later, a cardigan draped over her shirt, she was banging on Blackbeard's front door and praying that he was in and not along at the pub or something. And mercifully he was, and the reaction she had managed to stave off finally caught up with her, and she blurted it all out in a single breath before the poor man had scarcely had time to see who she was.

'... And I'm sorry,' she said. 'But I can't go back there. Not till daylight. Can I have your sofa, please?'

CHAPTER 8

Sergeant Blake arrived at the cottage at eight o'clock the next morning, Thursday, the detective sergeant, Morgan, a half-hour afterwards. And, to her immense relief, both of them took her seriously. They didn't believe in ghosts either.

'You say you think he was wearing some kind of uniform, Miss,' said Morgan, sitting on one of her upturned tea-chests with his opened notebook on his knees.

'Sure he was,' she said. 'Khaki. It looked like the top half of an army battledress; buttoned right up to the neck, like they used to in the war. And a forage cap. I'm not sure about the trousers.'

'Can you describe him?'

'I've already told Sergeant Blake: he didn't seem to have any features. His face was just a shape. A bit like an egg.'

Morgan made a note of that. 'Could he have been wearing a stocking over his face, d'you think?'

Of course! She hadn't thought of that. 'Yes,' she said. 'I'm sure he was, now you say so. It never occurred to me.'

'Don't expect it would, Miss,' said Morgan. He had the same Dorset buzz in his voice as Sergeant Blake. He smiled. 'Can't all have criminal minds, can we, after all? How tall do you think he was?'

She had no idea. It had been dark and she had seen only the top half of the battledress jacket in the dull glow of the torch. She held the edge of a hand across her chest.

113

'From about here upwards. And his face, and the cap. So I couldn't relate the rest of him to the ground. And I suppose he was carrying a torch to light his face with.'

Blackbeard, the perennial Boy Scout, brought in four mugs of tea on a tray from the kitchen. He had put clean sheets and pillow cases on his bed for her last night, and slept on the couch in his parlour, which in his cottage was his studio, so there had not been a lot of room.

'Thank you, sir,' said Morgan, taking one of the mugs and briefly testing its contents before setting it down on the tea-chest beside him, then continuing to jot his notes. 'Sergeant Blake tells me you chucked a mug at him.'

'I missed him. It broke on the rockery.'

'Pity,' said Morgan, with a sniff. 'A bit better shot and you might have done him enough damage to merit a couple of stitches. What happened then, Miss?'

'He just disappeared. Well, that's what it looked like; but I suppose it was just his torch being switched off. And I'm sure I heard feet scuffing through the grass, and then someone pushing through the hedge down there at the far end of the garden. And I think he might have got caught up in it. I heard a sort of gasp. As if he'd hurt himself.'

Morgan smiled grimly. 'We can only hope, can't we, Miss? . . . And that's the lot, is it? You didn't go chasing after him?'

She shook her head. 'No. I went straight along to Mr Cambridge's cottage. He put me up for the night. And phoned Sergeant Blake for me this morning.'

'How about tonight, Miss?'

'I don't know,' she said, and nor, at the moment, did she. Like most terrors, the events of last night had been reduced to little more than a bad dream by the bright sunshine of a new day. And she was damned if she was going to quit the cottage on the strength of some joker with a torch.

'It might get more serious than that, Miss,' warned Morgan. 'The next time it might not be a joke. If you take my point.'

Morgan joined Roper again in Dorchester at lunchtime. Roper had just come back from Brighton, where he had been to return Mr Newson's envelope of memorabilia. DS Morgan had burned several pints of midnight oil last night, and he had not been exactly idle this morning either.

With a half-pint jug either side of it, spread across the table between them was the six inches to the mile Ordnance Survey map of Newby Magna that Sergeant Blake had marked up for Roper with coloured pencils. The grounds of Box Cottage were shaded yellow, the drainage ditch behind it cross-hatched with red. And every other field and garden to which the ditch gave either access or egress – depending upon whether the owners were likely victims or likely villains – had the name of the tenant or landowner written across in red ballpoint in Blake's clumsy block hand.

But what Roper was currently examining more interestedly was a tuft of what looked like wool, in a small plastic evidence-bag that he was holding up to the light from the window. It was, unmistakably, a thread of khaki something or other, and perhaps even a fragment from a military uniform.

'Where did you find it?' asked Roper.

'The same place. The gap at the bottom of the hedge where we found the ladder marks. It was snagged up, about four inches off the ground.'

'Anything else?'

'Can't be sure,' said Morgan. 'But it looked as if the edge of the ditch had been disturbed. Definite signs of crumbling. As if somebody might have done a spot of climbing.'

'Which seems likely in the circumstances.'

'Right,' said Morgan.

At half past nine that morning, Morgan and Sergeant Blake had walked the full length of the ditch, from its origin behind the Carpenter's Arms all the way to the short length of concrete culvert through which the ditch discharged into Colnbrook Stream. But they had found nothing that might be construed as evidence, other than the tuft of khaki fabric. Blake was currently questioning all the villagers whose property backed on to the ditch, and that afternoon the tuft of khaki was going across to the Regional Forensic laboratory for a test or two.

'How about Army Records?' asked Roper.

'They weren't exactly eager,' said Morgan. 'The clerk I spoke to said all the records from the war were still on index cards in little green drawers. Hardly anybody refers to 'em these days. But he said he'd try to look up Thorn's and give me a ring back if he had any luck.'

Which might take weeks, thought Roper, and then might not turn up anything new.

At two o'clock, he finally tracked down Sergeant Blake, or, rather, his Escort parked outside a cottage, a few hundred yards up the lane from Miss Murcheson's place.

Roper wound down his car window as Blake, in his shirtsleeves, came down the garden path squaring his cap. 'Any luck, Tom?' he called.

Blake came across the grass verge, and rested a forearm on the car roof to look in at the window. His face was beaded with perspiration.

'For what it's worth, young Albert Harmer's wearing a bloody great bandage on his left hand today, . . . which he wasn't yesterday.'

'Now there's a thing,' said Roper. 'Did you ask him what he'd done?'

'Told me he'd been fitting a new fan belt on his car. The spanner slipped. And old Jake Haygarth reckons he saw someone flitting away across Saul Fox's field last night; with a torch. About ten o'clock.'

'The right time,' said Roper. 'Almost to the minute.'

'Aye,' said Blake. 'That's what I thought. But you can get into that field from almost anywhere, so it could mean anything or nothing.'

116

'These Foxes,' said Roper, recalling something he had read in Moxley's estate diary in a teashop on Brighton seafront at half past ten that morning. 'Would they be the same Foxes who were living here before the war?'

'From what I hear,' said Blake. 'Why?'

'Join me,' said Roper, leaning across for the doorcatch. Blake climbed in beside him and dropped his cap on the dash-shelf. Roper reached over to the back seat for the photocopy of Moxley's diary, a thick, heavy wad of foolscap held together with four treasury tags. He carefully turned the pages in the narrow space between his knees and the steering wheel. He remembered the year of the entry, 1938, but not the month. On the seafront opposite the West Pier that morning, he had spent an absorbing half-hour riffling through that diary.

'Here,' he said. '*June Two, 1938: Sergeant Clough called again today. There still seems to be no sign of Mrs Fox. She has been missing for nearly a month now.* And going back to May of the same year: *Christopher Leach tells me that Mrs Fox has disappeared, and not left as much as a note behind to let her family know where she has gone. Our first whiff of village scandal this year!*' It was Roper's guess that John Moxley had enjoyed stabbing in that exclamation mark.

'Before my time,' said Blake. 'Although I've heard gossip about old Fox being a bit of a bastard when he was a few years younger. And he's a tough old nut, now, mind: still runs his farm himself, and he's got to be ninety if he's a day.'

'So he might be worth talking to,' said Roper. A man could have a lot of memories crammed into ninety years.

'If you can get to him,' said Blake. 'He doesn't like visitors.'

Roper returned to the business in hand. 'How many more calls do you have to make?'

'Two,' said Blake. 'They'll take me about another half-hour. But they're both down at the stream end, which isn't the way Jake Haygarth saw that torch going last night. So they're probably both a waste of time.'

'How about this chap Harmer? With the bandaged hand. Whereabouts does he live?'

Blake jerked a thumb backward over his shoulder. 'About halfway between here and the Carpenter's Arms.'

'So the right direction,' said Roper.

'And he could have gone straight home along the ditch,' said Blake. 'His mother's garden backs right on to it.'

'So perhaps he's the villain?'

Blake shrugged. 'Could be,' he conceded. 'D'you want me to go back and talk to him again?'

'No,' said Roper. 'I will.' He tipped his wrist and glanced at his watch. 'Where will you be at half past four?'

'My place,' said Blake. 'I usually call in for a cup of tea. I'll get the missus to put out another cup and saucer.'

Blake climbed out again, and got into his Escort while Roper did a three point turn in the narrow lane. He had little difficulty finding Harmer's cottage. A faded sign nailed to the fence beside the front gate read: A. G. Harmer, Plumber and Electrical Contractor. Free estimates given.

Roper pulled in beside it. The hedge needed cutting, a couple of slates were missing from the roof and the rainwater gutter sagged ominously here and there. Further testimony to the fact that Mr Harmer did little work for his own mother was provided by the jammed front gate that needed a firm shove and a sharp kick from the side of Roper's foot to open it. Weeds sprouted between the concrete blocks of crazy paving between the gate and the front door.

And Albert was not in. He was working. Across at the vicarage. Putting in a new pane of glass for Mr Moxley. Had been for the last hour.

' . . . Why? What d'you want him for?'

Roper had known that Mrs Harmer was going to be

118

spiky as soon as her mean, pinched face had appeared round the edge of her door.

'I'd like to talk to him, Mrs Harmer.'

'I know what you are,' she retorted. 'Bloody police, aren't you? Well, Sergeant Blake's already been, and frankly I don't know what all the fuss is about. My Albert's only met the new woman once. And he's a good boy.'

'Do you know where he was at ten o'clock last night, Mrs Harmer?'

'Minding his own business, I expect. Same as he always does.'

Roper didn't pursue it. He didn't want to flourish his warrant card and he was on his way to the vicarage anyway, and could talk to Albert Harmer himself. And, when it came to the rub, there were few mothers who knew their own sons.

The white Cortina with the black vinyl roof parked on the verge in front of the vicarage could only be Harmer's. Polished like a mirror and with a stripe of 'go-faster' black tape stuck along each side, and with a dozen varieties of lamps, three of which at least were illegal, plastered around its radiator grille, it was patently a courting-car. Its open boot held a couple of bags of tools, with a rubber-cased torch sticking out of one of them.

The vicarage door stood open against the heat of the afternoon, and Moxley, stripped to the waist, was rollering a coat of white emulsion paint over the wallpaper at the far end of the hall. At the sight of Roper, he laid his roller back in the tray and came down his ladder and along the hall.

'Doing it yourself, are you, Mr Moxley?'

'Needs must when the devil drives, Mr Roper,' beamed Moxley, his eyes already lighting on his grandfather's diary and the thick swatch of paper under Roper's arm. 'Oh, how absolutely splendid. You've done it. Look, come in, won't you. Two more sweeps of the roller and I've finished that wall.'

'There's no hurry, sir,' said Roper. 'I'll have a word

119

with Mr Harmer first. His mother tells me he's doing a job for you.'

'Ah, yes,' said Moxley. 'One of my offspring put a ball through one of the conservatory windows this morning – for which she will lose about ten years' pocket money, I hasten to add. Young Albert's just replacing it. Round the corner, to the right.'

'Thank you, sir,' said Roper, and briefly left Moxley to finish his decorating.

With a mouthful of glazing sprigs, and a hammer tucked into his trouser belt, Albert Harmer was in the process of offering up the new pane of glass to the window frame of Moxley's conservatory. At the sight of Roper, his face stiffened visibly. 'Chlist,' he grunted, around his mouthful of nails. 'Not *another* gloody cocker.'

'Right first time, Mr Harmer,' said Roper amiably. He put up a hand to hold the glass pane in place. 'But don't let me stop you working.'

Harmer spat out a couple of sprigs and tapped them into the woodwork. The back of his black tee-shirt was wet with perspiration. Trendily long fair hair. A sword in a wreath tattooed on his left forearm above the bandage and the sour smell of beer in his body odour.

With the two sprigs tapped home, and the glass held safe, Harmer spat out the rest of them into the palm of his hand. 'Right,' he said, giving Roper the same belligerent stare as his mother had. 'Give. What's it all about this time?'

Roper glanced down at the grubby bandage around Harmer's left hand. 'When did that happen, Mr Harmer?'

Harmer lifted his hand and regarded it. 'I told Blakey,' he said, raising his eyes with studied insolence. 'Spanner slipped when I was changing me fan belt.'

'When?' said Roper.

'Last night,' said Harmer.

'When, last night? Exactly.'

Harmer tucked his glazing hammer back behind his

trouser belt. 'What's it to you? You could be anybody. Know what I mean?'

Roper reached into his jacket for his warrant card and held it up long enough and close enough to Harmer's nose for Harmer to read every word on it. 'When, last night, Mr Harmer?' he asked again.

Harmer clearly had no fear of policemen. He shrugged. 'About half past ten. Or maybe a while before. I'm not sure.'

Roper tucked his card away again. 'And *where* were you?'

'Up by Highview Farm. In the layby. Near the phone box.'

'That's Mr Fox's farm, isn't it? Highview?'

'So what?'

So everything, thought Roper. It had been across one of the Foxes' fields that the local grocer had seen someone making off last night.

'But you weren't all that far from home, Mr Harmer. What is it? A mile, say?'

Harmer hitched a shoulder. 'Yeah,' he agreed. 'About that.'

'So why didn't you drive home and change the belt this morning? In the daylight?'

'I had a delivery to make. Across at Bere Regis.'

'At half past ten at night?'

'Why not?' said Harmer.

'Where to? This delivery?'

Harmer didn't answer; but nor could he keep his eyes still, and more often than not that was more of an answer than an answer.

'Under age, is she, Albert? Had to get her home before her father found out? That it?'

It clearly was, or something very close to it. Harmer wilted a little, and shifted uncomfortably.

'I don't get on with her old man.'

'What time did you pick her up last night?'

'Eight.'

'And she was with you for the rest of the evening? Where did you go?'

Harmer had the grace to colour slightly. 'We didn't go anywhere. We just . . . well, talked. Know what I mean?'

'What time did you drop her off?'

'Eleven – half past. About.'

Which meant, unless the girl was a co-conspirator, that Albert Harmer had a cast-iron alibi for the events of last night.

'What's her name?'

'Look, if her old man . . . '

'I'm not interested in her father, Albert. Just the girl.'

Harmer bridled. 'Look, it wasn't illegal. She's seventeen, for Christ's sake!'

'Name, Albert. I want the girl's name.'

It took several minutes of argument, even then, before, piecemeal, Harmer reluctantly gave up what Roper insisted upon knowing, even if it took him the rest of the day. Shirley. Shirley Bignall. And if Roper really *had* to talk to her, well, could he do it while she was at work, like. Only her old man was a copper, see. A sergeant . . .

And Roper's gut told him that Harmer was telling the ungarnished truth. The lad was probably more terrified of Sergeant Bignall than he was of the rest of the Dorset constabulary all lumped together.

'You were going to do some work for Miss Murcheson. Along at Box Cottage.'

'I gave her a quote, that's all. She wanted her old range taken out and a new one put in. And a bit of gardening.'

'You've never been back?'

Harmer shook his head. 'No. . . . Honest. I haven't even seen her since.'

'What about talk? In the village. You heard any?'

'There's always talk when someone new moves in. Especially across at Box Cottage. Everybody wants to know about it, don't they? Know what I mean? There's some

122

bloody funny things happened over at Box Cottage. Ask anybody.'

'Like who?'

'Well, my old granny for starters,' said Harmer. 'She used to work up the big house ... the Moxley place. She was always in and out of Box Cottage in the old days. Before the war, like. She knew Ralph Thorn an' all. Personally. If you know what I mean. She's still got a picture of him, keeps it in her little box. Secret, like, you know?' With his own troubles over, Harmer was more than prepared to talk about his grandmother. Samuels, her name was. Mrs Maud Samuels. She lived just outside Dorchester. An old people's home, one of those council places, with a warden, know what I mean? Where the old biddies play Scrabble all day, and dance the Lancers on Saturday nights with all the old blokes. That kind of place, know what I mean, chief?

Roper stayed at the vicarage only long enough to accept Moxley's effusive gratitude for the photocopied diary, and at Sergeant Blake's cottage only long enough to share a cup of tea with him. At a quarter past five he was on the northern outskirts of Dorchester and driving into the flower-tubbed courtyard of the address that Albert Harmer had given him. The building was new, red-brick, two-storied. A few elderly folk sat about in wheelchairs in the sunshine, two old men were playing draughts in a glazed cloister, another, with a walking-frame, was weeding one of the tubs. From an upstairs window came the drone of a vacuum cleaner. It felt a busy place. And the keen-eyed warden was bearding him the moment he stepped from the car, a tall, military-looking woman in shirt and slacks who blocked his way so effectively that he couldn't move an inch from the car without forcibly pushing her aside.

'Good afternoon,' she said, riveting him firmly where he stood and daring him to pass her.

'Good afternoon, madam.' He was also about to give

his name and state his business but was given no time to utter either.

'I haven't seen *you* here before.'

'No, you haven't. Mrs Wing, is it . . . ?'

She melted slightly, perhaps recognising that she was face to face with the kind of officialdom that she herself represented.

' . . . The name's Roper, Mrs Wing. Detective Chief Inspector, County CID.'

'Not bad news for one of them is it?' she asked, suddenly anxious. ' . . . They hate that, you know, bad news. Deaths especially. It's bad for morale.'

No, it was nothing like that, Roper told her. And to be honest, he wasn't here in his official capacity. But there was a lady here, a Mrs Samuels, mother of a Mrs Harmer of Newby Magna . . .

Mrs Wing's face set hard again. '*They* never come, you know. Never. Mrs Harmer *nor* her son. Not in six months. Nobody bothers with old people any more. Tuck them away somewhere and forget about 'em. That's the philosophy these days.' But as quickly as Mrs Wing's face had turned to stone, so did it soften again. 'They have *so* much to talk about, you know. Do you have an identity card, by the way?'

Roper showed her his card. She returned it. 'Have to be sure, you see. Thank you. Give me five minutes. . . . They still have their pride, don't like being caught unawares. I'm sure you understand.'

The five minutes was nearer ten. And visitors were charged for a pot of tea and a few biscuits, Mrs Wing told him, as they went up to the first floor in the lift, five pence. The establishment was run on a tight budget, and for one of her charges to have tea in his or her room, well, that was regarded here as something of a treat. He could pay on the way out.

' . . . And we call them "flats", you know. And it isn't a "home".' This last injunction was whispered outside Mrs

Samuels's door as Mrs Wing rapped lightly on it. 'Visitor, Mrs Samuels,' she called cheerily. 'And a pot of tea's on its way. May we come in?'

Something bumped lightly against the other side of the door before it opened. Mrs Samuels was confined to a wheelchair, a blanket round her legs, a plump, cheerful-looking woman with a face that might have been pretty once and was still full of life.

'Oo,' she said, with twinkling eyes. 'A man in a *suit*. Don't get many of *those* in here, do we Mrs W.? Mostly the walking wounded from the Boer War. . . . Come in, dearie. . . . Mrs W. says you're a policeman. . . . So I can't come to a great *deal* of harm, can I? . . . Do sit down, lovie.'

'She flirts,' warned Mrs Wing. 'So don't say you haven't been warned, Mr Roper.'

'And when *you* come back with tea,' countered Mrs Samuels, 'you'd better *knock*. . . . Isn't that right, lovie?'

Roper smiled. At least the old lady had her wits about her, and however useless her legs were the rest of her looked very much alive. He settled himself in the wooden-armed chair by the window as Mrs Wing went off again to fetch the tea.

Mrs Samuels wheeled herself closer, clasped her hands comfortably over her ample stomach and appraised him lengthily with the twinkling eyes. 'Well, dearie, you're a turn up for the book, I must say. My first visitor since Heaven knows how long. And very nice, too. So what can I do for you, lovie?'

'A few memories, Mrs Samuels,' said Roper.

'Oh, I've got plenty of those, dearie,' she assured him. 'I could write a book, believe me. How far back do you want to go?'

'Newby Magna,' said Roper. 'When you worked at the Moxleys' house. Can you remember that far back?'

'Like yesterday, lovie,' said Mrs Samuels dreamily. 'The best days of my bloody life they were. Seventeen and six

125

and two evenings off a week and one weekend free every month. And a new uniform every year. He was a lovely man, old Mr Moxley. Dead now, of course. House is gone too, so I hear. It's a nursing home or something, so my daughter told me.'

'When did you go to work for Mr Moxley, Mrs Samuels?'

'Maudie,' she said. 'Call me Maudie. More friendly, eh, dear? ... It was 1929 ... I remember 'cause I was twenty-five that year ... I'd taken myself up to London before that. I had a nice little job. In Lyons. That posh Corner House near Marble Arch. I was a Nippy, a little white cap and a pinny – but you wouldn't remember them, would you, dearie? Anyway, my old mother died and I had to go back to Newby Magna to keep an eye on my dad; girls did in those days. And I had a nice young man in London too. Nearly engaged, we were. But I had to come back, couldn't leave my dad all on his own, could I?'

Like Mr Newson's, Mrs Samuel's digressions were frequent, but she never let them wander too far, and her memory, if it wasn't playing her tricks, seemed to be pin sharp. Her father had been one of Squire Moxley's gardeners, and it was he who had spoken up for her when he had heard that the job of second parlour maid was about to become vacant at the manor house. She remembered young Master Colin being born, the one who was the vicar now. 1935, that was, the year of old King George's Silver Jubilee, and how the butler had bigamously married the cook; the next year, that was ...

' ... Trumper his name was. Did time for it. Gave him two years, they did. And he looked such a gentleman too, you'd never have believed it.'

She ran through name after name, a few fondly, a few others with scorn, but never mentioned once the name that Roper was hoping for.

He rose as Mrs Wing brought in the tea and biscuits on a trolley. 'Who's going to be mother?' she asked.

'Me, dear, hopefully,' cackled Mrs Samuels. 'It's just a question of time, that's all.'

Mrs Samuels's preference was for chocolate biscuits, one already in her mouth as she poured the tea and handed a cup and saucer across to Roper. 'It was going six years without 'em in the war,' she said, belatedly offering the plate of biscuits to Roper. 'There were times when I'd have passed up me honour for a choccy bikky. Now where were we, lovie?'

Roper sipped at his tea. 'Can you remember anyone else who worked on the estate, Mrs Samuels?'

'Well, they used to come and go a lot in those days, domestics; the young girls especially. There was Gwen Buckle − or was it Buckley, just before the war? Took herself off into the ATS, she did. Never saw her again. The war did it, you see. Went off in every direction, they did.'

'How about the men?'

Mrs Samuels frowned thoughtfully. Then shook her head. 'No. Sorry, lovie. All the men I remember I've told you about.'

'Mr Moxley had an estate manager. He used to live along at Box Cottage,' said Roper. 'Do you remember him?'

And he could see that she did, even if immediately she didn't say so. A sudden touch of affection joined the twinkle in the eyes, a few precious moments were bought by slowly stirring her tea again, then her hand stretched out for another chocolate biscuit to buy a few seconds more. She sat back in her chair and looked wistful.

'I've never forgotten him, lovie,' she said at last. 'But he died, you know. The war. Like young Mr Moxley.'

'You knew him well then, Maudie?' asked Roper, although really it wasn't a question so much as a prompt. That faraway look that had suddenly sprung into Maudie Samuels's eyes was born of something more than mere nostalgia.

'All the girls did, dearie,' she said dreamily. 'Rat-bag though he was.'

Roper, on the surface at least, let that pass. He took another sip of tea. And waited.

'I was coming up for thirty,' she said. 'On the shelf, that was, in those days. And he was such a big handsome bugger.' She fell to silence for a moment and bit a corner from her biscuit. She chewed it meditatively to extinction and washed it down with another sip of tea.

'I think we all had him,' she said. 'Young Ralph. All the girls. All the good-looking ones, anyway. And I was pretty myself in those days. I wasn't always like this, lovie ... hard to believe, I know. But I had a bloody good figure, even if I do say so myself, and lovely long hair. Blonde, I was. He used to like the blonde ones best, did Ralph.'

'Lovers, were you, Maudie?' asked Roper. 'Was that it?'

She downed another nibble of the biscuit and a swig of her tea.

'Lovers?' she said quietly. 'Gawd, lovie, I couldn't keep my hands off him. I used to sneak out of the big house at one o'clock in the morning sometimes and creep up to that Box Cottage and me legs used to be like two jellies. And creep back again at half past five before anybody else was up; and back in me cap and pinafore and looking as if butter wouldn't melt in me mouth while I served up the family breakfasts at eight o'clock. That was my life in those days, dearie, and I wouldn't have swopped it for *ten* pounds a week, take my word for it.' She leaned forward confidentially, slopping some of her tea into her saucer. '*She* don't know, mind.' Her mouth twisted distastefully. 'I never told *her*. Po-faced bitch. Wouldn't know what a proper man was, even if she had one, which she hasn't, of course.'

'Who's that, Maudie?' asked Roper.

'Her. My daughter.' She sat back again. 'I *never* told her. Well, I couldn't could I? And you could fool men in

128

those days. Old Samuels just thought she was a couple of months early. And if I'd told her, I'd have had to have told him, wouldn't I? And what the mind don't know the heart don't grieve about, as we used to say. Eh, lovie?' Smiling smugly, Mrs Samuels tipped the tea she had spilled back into her cup. 'I've *lived*, dearie, believe you me.'

Roper, by now, did not doubt it. It seemed that a lot had gone on under John Moxley's nose that he had never committed to that diary.

'November the fifth, 1932,' said Maudie Samuels, dreamily again. 'Firework night. That's when I started her. In front of the fire at Box Cottage, while all the others were up at the manor watching the bonfire. More tea, lovie?'

Roper declined. 'Did you ever think of sueing him, Maudie? Breach of promise, anything like that?'

Mrs Samuels laughed heartily. 'Breach of *promise*, duck? He hadn't ever promised *anything*. And it was *me* who did all the chasing, wasn't it? No, dear, I made me bed, as they say, so I had to lie on it.'

And then the late Mr Samuels, the Foxes' cowman in those days, had opportunely happened along . . . well, not exactly *happened* because he'd fancied Maudie since she was sixteen, so all Maudie had had to do was to fan a twelve-year-old spark back to life with a few flaps of her skirt.

'But he was a good man, when all was said and done, and he was very fond of me in his way. Older than me, of course. Been dead years now, he has, poor old Samuels.'

She bore no grudge. Every Christmas, Ralph Thorn had sent the child, now Mrs Harmer, a present. ' . . . And nothing cheap, dearie. The Christmas before the war it was a proper doll's house from Hamley's in London. Two or three pounds it must have cost him, and it was furnished an' all. I tell you, dearie, he was a *lovely* man. Educated. And he had this lovely voice, a mouthful of big strong white teeth and black curly hair. Here . . . ' She put the cosy back on the teapot. 'Top drawer. Over there by the bed. I'll show you his picture. In the toffee tin. My secret hoard, that is.'

Roper levered himself out of the armchair and went across to the institutional chest of drawers beside the bed. The picture on top of it was of grandson Albert, taken when he was young enough to be in his school's football team.

The drawer was full of sensible woollen underwear and thick lisle stockings. It smelled of old-fashioned lavender bags. The toffee tin was in the front left-hand corner under some nightdresses, George V and Queen Mary in profile on its gaudily printed lid, a relic of the Silver Jubilee of '35. The tin was in mint condition, and the antique buff in Roper valued it at about ten pounds, perhaps more.

Mrs Samuels opened it on her knees. Her will, her insurance policies – for her funeral expenses, they were; well, funerals cost the earth these days, didn't they, dearie? Her Post Office savings book. Fifteen hundred pounds in there, she confided. For Mrs Wing, although Mrs Wing didn't know about that. More thoughtful than any daughter, Mrs Wing was. A batch of old letters held together with an elastic band. A wedding photograph in a brown folder with tarnished silver tooling on the cover. Her and old Samuels, that was. January 20th, 1933. Maudie in a short white wedding dress with her lace veil thrown back, and old Samuels – he looked a good fifty then – looking as if he were being strangled half to death by his high celluloid collar, in his Sunday-best suit with baggy, crumpled trousers. And Maudie Samuels had been right. She had not always been the way she was now.

And then a faded photograph of her mother and father, mother standing behind bearded father who was sitting patriarchally in a high-backed wooden chair; and then a group photograph of all the Moxley family and their domestic staff, taken on the lawn in front of the manor house on May 12th, 1937.

' . . . Coronation day, that was, dearie. George the

Sixth's. Mr Moxley got a man down from Dorchester to take that. That's me, third from the left in the front row, in me cap and pinny. And next to me, that's the butler, the one that came after Mr Trumper went to prison, and next to him, that's Ralph Thorn. You can see what I mean about him, can't you, lovie?'

Mr and Mrs Moxley, son, daughter-in-law and grandson, sat in the middle of the front row, but it was Ralph Thorn, somehow, who dominated the photograph. He sat with folded arms and knees apart, and was smiling the smile that Roper had last seen on the photograph of him taken outside the Steadman house in Brighton a few years later. He wore a shooting jacket, breeches and riding boots, and even sitting down was still almost as tall as the young servant girl standing behind him. It was devastating, that smile; Roper, even as a man, could see that.

And the most dreadful of all Maudie's secrets. Her greatest treasure. A full-face photograph, in a little leather holder, of Ralph Thorn, taken in the days of his late youth. Handsome, smiling, sure of himself.

A lady-killer, if ever there was one; and perhaps not entirely metaphorically.

CHAPTER 9

And the old boy in the cloth cap in the back row was Maudie's father, died a few weeks afterwards, he did, bless him. And that one was Agnes Creech, she was the kitchen maid, and next to her was Georgie Manners, the stable lad. Took up together, those two did. And that tall lad was Jake Haygarth, the one that has the grocer's shop now, but in those days he used to be Moxley's chauffeur and handyman. And that girl there was Winnie Fox . . .

'. . . Went doolally, she did. In the war. Kept seeing Germans coming down on parachutes, she did. Silly old bitch. Not that she was so old then, mind.'

Winnie Fox. Roper recalled the name. And the old crone's face on Cassandra Murcheson's drawing-board.

'Do you have a magnifying glass, Mrs Samuels?'

'Never without one, dearie. I like to read the obituary columns, to see if there's anyone I used to know.' Mrs Samuels reached down to a knitting bag on a low table beside her and brought out an elderly magnifying glass. The one old Samuels used to pore over his butterfly collection. Like an old miser counting his money, he was, with those trays of butterflies. When old Samuels had died, Maudie had burned them. She never could bear dead things. *Never.* Ugh!

Time had cruelly ravaged Winnie Fox. Nearly forty years ago she had been an exceptionally attractive young woman, dark-haired, dark-eyed and grave-faced. At the time the Coronation photograph was taken she looked somewhere around thirty, give or take a couple of years.

132

Roper moved the glass down over Ralph Thorn, the raffish, handsome face that was rapidly becoming familiar, sitting there in the front row with his arms implacably folded and flashing his teeth at the camera for perpetuity. Seven years and a few days after that photograph had been taken, he had died, but Roper could still feel something of Ralph's life force radiating from the old picture. If he had not known better, he would have said that Thorn had looked indestructible.

'Some scandals in that photo, dearie,' said Mrs Samuels. 'In and out of each other's bedrooms like one o' those French farces, they used to be. I was living out then, 'cause of old Samuels and the baby, but I still heard all the gossip. My ears used to flap like taxi doors. Like I said, I could have written a book. Would you like this last digestive biscuit, dearie?'

Roper shook his head. When it came to tea and biscuits, Mrs Samuels was clearly a woman of no mean capacity. He waited while she drained the teapot into her cup and arranged the last of the biscuits on her saucer.

'When did you last *see* Ralph Thorn, Maudie?' he asked. 'D'you remember?'

Mrs Samuels briefly closed her eyes to give the matter its due and proper consideration. 'Well, to be honest, I don't, dear. Not exactly. In 1943, I got m'self a little job across at Poole. War work. Putting rivets into aeroplanes. It paid more, you see. Nearly six pounds a week, with overtime. . . . So I wasn't in the village much, except late at night and Sundays. And I don't think Ralph came home on leave much. . . . He was at Dunkirk, you know. And Crete. And Egypt for a while, with the Eighth Army. But I did hear . . . ' Maudie Samuels broke off momentarily to put her cup back on its saucer and to lean a little closer, and to cast a quick glance at the door. 'Course, it's only village gossip, and, as God's my witness, I never was one for gossip . . . except to listen to it.' She leaned closer still and dropped her voice to a conspirator's whisper. 'But I did hear that Jake Haygarth went along to Box Cottage one night . . . when Ralph *was* on leave, and waved his Home Guard's rifle at him. He was drunk, of course, Jake was, but it was something to do with Winnie Fox. Well, that's what I heard. But don't repeat that, will you, lovie, because it was only a rumour in the first place. And she was *years* older than Jake, too, and a hot little piece an' all, for all that she went to church twice on Sundays.' Maudie leaned back again in her wheelchair, her wickedly knowing smile taking cover behind her cup. 'Although she hadn't gone doolally then, you see.'

Roper took out his notebook, and on a new blank page wrote the names of Haygarth and Fox and followed each with a question mark. Not that he knew yet what questions he would ask, but they would spring to mind eventually. If Mr Haygarth had been given to waving guns about, drunk or sober, there must have been a reason of some sort.

'Can you remember what year that was, Maudie?'

Mrs Samuels puffed out her cheeks. 'Well,' she said, meditatively. 'It was Christmas and it was snowing. When was D-Day?'

''Forty-four,' said Roper. 'June.'

'It was the Christmas before, then,' she said. 'So it must have been the Christmas of 'forty-three.'

Roper flipped back a few pages of his notebook. Colin Moxley had also stated that Thorn had been back in the village that particular Christmas.

'So this Mr Haygarth didn't go into the army?'

'Flat feet, dearie,' said Maudie. 'At least, that's what he told everybody. They didn't take 'em in the army with flat feet, y'know. So he joined the Home Guard instead. Nice man, though; well, he was only a boy then, really. Twenty-two or three he was in those days. He liked his booze, mind.'

Roper continued to listen to Maudie Samuels's steady outpourings of potted histories. To Mrs Samuels, folk were mostly good; and the bad ones were only bad because of extenuating circumstances, which she went to great pains to point out. Only Winnie Fox, who went doolally, poor soul, could not be explained away within the framework of Maudie Samuels's experiences . . .

' . . . Probably living with those two men did it. Funny bloke, old Saul Fox. Always was. And that brother of hers, he was always a rum 'un an' all. *And* the war, of course. It had a lot to answer for, that war.'

'Did you ever hear any talk about Ralph Thorn getting married, Maudie?' asked Roper.

'No, dear, I never did. I wouldn't have thought he was the marrying kind. Love 'em and leave 'em, that was more his style.'

'He married a Brighton girl. A couple of weeks before he was killed.'

Maudie Samuels was momentarily stunned to silence. Then she threw back her head and burst into a cackle of wheezy laughter, so that her great body shook and the cup on her lap rattled about on the saucer. It was a good minute before she finally managed to recover herself, plucking a paper handkerchief from the cuff of her print dress and dabbing her eyes with it.

'Oh, I'm sorry, dear,' she gasped. 'That's a much better story than *all* of mine. So some poor little girl finally trapped him, did she? . . . You sure? I mean, I believe you, lovic, honestly. But Ralph . . . ? I wouldn't have thought it was possible.'

Roper assured her it was true. ' . . . I thought you read the newspapers, Maudie.'

'Not the newsie bits, dear. Just the gossip and the obituaries.'

So Roper told her of the recent events at Box Cottage, and Maudie Samuels was enthralled. From time to time she popped her eyes in horror, or quivered with delight. Maudie had heard of many strange doings in Newby Magna. But murder, no. *Never* a nice juicy murder. And Roper did not doubt that, by late tonight, there would not

135

be a single resident in Mrs Wing's home who had not been regaled with the latest tale of Box Cottage by the redoubtable Mrs Samuels. And Roper could borrow both of the photographs, the Coronation one *and* the picture of Ralph Thorn, provided, of course, that he took care of them, which she was *sure* he would. And, yes, she *did* like chocolates, but what she would rather have – Maudie cast another quick glance at the door and dropped her voice to a whisper again – what she would rather have was a quarter bottle of gin. Gordon's, dearie.

'Only keep it in your pocket until Mrs Wing has brought you up, lovie. Don't need her to know, do we?'

Roper and Colin Moxley sat together in the rear pew of the old Saxon church. From the vestry door, down by the altar rail, came the muted sound of a piano and the trills of choirboys practising the hymns for next Sunday. On Moxley's lap was the Coronation photograph. It was half past eight in the evening.

'D'you know, Mr Roper,' said Moxley, on a wave of nostalgia. 'I remember this picture so well, but I haven't seen it since grandfather sold up after the war. Frankly, I'm *astonished*. I never *ever* thought I'd see it again. I knew almost all of these people. . . . I don't suppose I could prevail upon you, could I?'

'I was going to get it copied for you anyway, Mr Moxley,' said Roper.

For a second or two, Moxley was beset by a great and overwhelming emotion. 'Well, bless you,' he said. 'Thank you, Mr Roper. I don't have many photographs of my father. I'm sure you understand. . . . If there's any way I can make recompense . . . '

'Well, yes, sir, there is. Could you fill me in about a gentleman called Jake Haygarth? He's someone else I'd like to talk to.'

'I know him very well indeed,' said Moxley. 'Jake's the secretary of the church committee. My secular right arm, you might say. He used to be my grandfather's chauffeur and odd-job man. – Here. This is Jake in the old days.' Moxley's forefinger circled the face of young Haygarth in the photograph. 'Why? Can he help you, d'you think?'

'Mrs Samuels told me he was in the village all through the war. He might be useful.'

'Yes, that's true,' said Moxley. 'As I recall, he was a sergeant in the Home Guard.' He slid back his shirt cuff and glanced at his wristwatch. 'You could speak to him now, I should think. He's just about shutting up his shop. If you hurry, you could catch him before he goes home.'

Jake Haygarth was just closing his shop door with his keys in his hand, ready to lock up for the night, a well-fleshed, burly man, and a far cry from the stripling boy of Maudie Samuels's photograph. At Roper's footfall behind him, he glanced back over his shoulder and switched on his shop-keeper's smile. Mr Haygarth was clearly a man with an eye to business.

'Something we can do for you, sir?'

'The name's Roper, Mr Haygarth.'

Into Haygarth's eyes came a sudden flicker of recognition, or perhaps it was wariness. 'Aye,' he said. 'You're that detective who's been working along at Box Cottage. I've seen you driving about with Tom Blake. What can I do for you?'

'Just a chat, sir,' said Roper. 'I'm not here officially. If you like we could talk over a beer along at the Arms.'

'I don't drink,' said Haygarth. 'Teetotal. Have been for years. And I was just on my way home.'

'I do need to talk to you, Mr Haygarth,' persisted Roper. 'I'm told you were about here during the war.'

'Aye,' said Haygarth guardedly. 'I was. . . . But I don't know anything about what's been happening along at Box Cottage.' He sent a covert look towards the forecourt of the Carpenter's Arms, outside which half a dozen locals

137

were chatting over their beers. Mr Haygarth evidently had a reputation to maintain and had no wish to be seen consorting with a policeman. A bell tinkled as he opened his shop door again. 'You'd better come in,' he said gruffly. Once inside, he locked the door behind them. 'Office is behind the counter,' he said, pointing.

Roper made his way between bags and boxes of greengrocery, and then between an aisle of display shelves, then through the open counter flap. Haygarth's muddly office had a sink in it and looked as if it had once been a scullery. The window was steel-barred, the desk a clutter of ledgers and invoices. Haygarth offered Roper his antiquated wooden swivel chair and pulled forward an old kitchen chair for himself. Roper waited while Haygarth plucked off his spectacles, breathed on them and then gave them a leisurely polish with the end of his necktie.

Unlike Maudie Samuels, it took some time for Roper to gain Haygarth's confidence and even then, he knew, he had not won it completely. Yes, Haygarth agreed reluctantly, he had worked along at the big house before and during the war. Chauffeur handyman. He had left the Moxleys' service in 1945. It was Squire Moxley who had lent him the two hundred pounds he had needed to buy this shop. He had been a good employer, had old John Moxley. They didn't make them like him these days.

The Coronation photograph was viewed with little reaction.

'Aye,' said Haygarth. 'That's me. Fourth on the right in the back row.'

'How about the others, Mr Haygarth? Any of 'em still about the village?'

Haygarth shrugged as he handed the photograph back. 'No,' he said. 'To be honest, if they were, I couldn't recognise them from that. Too long ago.'

It wasn't the truth. Roper could feel it . . . intuition, a gut feeling . . . something. Haygarth might be the Reverend Moxley's secular right arm, but he was also a liar.

'How about this lady? Maudie Samuels,' said Roper, leaning forward and tapping a forefinger over the young Mrs Samuels.

Haygarth's forehead puckered. 'Aye,' he conceded grudgingly. ' . . . Maudie. Maudie Whiteside, she used to be. Moved out, she did. Soon after the war. Went up to live in Dorchester. Haven't seen her in twenty years or more.'

'And how about this lady, Mr Haygarth?' Roper's finger slid across to Winnie Fox. 'I'm told she's still about.'

Haygarth shook his head.

'Her name's Fox, Mr Haygarth,' said Roper. 'Highview Farm.'

'It was a long time ago,' Haygarth grumbled. 'Coronation year, 'thirty-seven. I've forgotten what they all looked like.'

Roper doubted it. Haygarth and Winnie Fox had been in service together in the same house for several years, they had grown up together, probably went to the village school together, and both of them still lived in the same country village they were born in. They would have watched each other grow old.

'You know there was some trouble along at Box Cottage last night, Mr Haygarth?'

'Aye,' grunted Haygarth. 'Tom Blake told me.'

'And you told Sergeant Blake that you saw someone making off across one of Mr Fox's fields. About ten o'clock last night. That right, Mr Haygarth?'

'I'm not sure,' said Haygarth.

'You seemed pretty sure when you told Sergeant Blake, sir,' said Roper.

'I told him I saw a light; that's all.'

'A moving light, Mr Haygarth,' Roper reminded him. 'And lights don't move about on their own, do they, sir?'

Haygarth shrugged. 'I suppose not,' he said sullenly.

'Where were you exactly, Mr Haygarth, when you saw this light?'

'Here,' said Haygarth. 'I stayed late last night. Doing my books. I was sitting where you are now. I saw a light moving across the window.'

'Moving in which direction?'

'Left to right.'

'Towards Highview Farm.'

'Aye,' said Haygarth. 'It would have been. Can't say for sure, though.'

'Was it receding as well, d'you think? Or just moving from left to right?'

'Difficult to say,' said Haygarth. 'It kept going on and off.'

'As if whoever it was knew his way,' proposed Roper.

'Could have been,' agreed Haygarth. 'But I wouldn't really like to say. And I only know what Tom Blake told me. I don't hold with gossiping – nor false witness.'

'I'm sure you don't, Mr Haygarth,' said Roper patiently.

'Then why are you here at all?' asked Haygarth irritably. 'I've already told you I can't help you.'

'You lived in Newby Magna all through the war, sir?'

'Aye,' said Haygarth. 'So I did.' He jerked his head towards the photograph on Roper's knees. 'And so did most of those people.'

'But you just told me you didn't recognise any of them, Mr Haygarth,' Roper insisted quietly. 'So how do you know?'

'All right,' retorted Haygarth crossly. 'I remember all of them. Very nearly. But they're either dead, or I haven't seen them for years.'

'Let's start from another direction, shall we, Mr Haygarth?' said Roper, tucking the photograph into a foolscap envelope that Moxley had given him. 'I'm interested in a few things that went on around here about the end of the war. The manor house had been turned into a convalescent home for wounded officers. That right?'

Haygarth nodded.

'And you were still working there?'

'Aye. The Moxleys were still living in the south wing.'

140

'Do you remember Ralph Thorn, Mr Haygarth? John Moxley's estate manager?'

The question drew another grudging dip of Haygarth's head. 'Aye. Just about.'

'Can you remember when you last saw him, Mr Haygarth?'

Haygarth's plump, ruddy face stayed studiedly expressionless. 'No, of course I don't remember. It was over thirty years ago.'

'Try the Christmas of 'forty-three, sir,' prompted Roper, loosing a chance shaft. 'Perhaps that was the last time.'

It clearly was. A brief downward shift of Haygarth's eyes, quick as a camera shutter.

'It may have been,' he said. 'You can't ask a man to remember a particular Christmas. Not after all these years.'

'So it *was* a Christmas, Mr Haygarth?'

Haygarth at last conceded defeat. 'Aye,' he agreed. 'It was Christmas. I went along there.'

'Box Cottage?'

'Aye,' said Haygarth. He folded his hands together on his knees and spent a few moments contemplating them. 'Christmas Eve, it was. Thorn was on leave.' His left thumb massaged the back of his right hand as if it irritated him. 'He'd come home from Italy. For some sort of officers' training course.'

Roper waited. Haygarth was definitely a man with something on his mind.

'I was engaged to a village girl,' said Haygarth. 'Or I thought I was,' he added bitterly. 'The November, that was. We'd planned to get married the Easter of 'forty-four.'

Winnie Fox, probably; if Maudie Samuels had got it right.

Haygarth raised his head. 'The night before Christmas Eve, we were going to the pictures. Across at Dorchester. I had a motor-bike in those days. It was our evening off; we were both still working at the manor. But in the afternoon, she told me she couldn't come out that night.

141

Told me some cock and bull story about her father being ill . . . although I didn't know she was yarning me at the time, had no reason to, you see. Mind you, I didn't know Ralph Thorn was home on leave, either. He must have arrived back in the village the night before.'

The new, wry note in Haygarth's voice made it evident that he had seen Ralph Thorn as a rival, and had, perhaps, for a long time before that Christmas.

In the event, Haygarth had spent that evening along at the Carpenter's Arms with a few of his cronies, mostly the old ones because the lads of his own age were in the army. Also in the bar that night was the girl's brother . . .

'We didn't get on,' said Haygarth. 'They were a funny lot, her father and her brother. But it was Christmas . . . and I'd had a few too many . . . I drank like a fish in those days. I went to the bar. We had a drink together. And I asked him how the old man was. It turned out he wasn't ill at all. Made me angry, that did. Especially in the state I was in. I asked where *she* was. He told me she was along at the manor. Working.'

'And you knew she wasn't.'

Haygarth nodded. 'Aye,' he said. He did not remember the time when the landlord had finally turned him out of the Arms that night. Out here in the wilds, the licensing laws were scoffed at in those days and one of the last customers out of the pub was more often than not the village bobby.

'I woke up in a snowdrift somewhere,' said Haygarth. 'Frozen stiff and as drunk as a lord. Couldn't even work out where I was for a while . . . or why I was there. There were no street lights, you see. We had the blackout. Because of the air raids.'

'I remember it,' said Roper.

'Aye,' said Haygarth. 'I suppose you would.' He broke off for a few moments and examined his hands, fronts and backs. 'When I'd got myself warm again, I realised I was up by her place. Her father's place. If it hadn't been so

142

cold, maybe I'd have gone up there to sort her out. I had a terrible temper in those days. Terrible.'

In the ensuing silence, someone outside rattled the shop door. Haygarth didn't even look up.

'Anyway,' said Haygarth. 'Like I said, it was cold, so I made tracks back to the manor.'

Which wandering tracks had taken the young Jake Haygarth past the hedge of Box Cottage. And he had glimpsed a light at one of the front upstairs windows, and even in his half-stupor had realised that something was amiss.

'It was a sort of shimmering light,' he explained. 'Sort of orange. Kept coming and going. Very faint.'

For a moment, Haygarth had stood there trying to focus, trying to puzzle out what the light was. Then it occurred to him. It was a fire. Box Cottage was on fire.

'Well, I didn't like Ralph Thorn, but it was Squire Moxley's cottage, not his, so I worked out that I ought to be doing something about it, I suppose. It was thatched, the roof was, like it is now, and if that went up, even with all the snow on it, the cottage'd be gone. So in I went . . . didn't know what I was going to do, mind. Took one of my shoes off and started smashing out at the parlour window. Then all hell broke loose. Lights started coming on, then the front door opened, and there was Ralph Thorn, nothing on but his army boots. He got me . . . ' Haygarth gripped the lapels of his jacket. ' . . . here. And lifted me off my feet and chucked me down in the snow and beat the hell out of me . . . before he'd even seen who I was. And when he had, he dragged me back on my feet . . . and then I saw *her*. Halfway down the stairs. In a man's dressing gown. I went mad. But I was no match for *him*. Before I knew where I was, I was out in the lane again. On my back, with two of my teeth missing.' Haygarth opened his mouth and drew two of his upper front teeth fractionally downward to demonstrate that they were not his own, and had not been for many years.

143

'I *knew* I was going to kill him,' he went on, a quiet anger in his voice. 'I don't mind admitting it. She'd told me it was over, you see. Between her and Thorn.'

'But you didn't kill him?'

Haygarth slowly shook his head. 'No,' he said. 'But, God forgive me, I wanted to. And I wasn't the only one, mind. There was many a young man around these parts in those days who'd have taken a shotgun to Ralph Thorn.'

Roper's ears pricked sharply. 'A shotgun, Mr Haygarth?'

'Aye,' said Haygarth. 'We all had shotguns then.'

'But in your case, you had your Home Guard rifle as well, didn't you, Mr Haygarth?'

'You've been listening to too much gossip,' said Haygarth. 'I've heard that story, too. All the Home Guards had *rifles*. But we never had *ammunition*. When the Germans came, we were supposed to collect it from the village bobby's cottage. He kept it locked up in his kitchen cupboard. . . . No. It was a shotgun I took along to Ralph Thorn's on Christmas Eve morning. A twelve-bore. Knock a panel out of an oak door at six feet. Twin barrels and a cartridge in each of 'em. That's the mood I was in that morning.'

When Thorn had opened his cottage door, he had found the barrels of Haygarth's shotgun, the safety catches of both barrels thumbed off, thrust up under his chin.

'And, d'you know,' said Haygarth, with something close to admiration, 'Ralph Thorn didn't bat an eyelid. I could have blown his head off. I wanted to, believe me. Oh, yes, I dearly wanted to, God forgive me.' Haygarth shuddered briefly at the memory of all those years ago, and what he might have done to Ralph Thorn.

'It wasn't worth my while, he told me. You'll hang, old boy. That's what he said. I've always remembered that. You'll hang, old boy. He'd got an officers'-mess voice by then. Real BBC. She's gone to work, he said. If I wanted her, she was back at the manor. And I said, it wasn't her I was after, it was him, Thorn. But I knew already I couldn't do it. . . . And he knew, too. And he

144

laughed, and took hold of the barrels and pushed them to one side. She wasn't worth it, he said. No woman was. When I was older, I'd find that out. Then he broke the gun open and took the cartridges out.'

'And that was it?'

'Aye,' said Haygarth. 'That was it. And I still thank my lucky stars that it was. Or I'd have finished on the rope in Dorchester gaol. . . . And I'm not proud of it. I went up to the manor, gave my gun over to John Moxley and spent an hour crying on his shoulder. He was like a father to me, that man. He took me across to see Mr Leach . . . he was the vicar here then. I never took a drink after that. Never. I saw the light, you might say.'

'How about the young woman, Mr Haygarth?'

But Haygarth declined to commit himself further on the subject of the young woman who had been standing on the stairs that night.

'I think the less said about her the better,' he said. 'And it was no fault of hers. It was Ralph Thorn's. All of it.'

'Is she still living in the village, Mr Haygarth?'

'I'm sorry,' said Haygarth. 'I'm not going to tell you that, either. I've told you. It was Thorn's doing. He was an evil man. I know we aren't supposed to speak ill of the dead, but he was. A devil. And the body of that poor girl in the wall of Box Cottage, that was Thorn too. I'd lay odds on it, if I were a betting man.'

Roper rose to leave, and Haygarth was plainly relieved to see him go. He probably thought that his reply to Roper's last question was a suitable smokescreen, but so far as Roper was concerned it was evidence enough that the young woman was still living in Newby Magna, and perhaps across at Highview Farm.

Roper followed him back through the shop. Haygarth shot back the bolts and held the door open.

'I'd practically give an arm to know where you'd got the picture from,' he said. 'Don't suppose you're prepared to tell me, of course?'

145

'I'm like you, Mr Haygarth,' said Roper. 'I don't tell anybody anything I don't want them to know.'

Haygarth stood aside, holding open the door. 'Ralph Thorn killed that young woman along at Box Cottage. And he paid for it. God's will, that was.'

'And he's still coming back to haunt the place,' said Roper. 'Why's that, I wonder.'

'Because he still hasn't paid *enough*,' said Haygarth fervently, and for a moment Roper thought he was joking. 'He's still looking for somewhere to lay down his soul. That's my opinion.'

And, if Roper read Haygarth aright, the grocer was deadly serious.

At half past nine, Roper was back in his office and writing up a resumé of his day. He was in his shirtsleeves, his jacket over the back of his chair. The evening had turned muggy, and even with both the windows open not a breath of air stirred anywhere. It felt like storm weather.

At ten, the resumé committed to paper, Roper realised that he was really no further forward. He had learned a lot about Newby Magna in the years before and during the war, but he was still no closer to finding out who had killed Marjorie Steadman/Thorn on May the 27th, 1944, and perhaps he never would. Ralph Thorn seemed the likely villain, although it was unlikely that that could ever be proved thirty years on, which was a pity. All that could be said of Ralph Thorn, with any sureness, was that he had been a womaniser of some speed and stamina. And perhaps Albert Harmer's mother wasn't Thorn's only by-blow. Between Maudie Samuels's seduction and Winnie Fox's – Roper was fairly certain that the young woman Haygarth had seen on Thorn's stairs that night had been Winnie Fox – some eleven years had elapsed. And in eleven years a man of Thorn's repute could have sown a crop of bastards all over the county. And beyond. Marjorie Steadman, Roper recalled, had also been pregnant at the time of her death, and she had come from Brighton. When it came to sex, Ralph Thorn seemed to have been unstoppable, and his lady friends more than willing. The local lads must have hated him. And that was surely a motive for something or other.

The storm broke at ten thirty, with flashes of lightning over the downs and the gun-bursts of thunder gradually drawing closer until they were right overhead and rattling the windows.

On a fresh sheet of paper, Roper wrote a few names. Steadman. Thorn. Moxley. Haygarth. As an afterthought he added another. William Monk, retired civil servant, late of Streatham, London, later still of Box Cottage, Newby Magna. Because if Blake's intuition was right, and it probably was, William Monk had also been murdered at Box Cottage. And now a young woman, Cassandra Murcheson, was having the frighteners put on her at that same cottage. Why? What secret, after thirty years, could Box Cottage still hold? And for whom? Because it was certainly someone who was still very much alive. Unlike Jake Haygarth, Roper was inclined to the belief that Ralph Thorn's soul, together with the rest of him, had been blown to pieces in Normandy a few days after D-Day.

A mighty crash of thunder seemed to suck all the air out of the room as Roper lit a cheroot. There was someone in Newby Magna with something to hide. Someone who had lived there for all, or most, of a lifetime. Someone to whom something in Box Cottage still offered a threat. The threat could not have been the corpse of Marjorie Steadman, because the soldier in the garden had appeared *after* the body had been found in the wall. Ergo: there was something else . . .

But what?

Whatever it was, the late Miss Gomersall, the tenant of Box Cottage for the twenty years after the war, had been disregarded as its potential discoverer. The hippies who had camped there had been driven out, and so had the couple who had lived there after them, and so had been William Monk, although he had left feet first in a box.

Thunder flapped again and resounded away into the distance, and it was that which had masked the brisk rap of knuckles on Roper's office door. When he glanced up, DS Morgan's face was peering round the edge of it.

'Thought you were supposed to be on leave,' said Morgan. 'I've been trying to phone you at home all evening.'

'Something come up?'

'Could be,' said Morgan, cautiously. He came in all the way and shut the door behind him. Roper stretched out a foot under his desk and kicked his visitor's chair back a few inches.

'You don't sound all that sure about it.'

'I've had my knuckles rapped,' said Morgan. 'Superintendent Mower. Army Records rang. They wanted you. And since you weren't here, they wanted the next ranking officer . . . upward. Which was Mower.'

'So you copped it.'

'Bloody right,' said Morgan, gloomily. 'And it's your turn tomorrow. He wants you in his office at first light, leave or not, that's what he said. He wants to know, I quote: what the hell does bloody Chief Inspector Roper think he's buggering about at? End of quote. I think what got him was the call from the Ministry of Defence – it sort of caught him with his pants down.'

'I'll sort it out with him in the morning,' said Roper. 'What did Records have to say?'

Morgan reached into his jacket for his pocket book. 'You're in for a surprise, guv. Ralph Thorn *wasn't* killed in France. Or if he was, the Army doesn't know about it.'

'Where was he killed then?' asked Roper, with quickening interest.

'He wasn't,' said Morgan, opening his notebook and flipping back a couple of pages. 'On paper, at least, he's still in the army. He was given a four-day pass to get married on May 26th, 1944. He never went back. He's still on the records as being absent without leave.'

'So who sent that telegram to old Squire Moxley?' asked Roper.

'It wasn't the War Office,' said Morgan. 'Definitely.'

But somebody had, thought Roper. Definitely.

CHAPTER 10

In the dream it was a sandstorm, hot and choking and blinding, the wind screaming in her ears and cramming her head with noise. The waking was equally terrifying, her fingers scrabbling at her throat to loosen whatever it was that was so tightly tied around it, her breath sawing in and out, the muscles of her chest paralysed, a tremendous weight pressing down on it, the thunderous roar of pumping blood coursing through her ears. Only there was nothing around her throat and only the weight of a sheet pressing down on her chest and she knew that if she didn't move soon she would die, and she was on her knees on the floor and crawling across it, and cracking her head on something which made her dizzier still, and it was tempting simply to lie down and surrender to it, only her old Dad was telling her to fight it, Cass, whatever it is, girl, fight it! And he was there, her Dad was. Somewhere in the black and all-enveloping dark. Only she was choking to death and he couldn't seem to understand that. Her fingers found the leg of a chair. She had crawled the wrong way. The chair was by the window, and she had set a course for the door. Dear God, where was the door? For a moment, the chair was an anchor, a base, a point of reference in the midst of this airless choking dark that would eventually engulf her . . .

Hand over hand, she found the top of the chair leg, the seat, the back, her will slowly receding and her consciousness with it. What gripped her chest now was like an iron vice. She caught a blurred glimpse of the moonlit

150

gap in the curtains, aimed the chair, once, twice. Heard glass shatter the second time, and again, and again, until she was finally exhausted and subsided, unconscious, still with the roaring in her ears, because it was so much easier to die than to fight it.

The deafening roar had become a gentle hiss, overlaid with voices calling to each other. A blue light flashed insistently through her eyelids, and it seemed to take an eternity for her to struggle up from wherever she was, like swimming up from the bottom of the sea with lead weights tied to her limbs. And she tried to tell someone that she was going to be sick, which she was, heartily and achingly and disgustingly, and again, and she mumbled that she was sorry, Christ, she was really sorry, and whatever had been over her face was pressed back again, and it hissed and smelled sweet and clean and fresh. And when she finally ungummed her eyelids and peered out through their two slits, she made out a white ceiling and a fluorescent lamp that started off as half a dozen and gradually fused into the one bright blur. And there was a woman crouching beside her, in an unbuttoned grey tunic and black necktie, and it was she who was holding the oxygen mask. And Sergeant Blake was standing over her as well, and good old Blackbeard from next door, and the flashing blue lights were coming from the cab-roof of a fire-engine parked behind the ambulance. And she was going to be sick again, sorry, and she was rolled on to her side and felt the chill of the steel bowl against her chin, and her shoulders heaved in convulsion after convulsion and she wished they had let her die in the first place, because it really would have been easier than this ghastly public performance.

Someone wiped her mouth. Someone else fed her cold water that tasted like nectar through a plastic straw, and all the air she had gulped down with it vented itself in a huge belch. And at last she became aware that she was being viewed by all and sundry with visible relief, and that she was wearing a hospital nightshift that she had never gone to bed in and that whoever had carried her out of her blazing cottage had seen her all, which wasn't much to shout about in any case, but it was hers and it was private, and she dearly hoped it hadn't been Blackbeard.

The ambulance went down on its back springs as someone else climbed aboard it. A white helmet and yellow leggings swam fuzzily into focus.

'What was it?' asked Sergeant Blake.

'Wet grass,' said the fireman. 'A bloody great ball of it, stuffed down the kitchen chimney.'

'Bastards,' said Blake.

'Bloody right,' said the fireman, vehemently.

With difficulty, Cassandra managed to bring him in sharper focus. 'It's not burned out, is it?'

'No, miss,' said the fireman. 'Another half-hour and it would have been but it isn't. We're just rolling up.'

'Rolling up?'

'Hoses.'

'Ah,' she said, and thought she was going to throw up again, but didn't quite. More of that delicious water. And a headache like a crazed dwarf racing round the inside of her skull beating his drum. More oxygen. Her lungs felt as if someone had lit a bonfire in them. It hurt her to breathe. It was just daylight. And she still had a cottage, not that she cared all that much. She briefly slipped away again, and when next she surfaced the ambulance was moving at some speed, the attendant was holding the mask over her face again and Blackbeard was standing by the doors at the back and holding on to the overhead rail. A length of white pyjama cord hung out between his moth-eaten pullover and his trousers, and looked faintly obscene and made her want to laugh only she knew that if she did she would be horrendously sick again. And it came to her, in passing, that a dozen bloody Stevens wouldn't even make half a Blackbeard, even on their good days.

★ ★ ★

152

Roper climbed out of the Escort on one side and DS Morgan on the other. Deeply impressed into the wet grass of the verge were the tyre marks of the fire-engine that had called here in the early hours of this same Friday morning.

Sergeant Blake let them into the cottage. He had finished his night's sleep on the chesterfield in the parlour and had still to shave and have his breakfast.

'How's Murcheson?' asked Roper.

'Making a bloody nuisance of herself,' said Blake. 'According to Ted Cambridge, she's discharging herself at lunchtime, whatever the doctors say.'

'Bully for her,' said Roper. 'What's the damage?'

'There isn't any,' said Blake. 'Mind you, if it hadn't been raining, given another half-hour, the grass in the chimney would have dried out and might have set the whole bloody roof alight.'

As Roper went into the narrow passage, Cambridge was just coming down the stairs with a small suitcase. Cassandra Murcheson's clothes, he explained. He was collecting her at midday, in the Mini, and what the hell were the police going to do about it all now? Because, in his book, what had happened here last night was attempted murder.

'I'd like a statement from you, Mr Cambridge,' said Roper. 'What you heard, what you saw.'

'Gladly,' said Cambridge, and if Roper was reading the auguries correctly there was perhaps more going on between Cambridge and Cassandra Murcheson than either of them was letting on.

While Blake took Morgan on a conducted tour of the outside of the cottage, Roper and Cambridge made themselves comfortable in the parlour. The ragged hole in the wall was still as naked as when Roper had last seen it. He took out his pocket-book and a ballpoint and wrote the time, 09.15, and the date.

'In your own time, Mr Cambridge. No hurry.'

Cambridge settled back on an old kitchen chair that

153

creaked ominously under his weight. He could remember the hour with reasonable accuracy, five minutes to four had been the time when he had finally turned into bed, and he had only been in it a couple of minutes when he had heard the sound of banging, and breaking glass, two, three times. On the off-chance that Miss Murcheson was the victim of another of those night visits from whoever it was, he had got out of bed again, stepped into whatever was at hand by way of clothes, and hared along there with a torch. It had been raining. At first he had seen nothing untoward, then, flashing his torch over the back upstairs windows, he had seen that the leadwork of one was buckled outward. Then he had trodden on glass shards underfoot. He had called up, hammered on the front door, and finally broken in through the parlour window because by now he smelled trouble, and when he had finally climbed in over the window sill he had smelled something more palpable. Coke fumes. The 'entire place reeked of them; by the time he had reached the landing, he had hardly been able to breathe himself.

Cassandra Murcheson had been lying huddled over the legs of an overturned chair, unconscious. Cambridge had carried her downstairs, opened the front door to let some air in, and laid her down on the passage floor with her head on the front step. It had taken some time, and a lot of hard work, before he had managed at last to breathe some life back into her and restore sufficient pulse in her for him to be able to feel it. From time to time, he had shouted for help. But no one had come.

' . . . So I had to leave her,' said Cambridge. 'I covered her up with my pullover and trousers as best I could, ran back to my own place, and took the moped down to Blake's house. End of story.'

Well, not quite, thought Roper. According to Blake's hurried telephone call this morning, Cambridge had gone in the ambulance with Murcheson last night and at the time Blake had contacted Roper – 8.45 – Cambridge had still not returned from the hospital.

154

'Did you hear anything before all this happened, Mr Cambridge?'

No, he had not. He had been working in his studio. When he was working he shut everything else out. But he *was* sure about the time he had heard the glass breaking. A few minutes after five to four. He was absolutely positive.

Roper dropped to a crouch beside Morgan and Blake at the far end of the back garden. Rain still dripped from the shrubbery round about, but the sun was out now and would soon boil it off. With the cap end of his ballpoint pen, Roper carefully tipped over the little black rubber box, hooked it out from under the hedge and drew it out into the light.

It was not rubber after all. It was a hard black plastic, ribbed on its bottom. Rainwater from its inside dribbled down the pen. It was an anti-slip pad, from the bottom of a ladder. And it had been lying only a few inches from the scarred bark at the base of the hedge that Roper and Morgan had noticed the other day, except that the plastic pad had not been there then. So this particular spot had been used twice now, for entry *and* egress, by whoever it was who was harassing Cassandra Murcheson. Only this time he had left something substantial behind; and taken with him a ladder, probably made of aluminium, because wooden ones were not often fitted with anti-slip pads, and aluminium ladders were lighter than wooden ones to carry about, and with any luck he had cached it away in a shed or an outhouse somewhere without examining it. In which case he was in for a surprise when the police came calling. Which would not be long now, because this investigation at last had the blessing of Superintendent Mower and the ACC and was going to be very official.

By ten thirty, Roper was in charge of three DCs seconded on detachment from County Headquarters, six uniformed constables and a sergeant, twelve gumbooted cadets armed with plastic bags and tweezers, two scene

155

of crime technicians and a scientific officer from the Regional Forensic Laboratory, who had already sniffed out with his gas-detector a higher than usual level of carbon monoxide still lurking in the less draughty corners of Miss Murcheson's kitchen.

Roper held the makeshift briefing in the parlour, his crew gathered about him either on the few chairs and tea-chests or on the floor. It was, he informed them, a full-scale investigation into an attempted murder, but he didn't want any fannying about just because there wasn't any body. Whoever the villain was, his land probably had access to that ditch behind the hedge in the garden. The cadets were to walk the length of it. And anything they found, from a cigarette end to a dead rabbit, was likely to be evidence so it was to be harvested with great care, put into a bag and labelled, and that bag was to be placed in a bigger bag to be sent to Forensic. By tonight at six o'clock.

Under the aegis of DS Morgan, the six uniformed constables were to pair off, start at the northern end of the village and work south. They were on door-to-doors. *All* the doors.

'You're looking for an aluminium ladder,' said Roper. 'An extension ladder that could reach the kitchen chimney-pot. That's about twenty-five feet. And it's missing one of these.' He held up the black plastic anti-skid block, now in a polythene evidence bag. 'When you find the ladder, say nothing. Just come quietly away and tell DS Morgan and DS Morgan will tell me. Sergeant Blake will hand out maps. – And if anybody refuses you admission, or insists on a search warrant, then I want to know about it. Have you all got that?'

They all had.

By eleven, Roper was nosing round the cottage on his own. He could still smell coke fumes in the fabric of the curtains, and in the cupboard under the stairs. In a confined space, which the cottage was with all its doors and windows shut, carbon monoxide was a certain killer. Given a few more minutes last night, Cassandra Murcheson's trip to the local infirmary would have seen her tucked up in the mortuary instead of a ward. Whoever had been here last night had meant business.

Her bed was exactly as she had left it, the solitary sheet with which she had covered herself trailed across the floor between the bed and the window. The leadwork of the left-hand lattice casement was bowed outward, four of its panes smashed out, another half-dozen cracked. It would have been easier for her to have opened it, but her brain had probably slipped out of gear by then. A chair lay on its side under the window, a tiny fragment of glass, twinkling like a diamond, adhering to one of the legs. So the chair had obviously been her battering ram.

There was a new picture on the drawing-board in her studio so she had clearly been working hard over the last few days. This one was almost finished, a metal-clad Superhero feverishly working at the controls of some kind of interstellar battleship. He bore, Roper noticed, a more than passing resemblance to Mr Edward Cambridge of this same parish, and perhaps it wasn't arty art, but it was meticulously observed and painstakingly executed.

At the side of the cottage, the boffin from the laboratory was hanging precariously sideways from an aluminium ladder and peering down the chimney that flued the kitchen.

'Found anything?' called Roper.

The man swung back to a more secure stance on the ladder, and glanced down. 'Could be,' he shouted back. 'A couple of flower petals. Blue ones. They could have got stuffed down with the grass. . . . And there's a black mark on the rendering . . . here.' He reached out and pointed to a smudge on the chimney stack a few inches from its top. 'It might have been scraped from the plastic block at the other end of that ladder. I'll run a few tests when I get back to the lab.'

157

'Bully,' said Roper. Because that anti-skid block, on its own, proved next to nothing. It could, for instance, have been thrown there by a youngster. But finding a mark left by identical material, twenty-five feet up a chimney stack, was what a jury would consider to be irrefutable evidence. And flower petals didn't drop into chimney pots on their own, as a rule, so the forensic officer was probably right: the couple he had found had been stuffed in with the grass last night. And if they could be identified, then their source might also be.

He moved on to the far end of the garden, past the rockery that had seen better days. A featherboard potting shed alongside the hedge looked to be in imminent danger of collapse. He dropped to his heels in front of the hole in the bottom of the hedge. The soil and grass around it had definitely been recently disturbed, certainly more so than when he had looked at it the other day. And a row of depressions in the grass between the hole and the flagged path were more than likely jack the lad's footprints, although last night's rain and this morning's sunshine had more or less obliterated their exact shape. If any muddy prints had been left on the path, and they probably had, the rain had seen those off too. Which was a pity. The weather had been singularly fortuitous for the villain last night.

Water sloshed nearby, the sound drawing closer. 'Sir,' a disembodied voice said. 'Down here, sir.'

A cadet, standing in the ditch, was peering up through the gap in the hedge. 'Sergeant Hume told me to bring you this, sir. I've just found it, down by the culvert.' He passed it up through the hedge. It was a crumpled, and very wet, black plastic rubbish sack. 'Looks as if it's had grass in it, sir.'

'Gloves,' said Roper.

The cadet took off his green rubber gauntlets and handed them through the hedge. Roper wriggled his hands into their warm, sticky insides and shook the bag into shape and opened it. It had definitely had grass in it, and still

158

had, here and there, adhering to its inside. And several wild-flower petals. Blue ones.

'Why?' asked Roper.

'They want her out of the cottage,' said Morgan.

'Why?' persisted Roper. 'We've found the body. So what else is hidden away up there?'

Morgan sipped at his beer. It was half past two in the afternoon. He and Roper were sitting at a ricketty iron table on the sunny forecourt of the Carpenters' Arms. 'Evidence,' he ventured. 'Something that might tell us who killed Marjorie Steadman.'

'Which means that somebody around here knows something that we don't.'

'Perhaps Ralph Thorn's still about,' said Morgan. 'Somewhere. Perhaps it's him.'

Roper doubted that. If Ralph Thorn were still alive, and if he had had any sense, he would have changed his name and be living miles away from Newby Magna. And if he had been living another life for the last thirty years, and had remained undetected, there would be little point in his coming into the open now to cover up an old murder when only a few years ago he might also have murdered William Monk.

'If he's anywhere,' said Roper. 'He's staying low.'

'Perhaps somebody around here has got some weird idea of protecting him. An old girlfriend.'

'Old's the operative word,' said Roper. 'She'd have to be rising sixty; and be tough enough to handle an aluminium extension ladder – as well as climbing in and out of a four-foot-deep ditch. It's a man. Bet your life.'

And Morgan had to agree with that. It had to be a man. A local man. Someone who had lived around these parts during the war – and still did. He would have to be between forty-five, say, and eighty-five.

'Eighty-five-year-old men don't nip up and down ladders in the dead of night,' said Roper.

159

'They're a pretty healthy lot around here,' said Morgan. 'Some of these old farmers.'

'Aye,' said Roper. 'But not that fit. Let's say he *could* be sixty. At a push. . . . But what's he trying to hide? And where is it?'

'Perhaps it's nothing to do with Thorn *or* the Steadman girl,' said Morgan. 'It could be something else. Perhaps the bloke's an old tea-leaf. And he buried his loot in the garden, and never dared to dig it up again.'

A glimmer of light shone . . .

'Jesus,' muttered Roper, almost choking on a mouthful of bitter. 'That's *it*! Dan, that's *bloody it!*'

And it probably was IT. William Monk, the elderly couple who had preceded him, the hippies, all of them had gone vigorously to work on the garden at Box Cottage. Miss Gomersall had not. Miss Gomersall had left the garden alone. Miss Gomersall, ergo, had been left in peace for twenty years. Miss Murcheson, on only her second day in Newby Magna, had told Albert Harmer that she wanted him to clear the garden for her.

And that was when her troubles had started. It was nothing to do with the body in the wall.

Whatever the real secret was, it was in the garden.

Nose down, tail down, the German shepherd sniffer-dog had dutifully quartered the garden for the best part of an hour. It had located nothing.

'Might do better if we knew what we were looking for,' observed Superintendent Mower tartly. The Superintendent had decided to grace the scene of the crime with a courtesy-call; which was a Mower euphemism for a hustling exercise. 'Any results from the door-to-doors yet?'

'No, sir,' said Roper.

'And still no sign of the ladder?'

'No, sir.'

Mower drew out a Georgian silver snuff-box from his waistcoat, and tapped it. Opening it carefully, he offered it

to Roper, which Roper recognised as a form of apology for
the tongue lashing Mower had given him at five past eight
this morning. Roper shook his head. Mower measured out
a pinch of snuff on to the back of his left hand. 'I want a
result here, Douglas. Sharpish.'

'Yes, sir.'

'Right, sir. Three bags full, sir,' said Mower, dipping
his head over the back of his hand, then sniffing daintily.
'We seem to have made several mistakes about this cottage
over the years. I want 'em tidied up.'

'Right, sir,' said Roper.

'Good,' said Mower, his eyes beginning to water. He
fumbled hurriedly in his jacket pocket for a handkerchief.
Why he never had the handkerchief ready beforehand
Roper had never found out, but the Superintendent was
always fractionally too late. His explosive sneeze ruptured
the silence of the sunny afternoon. He dabbed at his nose
with the handkerchief, then blew it noisily. 'Mind you,' he
said. Nobody could change his conversation in midstream
quite like Mower. 'It's an interesting case this, Douglas.
Thirty-year-old body; likely villain done a bunk from the
army; midnight hauntings. . . . *And* Mr Monk. I've been
taking a look at Sergeant Blake's old memos to the ACC.
Could he have been on the right track, d'you think, about
Monk?'

'I'd say it was very likely,' said Roper.

Mower gave a final blow to his nose before tucking
his handkerchief away again. 'So what's next on your
agenda?'

'I thought we'd turn the garden over,' said Roper, and
waited for Mower to erupt.

'So you'll want a few more cadets,' said Mower, mildly,
to Roper's surprise. He glanced at his wristwatch. 'I'll have
'em with you in half an hour. But what about the lady
owner? Want a warrant, will she?'

'I doubt it,' said Roper. 'I reckon she'll see it as a favour.'

Mower cast a jaundiced eye over the tangle of grass

161

and undergrowth. 'Yes,' he agreed. 'I see what you mean.
. . . But it's got to be quick,' he warned. 'Otherwise we'll
have the ACC on our necks. Follow?'

'Follow,' said Roper.

'Good,' said Mower, turning away before loosing his
parting shot: 'End of next week, Douglas, and I'll want
it wrapped up.'

Roper followed Mower's tall, hunched figure back up
the garden path, the Superintendent turning off beside the
cottage to return to his car, Roper going in through the
open door to the kitchen. Miss Murcheson was back from
hospital. She still looked groggy. Cambridge was in attend-
ance in the kitchen, chopping up something on a board,
it sounded like vegetables. He was obviously going to be
her head cook and bottlewasher for a few days.

'How do you feel now?' asked Roper.

'Lousy,' she said, tipping down her sunglasses and peering at him over the top of them. 'The mother and father
of all headaches. So please don't ask me anything I've got
to think about.'

'One question,' said Roper. 'Then I'll leave you in peace.'

She hitched her sunglasses back to the bridge of her
nose. 'Shoot.'

Roper perched himself on the corner of a tea-chest.
'Albert Harmer,' he said. 'He was going to do some
gardening for you.'

'Yes,' she said. 'He was going to make a start at the
weekend.'

'The entire garden?'

'Well, no, not exactly. All we talked about was scything
the lawn and clearing up that heap of rubble the estate
agent called a rockery.'

Roper lifted his head sharply at that. It had been the
rockery that William Monk had been about to refurbish
when he had, allegedly, shot himself.

'You didn't ask him to turn the ground over? You
didn't ask him to do any digging?'

She shook her head.

'You're sure?'

'Definitely.'

'But you *did* ask him to take down the rockery. You made a point of that?'

'Yes. I think so.'

Roper put his hands on his knees and levered himself upright. 'Do you mind if we do it, Miss Murcheson?'

'How much is it going to cost me?' she asked suspiciously.

'Nothing,' said Roper. 'It's down to the County Constabulary.'

'Great,' she said. 'You've got yourself a deal.'

CHAPTER 11

Mower was as good as his word. Four more cadets, boiler-suited and gumbooted, arrived in a van at four o'clock, their equipment ranging from a pickaxe to archaeologists' bristle brushes and dustpans, and with some conventional gardeners' spades and forks in between.

Roper gathered them around the rockery. It was to be dismantled, he explained, stone by stone, the soil and plants in it removed only with trowels, or hands, and put into plastic sacks, for a second examination if that proved necessary.

'And I don't want anybody charging in. You pick it all over. The big chunks of soil you put through the sieve.'

'Do we know what we're looking for, sir?' asked the brightest-looking of them.

'No, son, we don't,' said Roper. 'Could be anything. Housebreaker's loot, somebody's granny's bits of jewellery; a body. Might even be a weapon of some sort. But whatever it is, I want it. Intact.'

He watched them buckle to, arranging tarpaulin sheets round the base of the rockery to catch anything that fell, then levering out the scattering of large rocks on top and carefully brushing each one down before setting it aside on the grass. There were nearly five hours of daylight left, so the job might be done that day. If nothing was found, then first thing next morning Roper would set them digging up the lawn. It might all be a waste of time, but somehow he doubted it. There was something here, somewhere, and William Monk might have died because of it, and last night

Cassandra Murcheson had only just escaped a similar fate by the skin of her teeth because of it.

As yet, none of the door-to-door men had reported back about finding a ladder with a pad missing from one leg; nor had Sergeant Hume, in charge of the ditch party, found anything beyond that plastic sack with the grass cuttings in it, but he still had a good quarter of a mile to go in the direction of the village so there was still a chance.

At five o'clock, Cambridge brought out five assorted mugs of tea on a tray. 'How's it going?' he asked Roper, offering the tray.

'Thanks,' said Roper, slipping a finger into a mug handle. 'Nothing, so far. Just soil and rocks. And a 1968 ha'penny. How's Miss Murcheson?'

'Knocking back Codeines still. But she says she's feeling better.'

Roper sipped at his tea. 'Where's she spending the night?'

'My place,' said Cambridge.

'Good,' said Roper.

By six o'clock the rockery was only half the height it had been when the cadets had started on it, a levelled-off platform of dark wet soil, rocks and old bricks, only eighteen inches or so now above the surrounding soil, and the only recent find had been a cut-glass stopper that might have come from an old wine decanter. The cadets, Roper observed, were fast losing interest, and in all honesty he could not blame them. The most demoralising aspect of coppering was looking hard for hours and finding nothing, and it was always worse when you did not know what you were looking for in the first place. It looked as if tomorrow they would have to start digging up the garden.

Roper heard a van pull up in the lane in front of the cottage. A few moments afterwards, Sergeant Hume, capless and in his shirtsleeves, came clumping round the side of the house in his gumboots. The expression on his face looked promising.

165

'Found something?' asked Roper.

'Up behind the Carpenter's Arms,' said Hume, a hefty, fleshy man to whom the hot evening sun was doing no kindness. 'One of the lads found a sheared-off clump of grass in the ditch. When we offered it up to a likely patch on the lip of the ditch, it fitted like a bit of a jigsaw puzzle.'

'Which side?' asked Roper.

'The side opposite the Arms,' said Hume. 'I think you ought to take a look.'

'So do I,' said Roper. 'I'll follow you up in the car.'

At five past six, gumbooted himself, Roper was in the drainage ditch behind the Carpenter's Arms and checking that the waterlogged clump of grass and soil that the cadet had found did indeed fit, more or less, a scar at the edge of the ditch on its northern side. It looked recently done, and since both wet clump and gouged-out scar showed evidence of torn grass roots, the damage had not been caused by the mere onslaught of last night's rain. Something heavy. Like a skidding human foot, or heel. Or the end of a ladder. In the moonlight. Last night. Better evidence would have been footprints in the ditch, but if there had been any, either the rainwater would have washed them away or the cadets had trampled all over them. As it was, there were still a couple of inches of water at the bottom of the ditch now. At this point, the ditch itself was only two feet deep. The meadow land that bordered the ditch on the north side sloped gently upward from it. At the top of the rise a small herd of cattle grazed listlessly, tails occasionally twitching to drive off the flies. It all looked very quiet, very peaceful.

Roper moved a few paces upstream, where the ditch was shallower, and stepped up on to the grass, then walked carefully back in the hope of finding a shoeprint or two leading up to the meadow, knowing full well that after all the rain it would be a lost cause.

Or perhaps it wasn't . . . Luck came in the shape of

166

a cowpat. It had lain in the grass long enough for the sunshine to have put a hard crust on it, but before it had, someone had walked across the edge of it and left a shoeprint behind, as sharp as if it had been cast in plaster of paris. The outer half of a right shoeprint, from toe to heel; or rather, more strictly speaking, half of a print left behind by a passing gumboot, because both sole and heel had a barred tread across them. And since the grass had been grazed fairly short round about, and since the pat was not obscured in any way, the impression was unlikely to have been made during the hours of daylight. Ergo: it was more likely to have been made at night. And all the visitations of Box Cottage had been made at night.

'Any of your lads been up here?' called Roper.

None of them had. So the print had not been left behind by a police boot.

Roper lined up his right gumboot with the impression in the cowpat, and started walking up the slope in the same general direction, all the time looking for another pat with another print in it, although he knew that that was asking too much of a providence that might already have been too generous.

He was watched all the way by the herd of cows, until one of them took fright and spooked the others and they trotted out of sight over the rise.

He climbed only a few feet higher before a distant chimney stack came into view, then a grey slate roof, then a farmhouse with a haphazard clutter of dilapidated sheds and outhouses at its side and back, and a couple of dutch barns with corrugated iron roofs in the middle distance. The house itself was of Portland stone, a grey, dreary place with too few windows, none of which were opened despite the warmth of the evening. An elderly, rust-pocked Vauxhall Victor stood in front of the clapboard wooden porch, which was in an equal state of disrepair. He moved back out of sight as a wiry little man in a cloth cap, white shirt and baggy black trousers came out of the porch and opened the boot of the Victor. If it had not been for the car parked outside it, the farmhouse might have been frozen in time for the last eighty years.

Roper reached into his jacket for the map of Newby Magna that Tom Blake had marked up for him the other day, unfolded it and oriented it with the alignment of the ditch and the roof of the Carpenter's Arms behind him.

The house over the rise was Highview Farm, home of the Fox family, and Cassandra Murcheson's witch, a.k.a. Winnie Fox, one time lover, according to Maudie Samuels, of Ralph Thorn.

Roper called up Sergeant Hume. He wanted a photograph of the cowpat, with a ruler and a polar compass beside it, and a plaster cast made of it, because somewhere there was a gumboot sole that would match the impression in the pat.

'How about a warrant?' said Hume.

'Look innocent,' said Roper. 'Tell 'em you thought it was common land.'

'A cowpat?' one of the cadets muttered incredulously, as Roper sloshed back into the ditch and stepped out again on its other side. 'He's *got* to be bloody joking.'

'You can die laughing afterwards, son,' retorted Hume, tartly. '*After* you've driven back to County for the plaster. Come on. Get your skates on.'

The group of cadets huddled around the middle of the rockery broke apart guiltily as Roper appeared on the garden path behind them.

'Tea-break, is it, lads?' asked Roper, who had already observed that the rockery looked no lower than when he had last seen it. 'Or are we showing off our blisters?'

'Well, . . . neither, sir,' said the cadet whom Roper had already marked down as the team leader. He moved diffidently aside and pointed down at the newly exposed soil on top of the rockery. 'It's just that we think that white thing there might be a bone, sir.'

* * *

An hour later, the pathologist drew a more authoritative conclusion. It was a human thumb bone, the tip, although whether from a right hand or a left it was impossible to say.

'Were you expecting to find a whole body, Inspector?' he asked. He was Weygood's understudy. Weygood was over in Brittany for a few days' holiday. This man's name was Crabtree. Only a few years older than Roper, unlike his mentor, Crabtree exuded a lugubrious cheeriness, and an eager readiness to show interest.

'I've no idea, Mr Crabtree,' said Roper. He sketched in a few details of events to date, including the death of William Monk, and Crabtree was shrewd enough to put the rest together for himself.

'Well,' he said, 'Let's see what else we can find, shall we?'

After Weygood, Crabtree was like a breath of fresh air, constantly badgering the cadets to take care as they plied their bristle brushes and trowels across the top of the rockery. Within ten minutes, one of them found two more similar lengths of bone on the opposite side of the rockery from the first find. They were finger tips, and from the way they protruded, closely side by side, from the soil around them, Wilson prognosed them to be the tips of a first and second finger of a left hand. He took frequent photographs as more were revealed. A cluster of what looked like white stones glued together was a left wrist, a small brown disc adjacent to it turned out to be a china shirt button. An ulna, radius and humerus soon followed, then a shoulder joint and the upper part of a rib cage. More of those shirt buttons, down the centre line of the ribs, and fragments of fabric, black and wet and almost rotted away so that they crumbled at a touch.

With the sternum and clavicle exposed, it did not take Crabtree long to locate the skull and to clear the earth from around it. The skull was intact.

'Male or female?' asked Roper.

'Not sure.' Crabtree turned slightly and took in the newly exposed bones of the skeleton's toes and the slivers of rotting leather beneath them that might once have been the soles of a pair of shoes. 'From the height, I'd say it was a man. Can tell you for sure when we come to the pelvis. . . . Dig about just there, laddie, will you,' he added, to one of the cadets, pointing to the centre of the rockery. 'When you find a lump of bone, stop.'

Blackbeard came in with another mug of tea and she reached for it gratefully. She had been guzzling tea all the afternoon, and popping Codeines every few hours.

'Can you see what it is out there yet?'

'Yes,' said Blackbeard. 'But I wouldn't worry about it. Drink your tea.'

She flared angrily. Her head thumped, the police had roped off half her garden as if they owned it, and the last thing she needed just now was the overweening male protective-syndrome from Mr bloody Cambridge who, if he wasn't careful, would swiftly join the lower orders with bloody Steven.

'Whose garden is it, for Christ's sake? I want to *know!*'

'All right,' he said. 'Suit yourself. I think it's a skeleton.'

Her wrath subsided as quickly as it had risen.

'I've always wanted one of those,' she said. ' . . . And I'm sorry.'

'It's all right,' he said. And she wondered if he would be so calm and accepting if this were all happening along at his cottage, and she decided that he probably would. Bloody Steven used to practically run up the wall if a light bulb blew out.

'Perhaps we might do better to go for a walk,' he said. 'It'd help clear your head.'

'I'm scared to leave,' she said. 'In case something else happens.'

'The garden's full of coppers,' he said. 'It's hardly likely, is it?'

170

The rockery was down now to the level of the lawn, and the ribs and pelvis and leg bones of the skeleton were being brushed clean by two of the cadets as it lay stretched out on the earth. The gathering had been joined now by the Coroner's Officer. Crabtree was taking photographs and Roper was making a rough sketch in his notebook.

The skeleton was – had been – that of a male. Six feet one inch tall, and approximately forty years of age; give or take five years, Crabtree had suggested. And from the depth and width of the thorax and the thickness of the bones he had been a man in the prime of his fitness. Around his waist had been found fragments of a leather belt and, where his stomach would have been, a metal buckle. Three shillings and sixpence in old coins had been found corroded together in a clump where his left-hand trouser pocket would have been, and the cadet who had cleared the pelvis had, one by one, come across a vertical row of black china buttons. So the gentleman had died before the coming of age of the zip-fastener. He had died in his shirt, trousers, and shoes that might have been brown. And Roper did not doubt for a moment that he was looking at the mortal remains of Ralph Thorn, although he would probably never be able to prove it. And he had been shot from behind, with a shotgun, a few inches below and between his shoulder blades, and from only a foot or so away. Both his spine and the ribs either side of it had been shattered. From the interior of the rib cage some thirty tiny, distorted lead balls had been sieved, grey and powdery now, but clearly identifiable as shot. It might even be possible for Forensic to match them with the shot that Weygood had probed from the body of Marjorie Steadman, and if the two sets of samples were identical then it was likely that Steadman and Thorn had died by the same hand, and possibly within minutes of each other.

Roper turned aside as a hesitant click of heels came down the path from the cottage. It was Cassandra Murcheson, pale and drawn still, but a new Cassandra Murcheson in a white cotton dress and white sandals, and wearing a pink and nicely non-aggressive lipstick and her hair free from the plastic clip that usually restrained it.

'Mr Cambridge and I are going up to the Arms,' she said, drawing to a stop a few yards away on the path.

'I think that's a good idea,' said Roper, smiling at her. 'Enjoy yourself.'

She was not too sure what to do with her hands. She settled for clasping them behind her. Roper hoped she would leave: but she did not.

'Can I have a look, please?' she said.

'You wouldn't like it, Miss Murcheson.'

She shrugged. 'Perhaps not. But if I see it, it might go away. If you see what I mean.'

Roper weighed her. She was still in shock, but she was level-headed, and it was her garden, and if she needed some kind of exorcism in order to be able to stay here then it was not his place to deny it to her. He lifted the plastic tape strung between the iron stakes and she came across the grass and ducked under it. A waft of modest perfume came with her.

The cadets stood aside, like respectful mourners at a funeral in the presence of the immediate next of kin, as she stood over the grave.

'It's a man,' she said, after a moment or two regarding it.

'Right,' said Roper.

'What happened to the back of his ribs?'

'He was shot,' said Roper.

'Shotgun? Like the girl?'

'I'd say so,' said Roper.

She mulled that over. 'The same shotgun?'

'Possible. Can't be sure yet, though.'

She glanced up sideways at him, shrewd-eyed. 'And it's Ralph Thorn, I'll bet. Can't be anybody else, really, can it?'

Yes, she was smart all right, and could probably put

172

the rest of the story together as well as Roper could, although for the time being he would have to remain non-committal.

'Well, thanks for letting me look, anyway,' she said. 'At least I'll know what was there. Thanks. Really.'

Roper went back to the tape and lifted it again for her to duck underneath. Hopefully, her troubles were over now, and her tread back up the garden path was certainly a lighter one than when she had come down it.

The cadets and Crabtree got back to work again. It was one of the cadets who first revealed the length of rotting string behind the skeleton's neck and Crabtree himself who brushed more earth away around it and eventually prised out two plastic discs, a brown one and a grey one, through which the string had passed. Brushed clean in a bucket of water they proved to be identity-discs, army dog-tags. Erstwhile property of the War Office and Thorn, R. E., regimental number, and C of E, which meant that he should be buried according to the rites of the Church of England should he be killed in action. Except that he never had.

He had been killed here, at Box Cottage, by person or persons as yet unknown.

CHAPTER 12

The investigation did not move apace. It was Saturday midday before the Director of the Regional Forensic Laboratory telephoned Roper in his office, and even then he could hold out little promise.

The people at Kew had identified the blue petals adhering to the inside of the black plastic sack as originating from a basil-thyme plant. The particular genus was in flower from May to September and grew to a height of between four and eight inches. And, yes, regrettably, it was one of the commoner wild flowers.

'How about the grass, sir?'

'That's common too, I'm afraid. Rye-grass ... *Lollum perenne*, according to Kew. It's a fodder grass. Perennial. ... But I can tell you that all the clippings you sent us *were* cut lately ... very lately. And so was the basil, by the look of it. So if you can find a plot of newly mown grass with basil-thyme growing in it, you could be on to something. I'll have a photograph of a basil plant with you as soon as it comes down from Kew.'

It did, after all, begin to look promising. A patch of newly cropped grass with basil-thyme growing among it should not be difficult to find.

'And how about the shotgun pellets?' asked Roper.

'Well, if your lads had found the wadding patch with the second body we could be absolutely certain that the same make of cartridge had killed both victims. But we can say that the mass of equal volumes of each sample are identical within a gramme or two and the quality of

174

the lead . . . and the impurities of course, match exactly. So,' the Director added cautiously, 'it's *likely* that both victims were shot with identical cartridges, and *if* that was so, then you're definitely looking at a twelve-bore. Or *two* twelve-bores. Could have been two different guns, of course.'

But Roper doubted that. His hunch, and it was only that, was that Thorn and his wife were shot with the same gun and perhaps within minutes of each other.

'What about that tuft of khaki fabric, sir?'

'Twilled worsted . . . serge. Quite old.'

'Could it have come from a wartime army battle-blouse, d'you think, sir?'

'Anything's possible, but I'd hardly think it was likely after all these years. Mm?'

Roper, however, thought it was very likely indeed.

At one o'clock, Roper and Morgan were back at Blake's police house on the outskirts of the village.

'So far . . . ' Roper held up four fingers and bent them down one at a time. 'We have: a cowpat with a gumboot sole print in it, pointing in the general direction of High-view Farm; a boot print made at night, most likely. A handful of rye-grass cut with a motor mower of some sort. A few petals of what the experts tell us is basil-thyme; which was probably cropped at the same time as the grass. And the other thing that we *don't* have, namely one aluminium ladder with a skid pad missing. . . . Any ideas?'

Neither Morgan nor Blake had.

'We called on everybody locally about that ladder,' said Morgan.

'Including Highview Farm?'

'I went over that myself,' said Morgan. 'Me and three cadets.'

'And you looked all round?'

'Sheds, outhouses; the lot. We couldn't find anything like.'

'Who did you speak to up there?'

'The old man,' said Morgan. 'Saul Fox. He cut up a bit rough about us calling unannounced, but he didn't ask for a warrant.'

Roper turned to Sergeant Blake.

'Who's mown a field lately, Tom?'

'Practically everybody who's got one,' said Blake. 'It's the haymaking season. Especially with that spell of good weather we've had the last couple of weeks.'

So much for that, thought Roper. Thirty years suddenly seemed a very long time. From an envelope beside him he shook out twenty or so old scene-of-crime photographs. They concerned the suicide, or murder . . . or whatever, of William Monk. That the pictures were in old-fashioned black and white made them no less palatable.

William Monk, or, rather, his mortal remains, lying huddled on his right side as he had toppled from his chair, his knees drawn up, the top and back of his head missing, a length of nylon fishing gut tied to one of his big toes, the shotgun lying on the floor at the other end of the fishing line. The chair he had used, also lying on its side, a foot or so away. It looked right, had that ring of authenticity. It was little wonder that the investigating officers of the time had so readily accepted a verdict of suicide. Given the scene and the circumstances and without his present hindsight, Roper might have done the same himself.

The chimney-breast and the ceiling in front of it had been splattered with human débris. A close-up shot of the shotgun itself, the nylon gut still tied round its twin triggers, showed it to be a gun of quality. Roper was no expert, but a gun like that with chased metalwork and a butt polished to the sheen of silk had to be a collector's piece, and from its ornate scrollwork it probably pre-dated even the Boer War.

The shotgun itself, now wrapped in a polythene sheet, was also here in the flesh, brought out into the daylight from the County vaults for the first time since the inquest had closed on William Monk. Roper picked up the package and hefted it in both hands to feel its weight. It was lighter than most, a handsome weapon by any standards, and a little shorter in the butt than usual, and Roper did not doubt that it would cost him the best part of six months' salary to buy one like it; if, indeed, he could find another like it, which he did doubt. But it really was *very* light . . . the sort of gun that might be made for a woman . . .

'Can I see those firearms records, Tom?' he said to Blake, as he carefully laid the shotgun back across the desk.

Blake passed across his box file of firearms licence applications for the current year. To date, there were twelve of them, of which eight were renewals of existing certificates. Two of these were applications for .22 single-shot target pistols. Of the other six, all were applications for the renewal of existing shotgun licences. One that caught Roper's eye, and held it, was an application from Samuel Joseph Fox of Highview Farm . . . wherever Roper looked, and to whomever he talked, the name of Fox, one way or another, seemed to surface like bubbles of sour gas in a stagnant pond . . . a firearms licence had originally been granted to Sam Fox in 1943; not that that meant Fox had not been able to *use* one before that.

Roper closed the box file, sat back in Blake's chair and lit a contemplative cheroot. A lot of coppering was to do with chasing wild geese, or patiently turning over countless stones in the faint hope that something nasty might crawl out from beneath at least one of them. It was too early to swear out a search warrant for Highview Farm. There was no copper-bottomed evidence, no witnesses, except that Jake Haygarth had seen a few flashes of torchlight going in that direction the other night. Unless a gumboot could be found to match it, the print in the cowpat would be laughed out of court. And the aluminium ladder, until it was located, could only be listed among all the other ephemera that littered the case and which might come to nothing in the final analysis.

But evidence enough for a start might just be the close conjunction of rye-grass and basil-thyme, both of them recently mown.

But where?

'We'd be on a hiding to nothing,' said Blake. 'There are several thousand acres of mown grass around these parts just now, and by the time we get round to looking at 'em all the grass could be six inches high again.'

Roper had not thought of that. Looking for basil-thyme and rye-grass over a couple of thousand acres could take a week or more, and he might as well be looking for the needle in the legendary haystack, and even if he had the luck to find them growing together it still would not prove anything.

He took another draw on his cheroot.

'What have you got planned for tonight, Tom?'

'Not a lot,' said Blake. 'Paperwork mostly. Why?'

'I thought we could take a trip up to Highview Farm. You could introduce me to the Foxes.'

And talk to old Saul Fox, whose wife had disappeared without leaving even a note, in 1938, and whose son, Sam, had drunk with Jake Haygarth that Christmas of 1943, and perhaps even make the acquaintance of Winnie Fox, whom Haygarth had seen on Ralph Thorn's stairs that same night, and who, and not entirely metaphorically, might be another intimate connection with the late and very dead Ralph Thorn.

Blake drew the Escort into the layby beside the decrepit five-barred gate that was the main entrance to Highview Farm. Nailed to a stake a crudely painted sign proclaimed that trespassers would be prosecuted and to beware of dogs. The dingy grey farmhouse stood about a quarter of a mile along a rutted cinder track. In the last of the pearly daylight only one window showed a light in it.

178

Carrying the shotgun that had killed William Monk, Blake debouched from one side of the car and Roper stepped out of the other carrying a weighty briefcase. The two doors slammed one after the other, and set a distant dog barking.

The gate, when Roper went to open it, was padlocked and chained. Several flakes of the scabrous white paint that covered it came away in his hand.

'Is there another entrance, Tom?' he asked Blake.

'Not close,' said Blake. 'And if I know the Foxes, they'll all be chained up like this one.'

Roper stood on the bottom bar of the gate. It felt sound enough. He climbed over the top and dropped to the track on its other side. Blake followed him. The cinders crackled under their shoes.

The track was fenced off from the tracts of land at either side of it. On the right was a beet field; on the left grass, recently cut and the cuttings left to dry out in the sun. On the far side of the mown meadow stood the dark bulk of a tractor and some kind of trailer under a grey tarpaulin. Blake identified the trailer as a mowing-machine.

'Now there's a thing,' said Roper. He scanned the grass close to the fence where the mower had left a foot-wide band uncut. Wild flowers grew in profusion among it, but none with blue petals.

'We're never going to be that lucky,' said Blake, and he was probably right.

The distant dog was barking more frenziedly. Then against the dark silhouette of the house something moved, and briefly the dog was silent, but only briefly before the sound of it changed from a warning to a threat and the black bulk of it was launching itself out of the dusk and bounding towards them along the track. And when it finally skidded to a stop, its forelegs splayed and ready to spring, only a few yards away, Roper saw that it was a hundred pounds or so of square-shouldered and glittering-eyed black Rotweiler that clearly knew its business.

Roper held the briefcase in front of him and braced himself, and Blake had the shotgun ready to swing it. The dog shuffled closer on its belly, its teeth bared, its eyes watchful.

'That you, Sam?' called Blake, to the shadowy shape that had been beside the farmhouse but which was now advancing up the track towards them with what looked like a shotgun held diagonally across its chest. Closer to, it resolved itself into a man, cloth-capped, white-shirted, gumbooted.

'Aye,' the man called back. 'Who the hell are you?'

'You know bloody well who it is,' Blake shouted. 'Tom Blake. And if you don't call your bloody dog off I'll wrap this thing round its bloody neck.'

'Who's that with you?'

'Police, Mr Fox,' called Roper. 'Chief Inspector Roper, County CID.'

A sharp penetrating whistle had the dog springing up and loping back to Fox who had stopped some dozen paces away. Short, wiry and ferrety-faced, he was surely the same man that Roper had seen at the boot of the Vauxhall Victor yesterday afternoon.

'I'd like to see that gun broken too, Mr Fox,' called Roper. 'If you wouldn't mind, sir.'

Fox lowered the shotgun. There was a metallic click as he broke it open. 'You haven't said why you're here yet,' he grumbled. 'Been here twice already, you bobbies. And it's private, this land is. You got no business.'

'Routine enquiries, Mr Fox,' said Roper. He took a pace forward; the dog stiffened again and loosed another menacing growl from deep in its throat.

'Sit,' grunted Fox. The Rotweiler sat.

'We only want a word, Mr Fox,' said Roper, closing the last couple of yards between himself and Fox and holding out his warrant card.

Fox ignored the card. Perhaps he could not read . . . 'Don't have time for chatting. I'm busy.'

'Not at night, you're not, Sam,' said Blake, coming up beside Roper.

'If it's to do with that new woman over Box Cottage, we don't know nothing about it,' said Fox. He glanced belligerently at each of them in turn. 'We mind our own business here.'

'Sure you do, Mr Fox,' agreed Roper, tucking his card away and smiling equably. According to Blake, Sam Fox, his father and sister lived very nearly like hermits in that crumbling house past Fox's shoulder. 'May we come inside, sir; or would you rather join us back at the car?'

Neither choice roused Fox's enthusiasm.

'We have to talk to you, Mr Fox,' insisted Roper. 'One way or the other, sir.'

'Better be the house, I suppose,' conceded Fox sullenly. 'But quiet, see. The old man's gone to bed and he don't take kindly to being woke.'

'We'll be quiet, Mr Fox.'

'And it can't wait till morning?'

'No, sir, it can't,' said Roper.

For a few moments more, Fox stood four-square across the cinder track in the dying daylight; then without a word he turned about, his dog lurching to its feet and padding along beside him. Roper and Blake followed.

Apart from the one window the grey farmhouse was still in darkness. It looked as if it had run to seed fifty years ago and no one had spent a penny on maintenance ever since, sagging roof, peeling paintwork, lop-sided windows. At a guess, the Foxes might just be scraping a living off the place.

Roper continued to follow Fox and the dog. Blake had fallen behind. Closer to, the farmhouse was no more prepossessing. The Vauxhall Victor that Roper had seen yesterday, rust-pocked and down on its springs, was still parked outside. Beside the ramshackle clapboard porch, Fox paused briefly to clip the Rotweiler's studded collar to a length of chain stapled to the wall before opening the

181

porch door and leading the way inside. Tomato plants in plastic pots stood on a sagging wooden shelf behind the grimy porch window. Blake caught up with Roper again as he was wiping the soles of his shoes on the coconut mat just inside the porch door.

Roper felt something cold and moist being pressed into his free hand.

'Cop this,' muttered Blake. 'There's a whole patch of it growing out there.'

Roper closed his fist round it. It felt like the stem and petals of a small flower. Hopefully, it was basil-thyme . . .

The narrow passage that led into the house stank of sour humanity, musty and oppressive. A brass oil lamp stood on a wooden bracket at the foot of the stairs, its opalescent white bowl stained and greasy, its fitful glow revealing bare wooden stairs and naked floorboards. Above the lamp a patch of soot darkened the low ceiling.

Fox turned into the first room on the left at the bottom of the stairs, probably the room with the illuminated window that Roper had seen from the cinder track since another oil lamp glowed in it, this one hooked on a makeshift stand that looked as if it had once held a parrot cage.

This was evidently the Foxes' kitchen, so cluttered with furniture and junk that there was scarcely room to move, a table in the middle of the tiled, uneven floor, three old wheelback chairs at it and the relics of someone's meal on a red and white checked tablecloth that covered one end. In the brightest corner, under the oil lamp and to the left of the cooking range, stood a high-backed wooden armchair with a threadbare cushion tied to its seat. The corner behind it was taken up with a heap of old newspapers, and the pair of moth-eaten curtains at the window were too short and too narrow and makeshift. The rank smell of stale human-kind was even stronger in here, and despite the warmth of the summer night a dull orange glow showed through the bars of the range.

'Can we have some more light, Sam?' asked Blake.

'We don't have the generator on,' said Fox. 'Not in the summer. When it gets dark we go to bed. Besides, it'd wake the old man up.'

'Can we at least sit down, Mr Fox?' asked Roper.

'You can suit yourselves,' said Fox. 'Just don't plan on staying too long, that's all.' By the range, he closed his shotgun and thumbed on the safety catches, then stood it against the wall beside the wooden armchair. Still with his back to Roper and Blake, he took down a tobacco pouch from beside a chiming clock on the wooden shelf above the range.

Roper sat down at the side of the table nearest to the oil lamp, Blake in front of the discarded meal that looked like a congealed stew but might equally have been something made ready for the cat.

Fox, still wearing his cloth cap, fingered tobacco from the pouch, rolled it expertly in a paper and licked the edge of it, while Roper at last opened his fist and laid the flower that Blake had pressed on him on to the table. He could not be sure, in the poor light, but it certainly did look very like the photograph of basil-thyme that had come across from Kew late that afternoon.

Fox held a match to the frayed end of his cigarette. 'Right,' he said, shaking out the match and dropping it into the littered hearth behind him. 'What d'you want this time?'

'Don't know yet, Mr Fox,' said Roper. 'Not exactly. I'd like to show you something first, see if there's anybody here you might know.' He opened the briefcase and took out the Coronation Year photograph that had been copied from Maudie Samuels's print. 'Anyone there familiar to you, Mr Fox?'

Fox reached out reluctantly for it and tipped it towards the lamplight, and Roper was able to take his first good look at him. Fiftyish, sinewy, hollow-cheeked, greying hair growing untidily over his grubby shirt collar, the sleeve of what looked like a flannel vest just visible at the cuff of his left sleeve. And he was nervous, not that that was significant. An unannounced visit from the police was inclined to make most folk nervous, even the innocent ones.

'Well, Mr Fox?'

'No,' said Fox, shaking his head as he handed the photograph back again. 'Don't recognise any of 'em.'

'You surprise me, Mr Fox,' said Roper, standing up again and joining Fox by the lamp. 'The young lady third from the left in the back row's your sister, sir.' Holding the photograph close to the light, his finger circled the grave face of the young Winnie Fox.

'Oh, aye,' said Fox. 'So it is.'

'And this lady and gentleman here,' said Roper, 'they're Mr and Mrs Moxley. Mr Moxley was the squire, if you remember.'

'It were a long time ago,' said Fox irritably. 'I were only a lad m'self then.'

'And this young lady is Maudie Samuels. Remember her, do you, Mr Fox? She married your father's cowman.'

Fox shook his head.

'And Jake Haygarth, Mr Fox. You remember him, surely?'

'Aye,' grunted Fox impatiently.

'And how about this gentleman here, Mr Fox?' Roper's forefinger circled the head and burly shoulders of Ralph Thorn.

Fox's narrow face stiffened perceptibly. 'Died,' he said.

'Do you know where, Mr Fox?'

'Died in the war,' said Fox. 'The invasion.'

'Not quite, Mr Fox,' said Roper. 'He died here, in the village.'

'There was a telegram,' grumbled Fox. 'And his name's up on the war memorial. Look for yourself.'

'We dug him up yesterday afternoon, Mr Fox. Across at Box Cottage. I'm surprised you hadn't heard.'

'Well, I hadn't,' retorted Fox. 'Like I said, we keep

184

ourselves to ourselves up here.' He turned away, fishing in his trousers pocket for his matches to re-light his cigarette, and kept his back to Roper while he lit it.

Roper slid the photograph back into his briefcase. 'I saw some cattle grazing on your land near the Carpenter's Arms yesterday afternoon, Mr Fox.'

'Aye,' said Fox. 'Likely. What about it?'

'When were you last down in that particular field, Mr Fox?'

Fox had turned his back to the range again, shifty-eyed. 'Look . . . what's all this about? We don't know nothing, see? We don't know nothing. I keep telling you.'

'Relax, Mr Fox,' said Roper, sitting down again, and endeavouring to look relaxed himself. If Sam Fox knew anything at all he would crack soon, he was that sort. 'Why don't you sit down, too, sir?'

'Rather stand,' said Fox. 'Do what I like in my own house, can't I? Just you say what you want here.'

'We're looking for witnesses, Mr Fox,' said Roper. 'Somebody in the village saw somebody with a torch crossing one of your fields the other night. They were travelling this way. Somebody wearing a khaki tunic,' he added, garnishing Haygarth's story a little.

'Then he were seeing things,' said Fox.

'But you don't know that, do you, Mr Fox?' said Roper. 'I mean our witness might have seen this character and you didn't. Depends if you happened to be looking out of the window or not.'

'Well, I didn't see no soldier,' said Fox.

Roper smiled. Among Sam Fox's other negative attributes, it also seemed that he was not overly bright. 'We thought it might be one of the lads from Bovington army camp.'

'Aye,' said Fox. 'Probably was.'

'He didn't call in here, then?'

Fox shook his head.

185

'Only we found a bootprint, Mr Fox,' said Roper. 'Pointing this way.' He reached across the table for his briefcase and took out the plaster cast and unwrapped it. 'We think it was made at night,' he said, with an assuredness that he didn't think Fox was shrewd enough to question. It was not right, it was not fair, and if Mower were here he would rap Roper hard over the knuckles for conducting an interview like this; but there was something here, Roper was sure of that now, however tenuous, however vague. 'It's a cast of a cowpat, Mr Fox.'

'Aye,' said Fox. 'I can see.'

'Care to take a closer look at it?'

Fox reached out for it, using his left hand. As he did, the cuff of his shirt slid back over his wrist, and Roper saw that what he had thought earlier was the long sleeve of a flannel vest was a crudely bound and not very clean bandage. Fox looked briefly at the cast and handed it back again.

'Sprained your wrist, have you, Mr Fox?' asked Roper.

'Aye,' said Fox, quickly drawing his shirtcuff down again over the bandage. 'Did it this morning.'

'Doctor seen it?'

'No,' said Fox. 'Don't hold with doctors.'

'Fall over in the dark, did you, Mr Fox?'

'Told you,' said Fox. 'Done it this morning. It were daylight.'

'Perhaps you ought to let Sergeant Blake have a look at it,' suggested Roper helpfully.

Fox shook his head. 'No need,' he said.

But that filthy bandage, Roper had already decided, had been on Fox's wrist a damned sight longer than one day. And whoever had been wearing that army uniform in Cassandra Murcheson's garden the other night had hurt himself on his way out. Ergo . . .

'Do you mind kicking off your right gumboot, Mr Fox?'

Fox clearly did mind. 'Look, you got no bloody right,'

he blustered. 'Coming into people's places and asking questions. We ain't done nothing. I told you.'

'I'm only asking to look at the sole of your boot, Mr Fox,' said Roper patiently.

'It's just a boot.'

'I can see that, Mr Fox. . . . May I have it, please?'

For a few moments more, Fox did battle with himself, then he kicked off the boot and handed it to Roper who rose again and took both boot and cast closer to the oil lamp, then resorted to one of the first tricks he had ever learned after walking down the steps of Peel House as a fully fledged young copper.

'Tom . . . ' he said. 'Take a look at this.'

Blake joined him beside the lamp.

'What do you reckon?' muttered Roper.

'I'd say it was a dead ringer,' muttered Blake who had learned the same trick in the same school, just loud enough for Fox to hear.

It did, indeed, look like a dead ringer. Three letters of the maker's name in relief just behind the barred sole, both the O and the P with a piece hacked out of them, a definite wearing down on the sole's outer edge. In the final analysis it would need an expert witness, but it was still too early for that. A print in a cowpat was still a long way from proving anything.

'So would I,' muttered Roper. He turned slowly to face an anxious Sam Fox. 'What do you have to say to this, Mr Fox?' he said, holding out both boot and plaster cast for Fox's inspection. 'You've got some kind of explanation, I'm sure. If you look closely, sir, you'll see they match.' He smiled at Fox benignly. Fox drew little comfort from it.

'I don't know what you're on about,' whispered Fox. 'It's a bloody trick, that's what it is, it's a bloody trick.' He licked his lips, his eyes hunting from Roper to Blake and back again to Roper.

'Show Mr Fox the shotgun, Tom,' said Roper.

Behind Roper, Blake unwrapped the shotgun that had killed William Monk.

'What gun's that?' whispered Fox.

'It's the gun that William Monk was murdered with, Mr Fox,' said Roper, as Blake stepped in beside him with the shotgun displayed across both hands for Fox's closer scrutiny.

Fox shrank back from it.

'Never see it afore,' he whispered. 'Never. . . . And Monk didn't get murdered. . . . He shot hisself.'

'No, sir,' said Roper, quietly and insistently and never more sure of his ground. 'Mr Monk was murdered.'

Fox shook his head. 'No!'

'Yes, Mr Fox,' insisted Roper. 'He was shot. Like Ralph Thorn and his wife were shot. A twelve-bore. This might even be the same gun that killed them, too. We found a wadding patch in Mrs Thorn's body, you see, Mr Fox. That was a twelve-bore. And so's this.' Roper took the gun from Blake, broke it and snapped it shut again, then pointed it up at the ceiling and curled a finger round the triggers. Fox winced.

Click.

Click.

Fox's face slowly straightened again in the ensuing silence.

'Not loaded, Mr Fox. But an expensive gun, wouldn't you say? All this scroll-work? Cost a fortune these days, a gun like this.' Roper held it closer to Fox, but Fox still would not take it. 'Recognise it, do you, Mr Fox?'

'No,' whispered Fox, backing away until his heels met the brass fender behind him. 'No, I tell you! I don't know nothing, see! Nothing!'

There was a long and terrible silence. Then a floor-board creaked overhead, and then another, and whoever had caused both obviously held a greater terror for Sam Fox than Roper or Blake ever could. He was trembling now, his gaze riveted up at the ceiling as another creak sounded upstairs, and another, louder, along the landing.

'It were Da,' whispered Fox on a tremulous breath, plucking desperately at Roper's sleeve. 'Da and our Winnie. Both on 'em. It weren't me, I never done nothing. I swear to God . . . ' His terror-stricken eyes looked past Roper's shoulder as a slippered footfall began to shuffle down the stairs, slowly, slowly . . .

Roper watched the open doorway from the tail of his eye, saw the wavering shadow fall across it, briefly disappear, then reappear, getting longer as the halting footsteps came closer still.

The door went back against the wall with a crack like a pistol shot.

And there he stood, trembling on his stick. Old Saul Fox, tall and majestic and terrible in his wrath.

CHAPTER 13

Few men could muster that much dignity in an old raincoat, flannel combinations and carpet slippers. He took them all in: Blake, Roper, his son who still stood trembling on the hearthrug, his face drained of colour; while still ringing in Roper's ears was that dreadful indictment: it were Da, Da and our Winnie . . .

'What's going on here, eh?' whispered the old man, his voice choked with outrage, his bony knuckles stretched white about the handle of his stick. His inimical gaze fastened on Blake. 'Don't need police. You neither, Tom Blake. So out! All on yer!'

'I think you'd better sit down, Mr Fox,' said Roper.

The old man shuffled forward until he and Roper were eye to eye. 'My house!' he raged in the same cracked whisper. '*My* house! Be buggered if I'll be told what to do in it!'

'Da,' urged his son pathetically, still rooted to the hearthrug, one gumboot on and the other one off. 'For *Christ's* sake, Da! They're *police*.'

The old man's eyes flickered to his son. 'What have you been saying, boy? What you been telling 'em?' To Roper's astonishment, old Fox propelled himself towards his son, his stick rising and certain murder in his glittering eye.

Sam Fox backed away. 'They know, Da. They bloody *know*.'

'Know what?' hissed Fox, as he closed the last few inches towards his son who was cringing back with both arms raised to protect his head. 'What do they know, boy? 'Less you told 'em? Eh?'

Roper turned quickly and dropped the shotgun on the table and reached out for the ferruled end of the stick as it swung back further over Saul Fox's shoulder.

'That's enough, Mr Fox,' he said quietly. 'Please, sir.' But the old man found a surprising strength from somewhere and wrestled to free the stick, and Roper from the edge of his eye saw Sam Fox spot the chance he might have been waiting for for most of his life, but Blake was the quicker, springing forward and clutching the younger Fox round the arms and waist and binding him tightly and bundling him into the corner where the pile of newspapers were and holding him there while he snapped on one manacle and then the other while Sam Fox, tears of frustration in his eyes screamed all the while, 'You done her in, you old bastard! You killed our Ma! You did! You did!'

Some time had passed. The mayhem was over. Morgan and a couple of DCs were on their way, and a technician from Forensic, and Superintendent Mower was organising a search warrant back at County. Also on his way over was a doctor to see to old Saul Fox, because there had been a moment a while ago when Roper thought the old man was going to die of his terrible anger.

Out in the yard a generator puttered softly to life and the naked electric bulb above the kitchen table glowed fitfully then sprang to brightness and revealed Saul Fox, still wheezing, sitting in his high-backed chair and staring at Roper as if he were still prepared to do him to death.

'Feeling better, Mr Fox?'

The old man said nothing, one of his gnarled hands tightly gripping the arm of his chair, the other holding his stick and his breath still rasping in and out, his malevolent eyes still locked on to Roper's.

'We'll have a doctor here soon.'

191

'Don't need doctors,' wheezed Fox. 'I'll see *you* out, don't you worry.'

'Can I get you something? . . . A glass of water . . . ?'

'Bugger off.'

Game to the end, thought Roper. And it was very likely he would never talk. At ninety-odd he was still twice the man his son was, and what had been hurt more than his body was his pride. There could not have been many men who had usurped Saul Fox's authority in his own house. Roper heard the back door open and Blake and Sam Fox coming in from the generator shed. They turned into the office across the passage and the door of it closed behind them.

'What your son told us, Mr Fox. Right, was it? About your wife?'

The old man only stared, his fingers working around the handle of his stick.

'Where is she, Mr Fox?'

'She went.'

'Never came back?'

'She were weak. Didn't want her. Didn't need her.' The old man turned his face towards the fire in the range. In the electric light his eyes glittered like two grey buttons.

'So you killed her.'

The old man had lapsed to silence again.

'How about Ralph Thorn, Mr Fox?'

No answer. Roper had been right the first time. Whatever had happened all those years ago was locked away in Saul Fox's memory and was never going to come out again.

What little colour there had been was beginning to return to the old man's face, the fingers had stilled over the handle of the stick, his chest was rising and falling more evenly. He would probably live for ever, he was indomitable, and it could even be that he would never come to court after all these years. What was equally certain was that he would never be punished for whatever it was he had done. A home somewhere under close supervision until it was certain he was incapable of creating any more mischief.

'How about William Monk, Mr Fox?'

Saul Fox's eyes lifted, met Roper's contemptuously, then returned to the glow through the bars of the range.

In the distance, Roper heard the slam of car doors, and the Rotweiler started barking again.

It was five past ten and the house at Highview Farm was a hive of quiet and methodical activity. The warrant had still to arrive, but Sam Fox, who was no longer in a position to do otherwise, had agreed to the house being scoured from top to bottom. Two DCs and the Forensic technician were moving about upstairs, Blake was across in the kitchen keeping an eye on Saul Fox while the doctor looked him over and Roper was in the tatty room that served as the farm office and Sam Fox, still handcuffed, sat huddled in a chair in front of a battered desk. DS Morgan sat in a chair behind him with his pocket-book open, and Roper was perched on the corner of the table littered with ancient cashbooks, diaries, and heaps of papers and forms that looked as if they went back twenty years by the dust on them.

'You sure about this, Mr Fox?' asked Roper.

'I heard 'em shoutin'. Ma and the old man and Winnie,' mumbled Fox, eyes fixed on his feet.

'And where were you?'

'Bed,' sniffed Fox. 'I were in bed. The row woke me up.'

'What happened then?' asked Roper.

'I heard a chair go over,' said Fox. 'Something o' that sort.'

'You didn't get out of bed to see what it was all about?'

Fox shook his head. 'I were scared of 'im,' he said. 'I were always scared of 'im. He were a terrible man when he were upset.'

'Did you do anything at all?'

Fox shook his head. 'Just lied there,' he said. 'Hours and hours. It all went quiet after that, see. I thought it were over and Ma had come up to bed.'

'And had she?'

'No,' said Fox. 'Don't reckon. They took her out through the back door. In the kitchen rug. Him and Winnie. I saw 'em.'

'They were carrying something in a rug?'

'Not *something*,' wailed Fox. 'Our *Ma. I know* it were our Ma. I saw 'em both creeping out. Carrying 'er between 'em.' He lifted his head, his eyes brimming with tears of anguish. 'I put a coat over me nightshirt and followed 'em. I saw!'

'And . . . ?'

'There were a hole. The old man must have been digging it afore they carried Ma out. They dumped her in it, Winnie held the rug and the old man filled the hole in. Deep it were. The hole. Must have been because the next morning, he took out the horses and ploughed the field over so the grave didn't show.' Both hands rose to Fox's face to rub the tears away.

'And you say you saw all this?'

'Aye,' Fox sniffed. 'There were a bit of a moon and the old man had a lamp. I saw all on it.'

'But you never reported it?'

Fox shook his head. 'Scared, see. And I were only thirteen. He'd o' killed me too if he'd known I'd seen. I only got back to the house a couple of minutes afore they did. I lied there tremblin' all night. 'Cos *I* knew, see. Ma was never coming back. *They'd* done her in.'

Roper held out a handkerchief. Fox took it. The chain between his manacled hands clicked as he dabbed at his eyes.

'Will you testify to all this in court, Mr Fox?'

'Aye,' said Fox.

'And can you prove it?'

194

'Aye,' said Fox. 'I can show you where the two on 'em buried her.'

'But you don't know what the quarrel was about in the first place?'

Fox shook his head. The father wouldn't talk and the sister couldn't, so it was likely that the cause of the death of Mrs Fox would stay a secret for ever, but the scene that Sam Fox had described so inadequately was all too easy to picture. A sickle of moon, a terrified boy following his father and sister across fields and lying awed in hiding while he watched them bury his mother in the dead of a summer night. It must have been a terrible secret to keep for forty years, that.

'Would you like a cup of tea, Mr Fox?'

'Aye,' said Fox. 'Gaspin'.'

Roper nodded to Morgan, who closed his pocket-book and left it on the chair as he headed for the door. And as he went out, one of the DCs came in carrying a bundle of khaki with an army forage cap on top of it.

'Where did you find that?' asked Roper.

'The daughter's bedroom,' said the DC. 'Bottom of a chest of drawers.'

The cap was an officer's model, made not of serge but smooth barathea, the badge of the Wessex Yeomanry on it. 'And she's got a couple of cases up there too,' said the DC. 'One's a man's with a dress uniform in it and a load of army gear. And the other one's a woman's. A pair of white silk pyjamas and frilly underwear. All that sort of stuff. But it's all moth-eaten, sir. Old as the bloody hills, most of it.'

Roper took the bundle of khaki and shook it into shape. It was a wartime battle-blouse, moth-eaten like the underwear in the case upstairs, the three faded, embroidered captain's pips on each shoulder strap, and the smell of years rising from it. Roper felt the two breast pockets. Something in each. He cleared a space on the table and began emptying them. Ralph Thorn's army identity papers, a military railway warrant from Camberley in Surrey to Newby Magna. A leave pass, folded and almost falling into four pieces as Roper carefully opened it and read the to and from dates . . . which matched a few days either side of the date on Marjorie Steadman's marriage lines. As evidence, the sprig of basil-thyme on the kitchen table had paled into insignificance.

'Do you know who this belonged to, Mr Fox?' asked Roper, over his shoulder.

'Aye,' said Fox, his bright wet eyes lifting to take in the battledress. 'Ralph Thorn. She kept it. Couldn't ever part with it. She were daft about him. Even after he were dead. Loony, she is.'

'And it's what she wears to be Thorn's ghost, is it?'

Fox shook his head. 'That were always me. She's too little. . . . The old man's idea, that were.'

Roper returned Thorn's effects to the pockets of the khaki blouse. 'When Sergeant Morgan comes back, Mr Fox, I'll be asking you those questions again.'

'Aye,' said Fox. 'I don't give a bugger any more what you ask me.'

Morgan came in with a mug of tea. Sam Fox clasped it gratefully. Hot on Morgan's heels came the police doctor with his black case.

'How is he, Doctor?' asked Roper.

'Got a better ticker than I have,' said the doctor. 'Could go on for another twenty years. I've told him I'm going to call up an ambulance to take him across to the infirmary, just for observation. . . . He swears he's not going, but I've told him he is. I'll take it you'll see him aboard? He's going to put up a fight, mind.'

'Bloody right I'll see him aboard,' said Roper grimly. 'If I have to clap the old bastard in irons. Blake still with him, is he?'

'Keeping an eye on him,' said the doctor. 'And ready to spring at a moment's notice.'

'Good,' said Roper. 'Thank you, sir.'

'I'll bid you goodnight then, Mr Roper.'

'Night, sir,' said Roper. 'I'm much obliged to you.'

The door closed again behind the doctor and the DC who had found Ralph Thorn's battle-blouse.

Roper gave Sam Fox a few moments more to sip at his tea.

'Do you know where your sister is now, Mr Fox?'

Fox shook his head. 'Out,' he said. 'Nights she goes walking.'

'But you don't know where?'

Fox shook his head again. Morgan picked up his pocket-book and resumed his chair, and for the record Roper repeated his questions about the khaki blouse.

'Do you know how your sister came by it?'

Fox shrugged glumly. 'She just took it, I s'pose. A sort of keepsake. I told you, she were potty about him.'

'Do you know who killed Ralph Thorn, Mr Fox?'

Fox lifted his face from his mug of tea. 'Aye,' he said. 'I've always reckoned that were our Winnie. She killed him. *And* Thorn's missus. Both on 'em.'

'Know that for sure, do you?'

'Aye,' said Fox. He took a sip of his tea, the mug clasped between both hands. 'And the old man and me saw to the putting away.'

Roper perched back on the edge of the table and lit a cheroot, snapped his lighter shut. In his time he had found himself opening many a can of dirty worms, but none quite like this one.

'From the beginning, Mr Fox,' he said. 'All you remember. Take your time.'

It was a garbled tale that Fox told, tottering backwards and forwards over several hours on that May night of 1944, and even then it was incomplete because Sam Fox still did not know all of it himself. It had been early evening. Still daylight. Six or seven o'clock. It had been his sister's afternoon off from the manor house, and from a field that he was working with a couple of Land Army girls he had

197

seen his sister leave the house and cut across an adjacent field on her way to her evening duties. He had not expected to see her again until breakfast the next morning, but some twenty minutes afterwards, to his surprise, he had seen her returning, half walking, half running. He had called out to her, but she hadn't answered. A couple of minutes later he had seen her leaving the house again, only this time wearing a heavy coat, which she had not been wearing the first time, and she were hugging herself, like this, see? And still in a hurry. And Fox thought she had come back for the coat, which would have made her late for the manor, and that's why she'd been running. A while later Fox had heard two muffled shots, not that there was anything unusual about that. The rabbit population had been high in those days.

He did not see his sister return to the farmhouse, but obviously she had, because about half an hour later Saul Fox came striding out, took his son out of the hearing of the Land Army girls and told him to cycle along to the manor and tell Mrs Moxley that Winnie was sick and wouldn't be coming to work for a couple of days.

'But I just seen her,' had countered Sam.

'You've seen *nothing*, boy! *Nothing*! Just you do what I *say*! And don't you say more'n I just told you. Y'understand?'

Which Sam Fox had done, to the letter. He recalled Mrs Moxley wishing Winnie soon better and giving him her wages to take home to her. He had thought no more of it, there was a lot to do on the farm in those days, he still ploughed with a couple of horses and all the milking was done by hand. At dusk the Land Army girls had gone home to their lodgings and he had cycled back to the house. And had just been in time to see his father turning out of Winnie's bedroom – and locking the door behind him and pocketing the key.

There was no supper for Sam Fox that night. His father had ordered him straight into the parlour where the family Bible had been made ready on the table, thrust

198

Sam's right hand down on it and held it there and made him swear eternal silence on everything that had happened today and that was going to happen tonight. Not a word. If he did, it would be a mortal sin and Almighty God would know . . . and so would Saul Fox.

Then came the portentous words that Sam Fox had remembered for over thirty years. Still pressing his son's hand down on the Bible, Saul Fox had fixed Sam with his terrible eyes. 'We've work to do tonight, boy. And you'll do it willing, see? And no questions. You'll just *do* it.'

For the rest of the evening, Sam Fox had sat at one side of the kitchen fireplace and his father in his armchair, watching him, with never a word passing between them.

Towards eleven o'clock Saul Fox had several times looked at his pocket watch. Then on the dot of eleven he had risen, and told Sam to follow him. From the toolshed Saul Fox had taken a spade, a fork and a hurricane lamp. Still in silence, in the darkness, the two of them had started across the fields towards Box Cottage, Sam stumbling after his father's shadowy striding figure.

'Where we going, Da?'

'You be still, boy. We're putting right a wickedness. That's all you need to know.'

They had stepped from the field straight into the garden of Box Cottage. Neither the hedges nor the drainage ditch had been there in those days. The kitchen door to the cottage had been unlocked, its key on the inside. 'Now not a sound out o' you, boy,' old Saul had adjured, his hand on the doorknob. Only when they were inside did Saul light the hurricane lamp. He left Sam holding it in the passage while he went on into the parlour. Sam had heard his father rolling down the black paper blackout blinds at the parlour windows, then drawing curtains over them.

'In here, boy. And watch where you tread.'

And Sam, by now in a state of trepidation, had stepped into the parlour with the hurricane lamp, and all but tripped over someone lying on the floor. Ralph Thorn, in his army

199

trousers and shirtsleeves, on his face with a hole in his back the size of a saucer. And across the room, the body of a young woman lay sprawled across a leather armchair, not in it, mind. Across the arms of it, like she'd been blown there by a puff of wind, her legs dangling over one arm and her head over the other one.

'Dead, they were,' said Sam Fox, shivering at the memory of it. 'I were so scared I wet m'self. God's will, the old man said it were. They'd wronged our Winnie, that's all I needed to know, and we was going to hide their bodies away so's nobody else ever knew about it. It were our secret. Us Foxes.'

'What did you do with them, Mr Fox?' asked Roper.

'We carried Thorn out to the garden. And the old man said we was going to put him in the rockery. I had to hold the lamp . . . '

'Why the rockery?' asked Roper. A question that had been puzzling him ever since Ralph Thorn's body had been found. It would have been simpler, surely, to have just dug a hole somewhere in the garden.

'Couldn't,' said Fox. 'It were a proper garden then. One of Mr Moxley's gardeners came along every couple of weeks to keep it tidy. He might have noticed somebody'd been mucking about in it.'

So, in the darkness, his son shielding the lantern under his coat, Saul Fox went to work methodically taking the topsoil and stones down from Ralph Thorn's rockery and laying them out carefully on an old bedsheet. Then the hole. A tedious business, because the blade of the shovel kept striking stones and making a noise and there was always the danger of the stone shell of the rockery falling in and ruining everything. Besides which, every shovelful that was dug out had to be placed at one end of the sheet, carefully, so that it didn't spill over on to the surrounding grass. The mound of spoil grew slowly higher. Then came disaster. The spade struck metal. Two old rusty iron bed-ends, tipped into the rockery to lose them, the side of one under the heap of stones that formed the back of the rock-ery so that to attempt to move it would send the entire, by now frail, structure tumbling. And still the hole was not deep enough for two bodies, only for one, and that one had to be Ralph Thorn. Somewhere else would have to be found for the young woman.

'Then once we got him in, the old man had to fill the hole up again, and put all the stones and plants back to make it look right and there were a lot of soil and stones left over.'

'What did you do with those?'

'Dumped 'em,' said Fox. 'Bundled 'em up in the sheet and spread 'em all over our field next door. But that were next morning. Come sun-up.'

'And the dead girl?'

'Nothing,' said Fox. 'Not that night, anyway. The old man said we'd need things. Bricks, cement, plaster. All that. But we did get her off the armchair and covered her with a mat 'case anybody looked in.'

'Was she stiff? D'you remember?' asked Roper.

'No,' said Fox. 'She were all floppy. Except her arms. They was stiff. And her neck.'

'What time d'you think you moved her?'

'Oh, I don't know,' said Fox, frowning. ''Bout three o'clock in the morning, I s'pose.'

Which provided a time scale, not accurate, but near enough. Rigor mortis, as a rule of thumb, usually sets in between five and six hours after death, beginning at the extremities. Total rigidity is apparent after twelve hours. So Marjorie Steadman had not been dead for as long as twelve hours but certainly longer than five or six: six hours back from three o'clock in the morning would have made it nine o'clock the previous evening. Less another hour, say, because rigor had been advanced enough for Sam Fox to have taken note of it. So Marjorie Steadman had been shot at or around eight o'clock that evening. Say a half-hour either side. And Winnie Fox had been seen on her way to the manor, come back, then go out again, then, unseen this time, return again round about that time. She could have . . .

'Do you know if your father went out that afternoon or evening, Mr Fox?'

Fox shook his head.

'You sure?'

'He were building a new chicken run. And it were finished that day, so he couldn't have done.'

So Winnie Fox was the likely villain, and getting likelier.

Sam Fox had sweated all through the next day, thinking of that body wrapped up in a rug at Box Cottage and praying that nobody would go there. He was eighteen, an accessory to a double murder, he could hang. His father, for reasons unknown to Sam at the time, had spent that day knocking down a wall of an old pig-pen and chipping the bricks clean of mortar. In the late afternoon Saul Fox had taken the trap into Dorchester and come back with sand and cement and a bag of plaster. There was no sign of sister Winnie that day; Sam Fox had presumed that she was still locked in her room.

As soon as it was dark that next night, Sam Fox and his father had traipsed across the fields with a sack of sand and a sack of cement, and for three hours after that Sam had made journey after journey back to the farm, a bucket of bricks in either hand on each return journey. It soon became plain what the bricks were for.

'Why was she lashed to that baulk of timber?' asked Roper.

'She'd gone all limp again,' said Fox. 'And the hole weren't deep enough to put her in all huddled up. So we had to tie her to a piece of wood. Keep her upright, see.'

It sounded right. As rigor mortis takes about twelve hours to fully develop so it takes twelve hours or so to subside.

While his father had bricked up Marjorie Steadman, Sam had scrubbed the bloodstains off the parlour linoleum.

The leather armchair across which Marjorie Steadman had fallen was too stained with blood to be cleaned. It was taken back to Highview Farm that night on Sam Fox's back and broken up. The next morning, it made kindling for a bonfire in the yard.

'When you saw her lying across the chair, Mr Fox, was she wearing a coat?'

'Aye,' said Fox. 'A red one.'

'We didn't find much blood on it.'

Fox thought about that. 'She were lying sort o' tilted. The coat was over the front of the cushion. Sort of out o' the way, like.'

'And Ralph Thorn was flat on his face by the door?'

'Aye.'

'How was he lying?'

'Feet nearest the door,' said Fox. 'It was one o' them I nearly tripped over.'

Roper could now conjure up a possible scenario. On her way to the manor that night, Winnie Fox might have passed Box Cottage, seen signs of life in there, gone to investigate, put two and two together and then quickly returned here for a gun. Hell, after all, hath no fury . . . On her return to Box Cottage she had come across Ralph Thorn in the kitchen, prodded him into the parlour at the muzzles of her shotgun. Thorn had probably gone first, then his wife, perhaps as she had risen in terror from that same armchair . . .

It had been Saul Fox who, two weeks later, seizing the fortuitous opportunity of the Normandy invasion, had travelled up to London to send the telegram to John Moxley. Sam Fox had never been able to read or write.

'This wrong you were supposed to be righting, Mr Fox. Did you ever find out what it was?'

'Aye,' said Fox. 'There were a kid. Winnie had a kid. The old man saw to it.'

'Saw to it?'

'Aye,' said Fox. 'It were born dead. It's out there.' He

203

jerked a weary thumb over his shoulder. 'Under the old hen house.'

'After Thorn died?'

'Aye,' said Fox. ''Bout four months. I always reckoned on it being Thorn's.'

Roper did some quick mental arithmetic. Four months on from May would have made it September, and nine months back from September '44 would have been around Christmas '43, the very time when Jake Haygarth had seen his putative lady-love standing on Ralph Thorn's staircase. All of which took Roper's scenario from the realm of the possible into the domain of the highly probable.

'I'm going to have to talk to your sister, Mr Fox.'

'She don't talk,' said Fox. 'The old man told her never to . . . After . . . So she don't.'

'But she understands?'

'Aye,' said Fox. 'But she'd only nod or shake her head.'

And that, thought Roper grimly, would do.

'Where is she, Mr Fox?'

'Told you,' said Fox. 'I don't know. Just walking. She likes the dark best, see.'

'Which way; where does she usually go?'

But as Sam Fox opened his mouth to answer, a brisk rap came at the door and Tom Blake put his head round it.

'The ambulance is here for the old man,' he said. 'Just seen the blue light down by the gate. Your father says you've got the key to the padlock, Sam.'

Fox stood up. The keys were in his trousers pocket.

'Has he talked, Tom?' asked Roper.

'Not a word,' said Blake, fishing in Fox's pocket for the bunch of keys. 'Except to say we won't be taking him anywhere. God's will, he tells me. Says he'll die in that chair of his.'

'Then you'd better tell him he's got another think coming,' said Roper, but even as the words left his mouth an alarm bell was ringing in his head and he had the kind of image that only came to him in the worst of nightmares —

'—You didn't leave that other shotgun with him, did you, Tom?'

Blake stiffened. 'Aye,' he said. 'I bloody did and all. I'd forgotten . . . ' And hefty though he was, his turn of speed was commendable as he started back across the passage; but he was already too late, because the shot rang out before he had taken his first full stride out of the office. A single blast of sound that shook the house and rattled the windows and froze Blake in his tracks.

And when the sound had died, in the profound and terrible silence that followed, Roper heard the hushed voice of Sam Fox, who was the only person who hadn't moved an inch.

'Thank Gawd,' his voice whispered fervently. 'He's done it! Please *Gawd*, he's done it!'

CHAPTER 14

It was twenty to eleven. Roper felt as if he had been at the farm all night. The ambulance had driven away empty. The doctor had returned, and this time had brought the Coroner's Officer with him, and Superintendent Mower was also here now and what he had brought with him was official disfavour. Because Saul Fox was now beyond all earthly law, slumped in his chair, the shotgun halfway across the kitchen where the recoil had taken it and his head lolling over the back of the chair; if, that is, it could still be called a head, because really it was only a bloodied frontal mask now, the back and top of it a mess of bone and tissue fragments splashed redly over the ceiling above the inert body and on the whitewashed wall behind and the tatty curtains and the pile of newspapers. And even Mower, whom Roper had hitherto regarded as case-hardened, could only bring himself to regard it with some effort.

And self-accused, amidst the disorder, stood Tom Blake, shocked and pale and only a shadow of the man he had been a scarce twenty minutes ago.

'I shouldn't have left him with that shotgun. I didn't bloody think . . . '

'No, Sergeant, you shouldn't have,' agreed Mower tartly. 'And I'll expect a statement from you on my desk by two o'clock tomorrow . . . and you too, Douglas. Now fill me in. How did this all come about?'

And while the doctor acted out the formalities of pronouncing Saul Fox's life extinct, Roper sketched in the evening's work for the benefit of Superintendent Mower. And Mower listened intently, his head tilted to one side, and halfway through taking a pinch of snuff and forgetting his handkerchief again until the very last moment.

'You think the sister then?' he asked, when Roper had finished.

'Sure of it.'

'But you've only got the son's word, Douglas. And he's not very bright either, is he? I mean it could all be down to him, and he's just trying to hive off the blame on to his sister and father. I don't like instant confessions, Douglas. Life's never that bloody easy. Sounds to me as if the son's got an axe to grind. A lifetime of purgatory the old man gave him. Right?'

And Roper had to agree with that. Confessions were always dodgy items.

'What about Monk?' asked Mower. 'And all those bloody capers lately across at the cottage?'

'Not got that far yet,' confessed Roper.

'Well, do that now,' said Mower. 'I want to sleep easy tonight.'

The doctor had put his stethoscope away and was shutting his case. 'Single gunshot wound, self-inflicted. I'd have said he was in splendid health for his age. Still, I suppose he must have had a reason, poor man. . . . Would you like me to take a look at the son while I'm here? He could be in shock.'

'On the contrary, Doctor,' said Roper. 'He's delighted.'

'Good God,' said the doctor, swinging his case down by his side. 'No accounting for the bloody human race, is there?'

It was ten to eleven. Roper and Morgan were questioning Sam Fox again, although it was not so much an interrogation as marshalling Fox's confession into some sort of logical order.

The gun that had killed William Monk had been Winnie

Fox's, and so, probably, had been the gun that put an end to the two Thorns.

On the morning of Monk's death, Sam Fox had been cleaning out the section of drainage ditch behind Box Cottage, and through the bottom of the hedge had seen, to his alarm, William Monk apparently dismantling the stones at the front of the rockery. Fox had raced home to report this ominous sighting to his father. This was not the first time Monk had been observed working on the rockery, but it *was* the first time he had looked as if he were taking it down. Despite all the warnings.

'Warnings, Mr Fox?' Roper broke in. 'What warnings?'

'We tried to tell 'im,' said Fox. 'Tried to get him out, but he wouldn't take heed, see. *Always* working in the garden, he was.'

It had been Sam Fox who had cut through Monk's electricity lines and Sam, too, who had turned off Monk's water in the lane and smeared cow-blood over his windows. And the rabbit on Monk's front door . . .

And now William Monk was working on the rockery, taking it apart, and that could not be allowed to happen.

'He's got to go, boy,' had decreed Saul Fox. 'You got to stop him.'

'I can't, Da! I bloody *can't*! *You* got to do it.'

So it had been Saul Fox, well into his late eighties even then, who had been William Monk's ultimate executioner.

Using the Vauxhall Victor that Roper had seen outside, Sam Fox had driven his father as far as the Carpenter's Arms, driven back to the farm, then, on foot, cut across the fields to Box Cottage, by way of the drainage ditch, with his sister's shotgun tucked inside his coat. His sister's gun was easier to hide because it was a woman's gun, see, a lightweight, short one that the old man had bought special.

Saul Fox had approached Box Cottage from the front, his job to lure Monk in from the garden for a neighbourly chat, and keep him inside until his son turned up with the weapon, hopefully unobserved.

When Sam Fox had finally arrived, through the open kitchen door of Box Cottage, his father had already been to work.

'I thought he were praying.'

'Who?' said Roper. 'Your father?'

'Monk,' said Fox. 'He were sort of kneeling over a chair in the parlour. The old man had laid him out, see. With his stick. Hit him, like. On the 'ead. Bashed 'im while his back were turned.'

'I see,' said Roper, grimly. He had been puzzled from the beginning as to quite how Monk had been sat in that chair without some signs of struggle showing. With Monk unconscious it would have been easy.

Sam Fox had lashed Monk into a chair from the kitchen.

'. . . But I couldn't stay to watch, see. It were the *old man* who saw to the *killing* of him.'

'But you *did* tie him to the chair?'

'Aye,' agreed Fox. 'But that weren't the same as actually *shooting* him, were it?'

Sam Fox had slunk to the kitchen. He had heard the two reports, the second following so quickly on the first that it might only have been one.

'. . . Then the old man called me back in. He were shakin'. Told me to find some string and some rag, only I couldn't find any string, only a reel of fishing line. And the old man told me to untie 'im, but I couldn't do *that* either. Blood everywhere, there were, and the back of his head were all gone, see. But the old man said I'd *got* to. He'd done his bit and now I'd got to do mine . . . So I did. And he fell off the chair . . . and his legs twitched and put the fear of Christ up me . . . I thought he were going to come back to life, see.'

Saul Fox had then tied a yard of fishing gut to the triggers, then meticulously wiped every inch of his daughter's shotgun with the rag before tying the other end of the gut to Monk's toe.

And, of course, no one had ever known that Monk had

been clubbed on the back of the head first; because when his body had been discovered there had been no back to his head. Saul Fox might have been old, but he had been no fool.

Another knock came at the office door. This time it was Mower. He had a key on a ring in his hand. It was the key to the gun-safe bolted to the wall in Saul Fox's parlour. Mower had found the key on the floor, and the gun-safe had been standing open, two shotguns chained up in it and empty padlocks for two more.

'How many shotguns d'you have, Mr Fox?' asked Mower.

'Four,' said Fox.

And Roper had another of those fleeting nightmares. 'Two in the safe and the one your father's just used; where's the other one?'

Fox blinked. 'Dunno,' he said. 'There was three there last time I looked.'

The nightmare began to take substance . . .

'Where the hell's your sister, Mr Fox?'

'I told you,' said Fox. 'Out. She's been out a couple of hours.'

'Out where, for Christ's sake? What's she wearing?' Roper advanced quickly on Fox and shook him. 'What's she *wearing*, man!'

'A scarf. A yellow one. Round 'er 'ead.'

'And what else, for Christ's sake. *Think*, man!'

'. . . A coat.'

'What colour?'

'. . . Raincoat. Man's. Brown one.'

'Could she have been carrying a shotgun underneath it?'

'Aye. She might have been. But why would she want to do that . . . ?'

But Roper was not listening any more. Two strides took him out to the passage. 'Everybody down here in the hall! Sharpish!'

Blake appeared first, from the kitchen, the two DCs

practically fell over each other on the stairs, Morgan came up behind Roper from the office.

'How tall's this Winnie Fox, Tom?' he asked Blake.

Blake held the edge of his hand halfway between his trouser belt and his shirt collar. 'About here.'

'Note that,' said Roper. 'About five feet two. Winnie Fox. Man's brown raincoat, yellow headscarf. Anybody got a torch?'

One of the DCs produced one. Roper said to Blake:

'Tom, you take a car and drive the likeliest way by road to Box Cottage. Slow. And keep your eyes peeled for her. Me, and you two lads' – to the DCs – 'we'll cut across the fields. And Dan, you'd better stay here with Sam Fox. And keep your eyes open. If you see her coming back here, give us a call on your PR. She could be carrying a shotgun. And don't get carried away by the idea that she might be somebody's dear old granny; she knows how to use the bloody thing.'

'I'll go along with Sergeant Blake,' said Mower. Then, to all and sundry: 'Heads down and no playing heroic silly-buggers. And keep in touch.'

It was Blackbeard who called the meeting to order. She felt him brace himself and grip her upper arms and hold her away, and she had never felt more gauche in all her life.

'I'm sorry,' she said. 'That was my fault. Stupid.'

'Mine too,' he growled. 'Sorry.'

'You don't fancy me, that it?'

'On the contrary,' he growled. 'I fancy you rotten.' He reached past her and switched on the light in his cramped little hall. 'But I'd rather wake up in the morning and find we're still friends. We can work it out from there.'

'I loathe that bloody beard.'

'So I'll shave it off.'

'Do that,' she said. 'And we can work it out from *there*.'

He smiled, to her immense relief. She had come close tonight to making a fool of herself, and she hadn't even had the excuse of being drunk because she'd only been on fruit juices.

'Your place or mine tonight?' he said. 'I'm not having you go back there on your own.'

She had to think about that. In the last few days, for all her outward denials, the charms of Box Cottage had definitely begun to pall.

'Here, for preference,' she said. 'If that's okay by you?' His hands were warm still on her cold arms, the only two hot spots on her entire body.

'No trouble, Cass,' he said, and his eyes licked over her face like two loyal puppies. 'I mean that.'

'Thanks,' she said. Given a few more minutes in the dark just now she could have worked her wicked way with him, but she was glad now that the opportunity was gone. He was, all that hair or not, one of the best of the good guys, and he knocked bloody Steven into a cocked hat.

'I'd better warn you, though,' he said. 'I still fancy you rotten.'

It was her turn to smile, and for the first time in many a long month she actually felt happy. And perhaps she had been stupid tonight but those few moments of warm male cuddle in the dark had been one of acute need on her part and nicely restrained lust on his. Which made a pleasant change, and almost tempted her to revise her views on men in general.

'I'll go and get my things.'

'I'll come with you.'

'No,' she said. 'Really. You knock up the coffee.' Which is really why she had come into his cottage in the first place. 'I'll be back in five minutes.'

'If you're not, I'll be along there,' he said. 'And forget the feminist bit; any problems, you scream.'

'Don't worry, sport,' she said. 'I'll scream like hell.'

His hands dropped from her arms, so that she was cold all over again, and with the contact gone she began to have doubts about walking along to the cottage on her own, but thrust them aside, because she had been ridiculous enough for one night already without suddenly turning into the weak little woman . . .

'Take care,' he said.

'I'll be okay,' she said. 'Really. . . . Five minutes.'

She felt chillier still in the dark of the lane, the skin of her upper arms turning to goose-flesh. Behind her, footsteps sounded on the stone flags of the footpath and two men with loud boozy voices were talking football. She passed the streetlamp between her cottage and Blackbeard's, and, when they did, so the men's shadows lengthened and seemed to overtake her and she caught herself walking faster, which she knew was ridiculous, but all the same . . . She pushed open her gate with something akin to relief. The two men walked on by without even a glance at her.

She fumbled in her shoulder bag for her doorkey. Now cool it, she told herself, as she probed about in the dark for the keyhole with a shaking hand. Slow down. Nothing's going to happen.

With the front door closed behind her she felt safe again. The cottage was warm. She reached for the passage light, saw that the parlour door was open which wasn't important except that she seemed to remember having left it shut; but then she still hadn't gathered all her wits together after the business of the other night, so she probably *had* left it open. And anyway it didn't matter.

In the bedroom she quickly repaired her ravaged pink lipstick, and perhaps it wouldn't be ravaged again tonight but one never knew one's luck and the circumstances might again be made propitious if she chanced her arm a little. Codeine bottle into shoulder bag – the headache was still coming and going – and her only pair of pyjamas stuffed in on top of them. And then she began to feel the shivers coming over her again, and had to get out of the cottage, and wished to God that she had never left Ealing in the first place because however crummy that flat had been it didn't creak and groan after dark all on its own as if it were alive. Bedroom light out, down the stairs, but only halfway before she heard the shuffling footfall in the dark parlour and she knew that she only had to scream and Blackbeard would be here in a flash, only her feet were glued to the stairs and her hand to the bannister-rail and her mouth would only open far enough to whisper oh, Jesus, as the little hunched figure – and oh, dear God, was that really a shotgun she was carrying – shuffled to the bottom of the stairs and crooked a finger at her to beckon her on down. And she wished she could faint or something, just go limp and blot it all out, but she couldn't even do that.

The finger beckoned again.

Roper and the two DCs slithered in the darkness down the wet grass towards the drainage ditch, faster now because the parlour light was on in Box Cottage and Roper was convinced that he had caught a momentary glimpse of *two* people moving about in there; and, besides, the downstairs lights were on in Cambridge's cottage, which meant that he was more likely in there than not and the only other person Miss Murcheson would let into her cottage after dark was Cambridge if she had any sense. Which was a ramshackle rationale, but he had made it in haste to suit the circumstances, and if it was wrong it wouldn't matter a damn, but if it was right it would matter a great deal.

'Torch,' he whispered. One of the DCs passed it to him. With fingers splayed over the lens he raked the dull beam over the hedge on the Foxes' side of the ditch. No gap, but a couple of weak spots that he might be able to push himself through. He selected the most likely. The two DCs, one either side of him, sprang the hedge apart as best they could and he thrust himself through. One fifty-pound new suit to be charged to expenses. Clinging with one hand to the hedge and balanced precariously on the edge of the ditch he helped one of the DCs through after him. Time raced. He could feel it. Off shoes. Off socks. Sloshing water

214

under his feet as they found the bottom of the ditch. Up the other side, through the other hedge. Something scored painfully across his cheek. One of the DCs was in the ditch behind him.

He was through. He was in the garden behind Box Cottage. Then one DC and then the other, crouched one each side of him in the light spilling out from the parlour window. Roper quickly got back into his shoes.

'Which one of you's got the radio?'

'Me, sir.'

'You stay here then, and contact Mower and keep him posted. And if you hear shooting radio in for the heavy mob. – And you, lad' – to the other shadowy DC – 'you come with me. And don't do anything I don't tell you to do. Right, son?'

'Yes, sir,' whispered back the DC.

Cassandra sat frozen in her father's chesterfield while the witch of Endor gesticulated ferociously at the hole in the wall and then at the garden and tried to tell her something which Cassandra wouldn't have understood at the best of times, and now didn't even try to because there wasn't time. That the old girl was stark staring bonkers no longer mattered. She had a gun and she was going to use it, and even the voice that she could conjure up sometimes, the one that said, you know what I'd do, don't you, Cass, was silent and soon she would join it in the cold black void of wherever it was, and she wondered where the time was going because Blackbeard had told her he would be down here if she wasn't back in five minutes and surely that was at least half an hour ago.

'I don't understand,' she said, or she would have done if her voice had sounded, but that didn't seem to be working properly either and all that came out was a faint croak that was as near despair as she had ever heard. But *time* was the important thing. If only she could keep the mad old biddy hanging on for just a few more minutes and telepath a few

215

more desperate pleas to Blackbeard to get his skates on. *Please. Please . . .*

'I don't know what you're trying to say. *Honestly*, I don't . . . '

The witch continued to cavort and point, at the floor, herself, the gun, the hole in the wall, the window beyond which was the garden, and . . . of course, the rockery, and oh, dear God, there was a face at the window and she couldn't be sure but it looked like the detective inspector, but it was gone again before she had convinced herself exactly, because she had really only seen him with half an eye, and the barrels of that shotgun waving about were using up her entire concentration . . .

'You mean *you* killed him? You did?'

The witch nodded eagerly. Held up two fingers.

'Both of them?'

Nod–nod. Looked like Mrs Punch in a headscarf.

'Why?'

The witch beat her chest.

'He's not here. Not any more. . . . Th–they took him away. He's gone. Honestly.' But even as she spoke, Cassandra knew that she had said too much. The witch's eyes filled with hatred and both of her hands went to the gun and the two black holes at the ends of the barrels were like malevolent eyes. The gun was jerked upward, and again, then was flourished at the door. There was no mistaking that message. She, Cassandra Murcheson, late of Ealing, was going to die in the garden and Blackbeard wasn't coming and that face at the window had only been a mirage after all and there was no God and no justice and no tomorrow either, and she rose on buckling legs and shuffled backwards to the door with ice–cold death prodding into her belly and Winnie Fox shuffling menacingly after it.

Roper dropped to a crouch beside the DC in the shadow of the potting shed.

'Contact Mower on the radio. Tell him Winnie Fox is down here at Box Cottage, she's got a shotgun trained on Murcheson and he's to approach the cottage from the front and come up the side way, but only as far as the back wall. After that, he takes his time from me. Got that?'

'Yes, sir,' whispered the DC. 'And what do I do after that?'

'Nothing you don't have to,' hissed Roper. 'Just use your bloody loaf.'

Bent double, he started back towards the lit window of the parlour, but dropped low again when the back door of the cottage swung inward and Cassandra Murcheson stepped out backwards into the darkness with Winnie Fox following her. The kitchen was still in darkness, but enough light spilled from the parlour window to let him see what was happening. And that was that Winnie Fox was goading Murcheson towards the remnants of the rockery with the working end of a double-barrelled shotgun. In the background, he could still hear the DC muttering into his radio. And hoped to God that Winnie Fox's hearing wasn't all it might be.

They were close enough now for him to hear their feet scuffing through the grass.

'Look, this is crazy . . . what the hell are we doing this for . . . ?' he heard Murcheson whisper. She received no answer except another shove in the stomach with the barrels of the shotgun. The two of them were only a few paces now from the orderly piles of stones that had once been the rockery. Murcheson stumbled as the heel of her shoe caught one and took her momentarily off balance. . . . Roper waited, tensed, for the shotgun to blast out, but blessedly it didn't . . .

'Winnie,' he whispered softly. 'I'm over here, Winnie. Behind you.'

The silhouette of Winnie Fox stiffened.

'It's Ralph, Winnie,' whispered Roper. 'I'm over here, Winnie.'

She turned, with aching slowness. First her head, then her trunk, then her legs and feet in little shuffles and Roper offered up a short prayer that Murcheson wouldn't try to do anything clever like trying to grab that gun, because he wouldn't have put it past her, but sensibly she didn't.

'Over here, Winnie,' whispered Roper.

Winnie Fox was facing him now, her back to Murcheson, her head cocked to one side like an eager bird, the shotgun held diagonally across her chest.

Roper rose, slowly, knowing that if he moved too quickly all hell could break loose in a moment.

'It's me, Winnie,' he called softly. 'I've come for you, Winnie.'

The eager, querulous head tilted the other way. If the situation had been a fraction less fraught, if it hadn't been for that shotgun, he might have felt some compassion, but the chill hand clutching his gut precluded the finer emotions and he had eyes only for the shotgun and the shadowy whiteness of Cassandra Murcheson at Winnie Fox's back.

'I'm over here, Winnie.'

She began to shuffle towards him across the grass. Then stopped in the instant the footsteps sounded on the gravel path beside the cottage . . .

Roper dared to take a glance sideways. He had expected to see Mower, but it wasn't Mower . . .

He switched his gaze quickly back to Winnie Fox. 'Stay where you are, Mr Cambridge!' he shouted. 'Do *nothing!*'

The barrels of the shotgun had dropped menacingly down to the horizontal and Winnie Fox's glittering eyes were everywhere at once; and it wouldn't take much, a too hasty move on someone's part, a twig snapping underfoot to take her over the brink . . .

'Winnie,' Roper wheedled softly again. 'I'm here, Winnie. Over here.'

* * *

And still rooted to the spot, her heart thrashing about in her ribs and feeling giddy and sick, Cassandra Murcheson, with every second dragging like an hour, watched the awful picture of the witch of Endor shuffling through the grass towards the detective, the front of his jacket and trousers gleaming with mud and wetness; and from the corner of her eye Blackbeard's white shirt just in view at the corner of the cottage, only now he was talking to somebody, a quick whispered exchange . . . it looked like Sergeant Blake with him . . . and another man, in a raincoat and trilby hat . . .

'This way, Winnie . . . Can you see me now?'

The two figures were all but merged . . .

'I'm here, Winnie . . . I'm here . . . I've come back for you, Winnie.'

And then it was over. The two shadowy figures joined. The detective opened his arms and the witch of Endor stepped into them with a little cry and hugged him and Roper had the gun and was holding it out sideways and another man came out of the darkness near the shed and took it from him then moved back into the shadows and started talking into a radio. Then Blackbeard and Sergeant Blake and the other man were with her and it was too much to take in all at once, because it was all so sad, so immeasurably sad, and they couldn't understand that she wasn't having a weep for herself but for that poor old lady across the garden who thought that her long-lost lover had come back and that detective had to be another one of the good guys. That's why she was crying and not for herself at all.

'Shush,' said Blackbeard. 'It's all right, Cass. It's all right.'

And across the darkened garden, the other two lovers were still locked in their fervent embrace. Thirty years too late . . .

CHAPTER 15

The organ notes faded as Roper shook hands with Colin Moxley and stepped out into the bright sunshine. Saul Fox's mourners had been few. Cassandra Murcheson, Ted Cambridge, Mrs Moxley, Sergeant Blake and Roper; and of course Sam Fox and the plain-clothes warder with whom he had arrived manacled that afternoon.

Colin Moxley had mentioned other and more remote names during the service. A prayer had been spoken for Ralph Thorn and Marjorie Thorn, née Steadman; and Mrs Gwendoline Fox, whose remains had been unearthed a few feet from where Sam Fox had said they would be; and the remains of a child without a name whose pathetically tiny fragments had been revealed beneath the site of the Foxes' old henhouse. Mrs Fox had died of a broken neck, at her husband's hands most likely, although no one would ever be sure now. How the child had died would remain equally a mystery, or perhaps Sam Fox had been right and it had never drawn breath at all. Another find at Highview Farm had been an aluminium ladder, with a plastic pad missing from one stile, hidden away in a barn under bales of hay.

Roper joined the small knot of mourners around the few flowers laid out on the grass near the porch steps. On his way here this afternoon he had noticed that Box Cottage was up for sale.

'I had a job recognising you, Mr Cambridge,' he said.

Cambridge, smiling coyly, turned and stuck out a massive right hand. 'I suddenly noticed I needed a shave.'

Yes, I'll bet you did, thought Roper. 'And how are you, Miss Murcheson?'

'Fine,' she said. 'Great.' She shook his hand fervently. He would never know it, but if it hadn't been for Blackbeard it wouldn't have taken a great deal of effort on her part to be as potty about him. He had saved her life, and after giving her own evidence in court she had sat up in the gallery and listened to him giving his. How he had sat with Winnie Fox most of that awful night, and how she had not uttered a word but only held his hand and billed and cooed at him because she really had thought that he was Ralph Thorn raised from the dead and returned to her. And it had all sounded so sad that Cassandra's eyes had prickled again because he really was such a nice guy and hadn't sounded gloating or anything as he'd stood in the box. Winnie Fox, blessedly, had been found unfit to plead. Her brother would not see Highview Farm for five years at least.

'I see you're selling up,' said Roper, as she finally loosed his hand.

'I'm moving into Ted's place,' she said. 'We're starting a sort of workers' cooperative.'

'Bully for you,' said Roper. So the auguries had been right after all.

'. . . And we're getting spliced. The old-fashioned way. Saturday week.'

He smiled. Not his electric-light one, she noticed, but a proper ear-to-ear one, and she hoped earnestly that he had a nice woman of his own tucked away somewhere because that was the least he deserved.

'Congratulations,' he said. 'Both of you.' Further along the path, still chained to his warder, Sam Fox was walking towards the lychgate and the unmarked car that had brought him here.

'Look,' she said. 'If you like, you can come back to the cottage. A cup of tea or something . . . ?'

'No, thank you, Miss Murcheson. I'm on duty. And I've got a little job to do up in Dorchester.'

'Perhaps some other time . . . ?'

'Yes,' he said. 'Some other time.'

But she knew he never would, because it was the electric-light smile again but she couldn't let him go as easily as that because she was an emotional cow sometimes and before she really knew what she was doing she'd bobbed on her toes and reached up and hooked a hand behind his neck and dragged his face down and kissed his cheek the way she used to kiss her Dad.

'Thanks, Mr Roper,' she said. 'I think you're bloody gorgeous. You know that?' In her illustrations, he was also the model for the mighty Hu-Ra's sidekick, but that was something else he would *never* know.

'So are you, Miss Murcheson,' he said gravely, offering his hand again. 'Believe it.'

And then he was gone, down the path towards his car and joining Sergeant Blake at the gate, still wiping lipstick from his cheek.

In his car, Roper tilted his mirror and checked his left cheek for lipstick. Then slid his key into the ignition. Had he been a few years younger he might have fallen for Cassandra Murcheson himself. But for the time being he was off to see another lady for whom he had developed an affection; tucked in the glove compartment under the dash-board was a quarter bottle of Gordon's gin. Exactly as promised.

For Maudie Samuels, without whom the case of Box Cottage might never have got off the ground.

And tomorrow he was starting the leave he still hadn't had, and those quiet few days of *dolce far niente* he had promised himself . . .